WHERE IS SHE?

ROGER RAPEL

WHERE IS SHE?
by
Roger Rapel
Copyright © Roger Rapel 2016
Cover Copyright © Amy Parle Design 2016
Published by Black Hawk
(An Imprint of Ravenswood Publishing)

Ravenswood Publishing
1275 Baptist Chapel Rd.
Autryville, NC 28318
http://www.ravenswoodpublishing.com

Printed in the U.S.A.

ISBN-13: 978-1537152301
ISBN-10: 1537152300

Thank you to Amy Parle for the cover design amyparledesign.co.uk

To Nichola
With love
Roger Hughes
xx

CHAPTER ONE

Detective Sergeant Jim Broadbent was sat at his desk mulling over the files that were piling up; he was completing the normal end of investigative reports ready for filing. The end of case work had to be right; it had to include all the issues and conclusions. So that if someone came in cold and read the report they would immediately get the gist of the investigation.

Detective Superintendent Langton came out of his office requesting Jim to come in. Jim raised his eyebrows and thought 'what now?'

Jim went in saying 'yes guv?' 'Please Jim, sit down. I have just received this report from Central, I think we should take it on; have a read and see what you think?' Langton handed over the report as Jim skimmed through it; he took the file away with him to inwardly digest.

He sat at his desk as he began to read the report which highlighted a woman who had been reported missing by the boyfriend. He continued reading the background of the case; Janet Crosby a 25 year old shop worker who had moved in with her boyfriend Charles Sumner, then sometime later had gone missing. On the surface it appeared to have been a loving relationship of some 3 years; there appeared to have been no reason for her disappearance.

The police investigation appeared to have been thorough with the normal procedures having been adopted. He then picked up a report from the original investigating officer; who had concluded 'I'm not happy with Sumner, there is something about him, I don't know what, but he doesn't seem right to me.'

Jim knew too well about the sixth sense; as he would often get the same feelings when investigating cases himself, especially if matters didn't add up.

Jim picked up the phone and called the division where the officer worked and made an appointment for the following morning. He then made a list of witnesses to re interview.

Although he knew this would take some time, turning over stones looking to see what crawled out as the original investigation was now some 15 months old. There would be an acceptance of the inevitable that, Janet had either run off, or perhaps in hiding, or worse lying dead somewhere, but there had been no build up to this, nothing to suggest foul play.

Jim called it a day and went home to find Jackie in the kitchen wearing one of his shirts bopping from one foot the other as she listened to the radio preparing the evening meal. Jim as normal came up behind her lifting the shirt tail and patted her bum then wrapped his arms around her kissing her neck. Jackie raised her head to give him free access to the sensitive areas. She sighed and moaned at the sensation he caused. 'Stop it Jim, later, dinners nearly ready.' He patted her bum then went and got changed.

He came back out and opened a bottle of wine filling two glasses; he took a good mouthful of wine, he liked the selection that Jackie chose. 'Come and get it the plates are hot.' Jim carried his plate of hot stew and dumplings with a cloth to the table. They ate as they discussed their day.

They later went to bed early making the most of each other relishing in their favourite sexual preferences.

CHAPTER TWO

Jim arrived at Central where he met PC Cooke; they went to the canteen where they sat and discussed the issues of the case, including what he felt about Janet Crosby, and the feeling he had about Sumner. 'I can't put a finger on it, he just seemed so false,' Jim listened to the officer's thoughts and how he had conducted the investigation. Jim thanked him for his time then began the long slog of re-interviewing the witnesses and friends. He ticked off the list one by one as he slogged his way through.

There was nothing outstanding from the witnesses only that it was totally out of character for Janet to go off with no communication; she was devoted to her parents and her sister Lynne; there was no way she would have gone without letting someone know where she was going. She wouldn't have gone for all this time without contacting her family letting them know she was alright.

Jim knocked on the door of Christine Williams who according to the file was the best friend of Janet. The door opened slightly as he heard a voice say 'who's there?' Jim showed his warrant card. The door then half opened as he saw a really pretty woman. 'Yes how can I help you?' 'Sorry to disturb you, I am re-looking at the case of Janet Crosby and wondered if I could have a chat with you.' Christine nodded as she fully opened the door and stepped back inviting Jim inside.

Jim accepted the offer of coffee as he sat at the Kitchen table chatting about the area and the work she did. Jim

3

admired her body as she was making the coffee. He thought what a lovely bum. Then pulled his attention back to the reason why he was there.

'Okay Christine can you tell me about Janet, hold nothing back the full story, warts and all?' Christine then let him know about her relationship with Janet. He picked up on the fact that Janet had changed when she met Charlie. Jim noticed her eye's narrow as she spoke of him.

'Tell me about him why didn't you like him?' 'He was controlling her, he was so jealous of her; he kept her a virtual prisoner in the house he wouldn't let her out. We used to go out all the time for a girlie night out; sometimes just me and her and other times in a group. But then she stopped going out, she used to make excuses, but I knew he was controlling her.' 'Was he violent to her?' 'Not that I know of just emotionally abusive, but Janet wouldn't speak about it much.' 'Tell me about the emotional abuse?' 'When we met during the day for coffee, she would tell me how he would threaten her with eviction from the flat where they lived as he owned it. If he did evict her, she would have nowhere to live. She said he would sometimes raise his hand, but never hit her or so she said, I wasn't sure.' 'What makes you unsure?' 'Well, there was one occasion when I went to hold her arm comfort, as I took hold of her she winced and pulled away holding her bicep. I asked her what was wrong, she just said she had banged it against a door, but I didn't believe her.'

Christine offered more coffee Jim nodded as she got up. Jim looked at her figure more closely; as she leant forward to stand up her top to billowed open, it was then he noticed her full cleavage. He thought wow what a pair. Christine caught his gaze and inwardly smiled at his attention.

Coffee made she sat back down curling one leg under her as she sat on it; then continued. 'After that incident we never really met again, only the odd phone call. It appeared he was keeping her as his prisoner.' 'This is all good

4

background knowledge for me, thank you. Tell me do you know of any other friends that Janet had who I could speak to?' 'Not really they all drifted away as she stopped coming out.' 'Okay; what do you know about him?' 'I didn't know him before he met Janet; I'd seen him in pubs and clubs, he always appeared to be in the company of women, but that's all really.' 'Did you know any of the women?' 'Look I'm not sure where this is leading; do you think she is dead?' 'I don't know I've been asked to re-look at the case to ensure nothing has been missed so please bear with me.' 'Okay this never came from me right!' 'Okay go on?' 'There is one woman she was once his girlfriend, but she got out of the relationship and ran away.' 'Where did she run to?' 'This is the problem only a couple of people know, including me.' 'Go on?' 'More coffee?' 'Please.' Christine stood up again and over emphasized her lean showing on purpose her cleavage. Jim smiled as she stood up as she smirked and made the coffee washing the cups. She knew Jim was watching her so wiggled her bum as she washed the cups, her loose track suit bottoms moving with her motion.

The coffee served she continued 'look her name is Sandra she moved out of the area, she was really afraid of him, in fact shit scared of him. I think he had been violent to her as well.' 'Where did she move to?' 'This never came from me right?' Jim nodded as Christine got up and collected her handbag rummaged inside then took out an address book; she flicked through the pages as Jim was poised with his pen. 'Right here we go; her name as said is Sandra; Sandra Rose, she moved to 24, Smith Court, Winters Town; but promise, this didn't come from me?' 'I promise; have you a phone number for her?' 'No she just cut all contact with me when she went and changed her number.' 'How long ago was that?' 'Oh some three years ago; I haven't seen her for a long while, although she does ring now and again, but I haven't heard from her for ages, she refused to give me her number, she was so scared of him.' 'Okay Janet you have been a great help thanks for the coffee. I may need to call back at some time; have you a number I can call you on?' Christine then rattled off her mobile number. Jim then left as she opened the door saying goodbye.

Jim thought what a body she's got, fucking hell, I could give her one. Then drove back To HQ's where he researched the address, but no Sandra Rose listed in the voters register; although that wasn't unusual, especially if it was a rented property.

Jim then made a list of people to see the following day including the parents and sister of Janet.

Langton enquired as to the progress. Jim went into his office as he debriefed him on the conversation with Christine. Langton nodded saying 'any thoughts Jim?' 'Not at the moment to early, but PC Cooke had a bad feeling about Sumner and I'm starting to get the same feeling, a bit to early yet; perhaps after talking with Sandra Rose it may give me a better understanding.' Langton nodded as he reached for the bottom drawer and poured two fingers of scotch. Jim raised his glass as he nodded in appreciation.

CHAPTER THREE

Jim made his way to Winters Town, he found Smiths Court, which was a small mews of town houses in a row of similar houses; all with nicely kept gardens. He found number 24; he looked at the curtains, thinking it looked like a woman's house. He took a deep breath trying to work out how to approach the reason he was there and how he had found out about her address.

He pressed the doorbell, but there was no reply. He looked down the mews and saw the postman delivering the mail. He waited till he got closer. He identified himself showing his warrant card then asked if he was aware of the occupant of 24. Postie said 'as far as I know just one occupant; Sandra Rose, although I have never seen her; the house is always the same as it is now.' 'Okay thanks.'

Jim had no alternative so left a note for her to call him. He then saw a neighbour going next door. 'Excuse me love, I am trying to find the occupant of next door I have a message for her, do you know when she will be home?' 'Oh I'm so sorry, I hardly ever see her, she comes and goes at all different times, sorry I can't help much.' He thanked her then posted the message through the letterbox.

Jim then went to speak to the parents of Janet; they were so distant from the situation, Janet had left home to live with Sumner and she never came home or made much contact after she moved in with him, much to the parent's dismay they had been cut off from her and that hurt, they knew something was sadly wrong. They were now so worried for her, they couldn't sleep and her younger sister Lynne who Janet used to call her every day was so concerned for her safety as well, as she hasn't heard from Janet either.

'Is Lynne here?' 'Yes she's upstairs doing her course work for her A levels, do you want to speak to her?' Jim nodded 'yes please.' Mrs Crosby called upstairs asking Lynne to come down. Jim went into the lounge where he spoke with Lynne.

Lynne was a teenager who was hoping to get into university; she was studying hard to obtain the necessary grades for the prerequisite subjects.

'Look Lynne I'm here investigating the disappearance of Janet. Can you help in anyway? Anything no matter how small could help, did she confide in you about her relationship with Charles Sumner?'

Lynne was a little unsure then said, 'yes she told me about Charles and how he used to hit her, I told her to get out but, she was too proud, she didn't want to come home and admit she had been wrong.' 'Did she talk about the violence and what he did to her?' 'Not really although once she said he had slapped her face and then on another occasion he had punched her arm so hard, she thought he had broken it.' 'Did she have any friends you know of who might be able to help?' 'Her best friend was Christine, but I think you know about her?' 'Thanks, you have been a great help, if you think of anything else here's my card.'

Jim continued the rounds talking with her friends, but the same story was told, Charles Sumner had been dominating Janet, keeping her under his control. Jim was now nearly ready to have a session with him, he just wanted to talk with Sandra first as she may hold the key or certainly may have some ammunition to assist him in the interview.

There was nothing for it, unless she called him he would sit outside of her address I the morning until she left for work.

Jim got home where he saw Jackie in one of his shirts bopping to music as she cooked tea. She heard him come in, but liked the feeling that he was going to try and surprise her, so didn't acknowledge his arrival. Jim crept up behind lifting the shirt tail and patting her bum as he slid his hands up inside the shirt cupping a breast in each hand as he kissed her neck.

'That's nice Jim I like that.' She turned and kissed him saying 'get changed dinner is nearly ready.' Jim changed and opened a bottle of wine pouring two glasses as he laid the table. Jackie bought in two plates holding them with oven gloves. 'Mind, the plates are piping hot.' 'That smells really good babes.'

They chatted about their day and how each of them had heavy workloads. Jim helped with the washing up then opened his A4 book looking at the interviews trying to get his head around the possibility that Sumner had killed Janet, then dumped or buried her somewhere.

The hairs standing up at the back of his neck, if Christine was right then he could have had a fit of jealously and hit her; accidently killing her; he then started to think of all the scenarios. Then Jackie shouted at him 'give it a rest Jim and come here I need you. Jim went into the bedroom and saw Jackie standing in one of her Anne Summers outfits, his eyes were out on stalks as he walked up to her. 'Come her Broadbent and perform my favourite.' With that she sat on the bed dragging his head between her thighs, she moaned as she felt him performing her favourite oral; feeling his warm breath and tongue manipulating her, she quickly climaxed time after time with his expert attention on her. Jim loved and savoured her taste. They carried on through the night pleasing each other to the full.

CHAPTER FOVR

Jim arrived early as he sat outside of Sandra Rose' house; at about 7am he saw the upstairs lights come on. Well at least someone's at home he thought. He waited for some 20 minutes then knocked the door having seen the downstairs lights come on. The door was opened by a woman. 'Sandra Rose?' 'Yes, who are you?' 'From the police, I left you a note to ring me.' 'Yes what do you want?' 'Can I pop in for five minutes or make an appointment for another time?' 'I can only give you five minutes as I get ready for work.'

Jim was shown to the kitchen. 'How can I help you?' 'I am investigating a missing person called Janet Crosby and wondering if you may be able to help.' 'I don't know her; I don't recognize the name either.' Sandra started to brush her hair as she made coffee, then she placed a mug on the table for Jim, as he nodded in appreciation. 'Janet was a girlfriend of Charles Sumner; I believe you were close to him as well at some time is that true?' 'Who told you that?' 'I'm sorry I can't divulge that; I just need some background on him.'

Sandra looked frightened as she brought her hand to her mouth. 'Oh my god, I don't know what to say, he's an arsehole.' 'What does that mean?' 'Sorry I haven't got time now can you come back tomorrow as I'm off work.' 'What time would suit you?' 'Say 11am.' Jim finished his coffee then left. He was definitely getting one of those feelings again.

Jim went back to HQ's checking his in-tray. He sat thinking of his previous investigations where he had the same feelings as he had now. He knew he was right on the previous occasions, and even without speaking with Sumner he was getting the same bad feeling again.

He wanted to wait until he had spoken with Sandra before having a go at Sumner. He wanted to be on the front foot rather than the back one. It was whilst thinking of previous jobs that he remembered an investigation from another force where the boyfriend gave an impassioned television plea for his missing girlfriend to come home or make contact; when in fact, he had killed her. The SIO had shown the recording to psychologist who was also a body language expert, who stated in his opinion the boyfriend was definitely lying. It was at that point they turned all their attention on him and finally found the body whereupon he confessed.

Jim approached Langton suggesting the scenario of using a psychologist if his enquiries failed to turn up anything substantial; Langton thought and gave a nod of approval indicating he would research it.

Jim got home; Jackie had left a message on the answer machine 'going to be late; sort a dinner out for yourself.' Jim made a sandwich, then instead of working he sat and watched a film; it got to 10 o'clock and still no sign of Jackie. Jim tidied up and was just going to bed when he heard the door go, Jackie came in looking whacked out; she threw her coat over the chair and just flopped down on the sofa. 'Oh Jim get me a large vodka.' 'Had a hard day sweetheart?' 'Oh god I could kick it all in and get an office job somewhere; I'm sick of dealing with kids who have been abused; no one gives a fuck about those poor kids.' Jim handed over the vodka and poured a scotch for himself. 'You hungry Jack?' 'No thanks; I grabbed something on the hoof.' She lay on Jims lap and drifted off as Jim stroked her hair.' Jim knew her pressures so just let her lay there and relax.

11

Jim then helped her to the bedroom where he eased her out of her clothes then she flopped into bed the curled up into the foetal position pulling the duvet around her. Jim lay beside her spooning her till morning. They both woke up at about the same time Jackie looked absolutely knackered. He looked at her thinking she has to get out of the department and on to something else. 'You want breakfast Jack?' She nodded. Jim then cooked breakfast with all the trimmings. They sat and ate, then Jackie began to surface and show signs of life, there was no good talking to her till she was ready as she would only bite his head off; she was awful till she had eaten and had coffee. Jim looked at her as he nodded; she smiled and nodded back which meant she had surfaced.

'You look whacked out babes.' 'Oh Jim I am just about burnt out.' 'Okay babes let's have a week-end away somewhere just us, no phones.' She smiled 'perhaps we could go to that spa again?' 'Okay leave it with me.' Jackie got showered and dressed; then asked why Jim wasn't dressed; he indicated he had an interview at 11am; he would go straight there. Also would give him a chance to research the spa week-end. He arranged the same spa hotel they had been to before. He texted Jackie 'get Friday afternoon off as before I've booked same hotel.'

CHAPTER FIVE

Jim arrived at Sandra's address he was just about to ring the bell when the door opened; although he had noticed how attractive Sandra was when he first saw her, but now she was fully made up and dressed in casual but smart clothes she looked ravishing.

'Please come in, what shall I call you?' 'Please, call me Jim.' Sandra led the way to the kitchen, she clicked on the kettle; the mugs were ready with instant coffee in. The kettle quickly boiled then she poured the water in and bought the mugs over.

'Thank you Sandra very kind of you.' Jim then went through some rapport building questions which broke down some of the tension; it also gave him a chance to admire Sandra's body which was his favourite pass time, watching beautiful women. Sandra had brilliant blue eyes which radiated as she smiled.

'Now Sandra the reason I'm here.' 'Look Jim I know who told you about me, it was Christine wasn't it?' 'I'm sorry Sandra I can't confirm or deny anything that was given to me in confidence the same as I won't reveal anything you tell me.' Sandra nodded. 'Okay tell me about Charles Sumner?' 'Look Jim, he is a nasty piece of work, he had a real nasty streak inside him. Yes I dated him and moved in with him, but then he became controlling and began forcing his will on me, he wouldn't let me go out on my own and when I did, he would grill me as to who I had met and where. If I didn't answer he would hit me.' 'How long did this go on for?' 'I suppose about a year, I used to go out with Christine and some friends, but then he stopped me from doing that. I could only ring her. I decided to run; I'd had enough of his violence. I found this place and just ran when he was at work. I have never heard from him again I changed my phone number so no could reach me. I knew he was looking for me as Christina told me when I called her, she said he was asking where I was. That's about it really.' 'You were frightened of him?' 'Not frightened I was petrified. He had such a vicious streak in him. I had the thought at one time he was going to kill me, as the look of hatred in his eyes as he hit me was evil.'

'This has been really helpful Sandra, thank you very much. I may have to come back so take my card and if you think of anything else please call me.' 'You won't tell him where I am?' 'I told you, this is in the strictest confidence.' 'Thank you, I was worried but, you have been so kind.' 'Please call me anytime if you need to talk; can I take your number just in case something else comes up.' Sandra nodded as she wrote her number down; she looked knowingly at Jim; she had seen him admiring her body and had absorbed his attention. Jim got to his car and thought; no I can't, that would be a potential disaster; although she has got a lovely body.

Jim got back to HQ's then went to see Langton enquiring if he had made any headway on the psychologist for the broadcasted plea. Langton informed he had the go ahead to use one that had been used on many such occasions. Jim stated he was going to interview Sumner later when he would request that he should be part of the reconstruction and the plea for Janet to come home, or at least make contact; Langton nodded in approval.

CHAPTER SIX

Jim knocked on the door of Sumner's house, the door opened there stood Sumner, Jim looked at him; he knew him from somewhere. He tried to wrack his brain, but had to let it go for the moment. 'Yes what you want.' 'Charles Sumner?' 'Yes who wants to know?' 'I am detective sergeant Broadbent I am reviewing the case of Janet Crosby can I come in and have a chat.' Sumner looked at Jim also with a hint of recognition.

Jim sat down and went over the normal questions in relation to his relationship with Janet including their friends, parties, nights out, including favourite restaurants. He wanted to get him on his side, but he didn't like him, there was something about him, he had a devious look in his eye, which Jim picked up on.

'Okay thanks; have you any idea where she might have gone?' 'Not a clue I went to work when I came home she had gone and haven't seen or heard of her since.' 'Okay thanks; we are considering a televised appeal for her to make contact or for anyone with information on her whereabouts to come forward; we would like you to be part of the appeal as it would give an impact to the audience; would you do that for us please?' Sumner had no choice as he looked at Jim. 'Of course I would be glad to help all I can.' Jim took a contact number for him.

Jim got back in his car and thought where the hell do I know him from, his mind was doing summersaults as he jumped from one thought to the other, but nothing came to the fore.

As soon as he saw him he got that sixth sense feeling, as the hairs were standing up on the back of his neck again; he kept saying to himself 'he is definitely not right, there is more to this.'

Jim went back to his old division and checked through the records for Sumner, but found nothing; he was clean. He then chatted to his old team; then he took Vicky to one side 'hi Vic how's Tim doing?' 'Yeah really good, he's put up some really tasty work lately.' 'Good well done; can you get him to check out the name Charles Sumner, he was the boyfriend of missing girl Janet Crosby, I think he might have done her in?' 'Okay will do.'

Jim then called it a day and went home and saw Jackie bopping in the kitchen again as she listened to music and cooking, she turned around hearing the door, and went to meet him planting a big kiss on him. 'Come here Jim' as she hugged him tightly 'right get changed dinners nearly ready.' She turned as she went back to the kitchen he patted her bum as she wiggled in response.

Dinner eaten Jim sat feeling full as they discussed their day's work. Jim then said 'don't forget tomorrow be here for 3pm, then we are on the road to the hotel.' 'Oh Jim good job you mentioned it I nearly forgot.'

Jim then sat at the table looking over his notes but, he just kept coming back to Sumner and where had he known him from but, he kept drawing a blank.

He then heard Jackie call him 'Broadbent get in here now.' Jim closed his book stretched and went into the bedroom where Jackie stood in her black Anne Summers kit, then another night of passion commenced. Jim had his head pulled between Jackie's thighs again, which was her favourite. The night was full of lust which ended in them both crashing till the morning.

Jim arose feeling exhausted from the night's exertion, but satisfied, he patted the bed but Jackie had already gone to work; she left a note saying she had forgotten to ask for the time off so had gone in early.

Jim looked at the mess in bedroom as he picked up the Anne Summers kit as he remembered the night. Then he showered and shaved and dressed as he made toast, he sat drinking coffee. He still couldn't get Sumner out of his head.

He went back to Sumner's house and made sure he was out, then went around the back and emptied paperwork from the dustbin. He hoped that his visit may have panicked him to throw something away. He put all the papers into a black sack then got into his car and drove to a quiet location; he sifted through the contents. It stank of decaying odours; then he found a piece of paper outlining some common land with a number of small wooded areas. Jim knew of it, it was on the edge of the Larches estate, popular with courting couples, dog walkers and ramblers.

Jim went back to HQ's he looked through the papers in the file of Janet Crosby to see if the previous search had included the common. He shuffled through the papers and discovered the search just fell short of the common. He went into to see Langton explaining his findings. They sat and poured over the benefits of undertaking a search of the area. Jim then said 'let's do the appeal then do the search afterwards, especially if the body language expert confirms Sumner is lying.' Langton nodded. 'Just to let you know guv I need to be away early as I'm taking Jackie away for a week-end, is that okay?' 'Bugger off then, see you Monday.' Jim smiled nodding; just as he was about to leave, Langton went for the scotch drawer Jim put his hand up stating he had a long drive. Langton nodded as he pulled out a glass, pouring himself one.

Jim arrived home and packed a track suit, tee shirts and a pair of slacks just in case they went out; but, knew it was unlikely. With that Jackie came home huffing and puffing

having run up the stairs. Jim said 'woe slow down babes.'
'Come on lets go Jim, I've escaped.'

The town roads were busy, but moving; then they hit open road which meant he could open it up a bit. The long meandering drive down to the hotel was like Déjà vu; the same girl was at the reception desk, she smiled welcoming them back. Once the itinerary was sorted they went to their room and unpacked the few clothes they had, then they went down for a quick swim before the evening buffet. The coolness of the water washed away some of the cobwebs. The evening meal consumed they had a quick drink then to bed, they were both knackered.

The morning came with a light fruit breakfast eaten; they had a massage. This was Jackie's favourite just being pampered under professional hands. She was pummelled and squeezed as she felt the tension leaving her shoulders.

Jim was undergoing the same procedure, but his mind was still on Sumner, he had to be the killer of Janet; he also kept thinking where he knew him from. The young masseuse said to him 'please try to relax sir, you're so tense.' Jim took the advice as he drifted off under the young expert hands. The masseuse then said 'that's better.' He could feel the tension being worked out of him. The hour was soon up the masseuse said 'please stay still for five minutes then drink a glass of water.' Jim lay there just day dreaming then got up, as he did so he felt light headed so did as he was told and drank a full glass of water.

He sat outside in the communal area waiting for Jackie; he sat marvelling at the wood panelling. He thought if only walls could speak. The old stately home must have seen some sights.

As he was day dreaming; Jackie came out of her treatment room. She looked completely different as she saw Jim she gave a relaxed radiating smile. They exchanged a kiss then, they both went for a swim releasing all their cares as they swam gently through the warm water; they hugged in the shallow end; then into the sauna room. They sat soaking up the steam and glowing. After the hot steam they had another swim before a shower then a casual walk around the grounds before lunch.

Jim checked the itinerary as he said 'you've got reflexology and I've got a sports massage; now that is going to hurt.' Jackie laughed 'good job; they wouldn't touch your feet.'

They went to lunch as they sat talking about their sessions and how relaxing it had been so far; they walked around the grounds admiring the well-kept gardens, Jim checked his watch, "oops better get going babes, see you later."

Jim arrived at the treatment room where he was met by a slender woman. Jim said 'be gentle with me please.' The woman laughed as Jim slipped off his track suit. Then lay on the treatment table in his shorts as the masseuse began her massage, slowly and gently at first then, she really kneaded the deep underlying muscle groups. Jim groaned under the pressure of the power being exerted on him. He wondered how such a slim girl could exert so much power. When she had finished he felt like he had done ten rounds in the ring. The masseuse again instructed him to lay still and to drink water before he stood up.

He met Jackie who looked radiant, 'wow I've never had one of those before; that was good, I never knew the feet could be so relaxing.' She looked at Jim who was really suffering from the massage, then she burst out laughing, 'oh Jim you look awful babe's.' 'Oh man she pounded me, she said in a couple of hours I would feel the benefit.' Then he burst out laughing as well.

The weekend went by too quickly. No sooner had Sunday arrived they were on the road home again. The journey back was relaxed as they chatted about all and nothing. When they arrived close to home the sun was setting and just getting dusk. Rather than cooking they grabbed a takeaway from their favourite Indian; then went to bed with a sense of satisfied exhaustion.

CHAPTER SEVEN

Langton had been utilising the force press officer making the most of his contacts to set up the date for the televised appeal. The media circus always liked these events, as it sold papers also the television viewers got to see the distraught family, and in this case the boyfriend as well.

Jim went to see Janet's parents; albeit they weren't too happy about sharing the platform with Sumner, but if it helped to make an impact they would; hoping beyond hope it might jog someone's memory and get them to come forward with any information or that Janet might see the appeal and make contact herself.

Jim and Langton had sat down with the psychologist and the press officer; he discussed the way the appeal should go. The psychologist suggested that the parents go first to make their own heartfelt appeal then let them go; once they had left the arena, get Sumner to make his appeal; he wanted certain questions asked, not direct impact questions, but subtle ones which should unnerve him which, if he was lying, the tell signs would show through.

The day of the appeal came, the seating arrangements were made with the parents on one side then Langton and lastly Sumner furthest away from the parents. Langton would open the proceedings then introduce the parents; he would let them go after their appeal, as the emotion would be too much for them to remain. Then he would introduce Sumner to the press where he would make his appeal.

The awaiting press were present with TV cameras; there were cables running everywhere attached to numerous microphones on the desk. The press officer then directed Langton on a countdown 3, 2, 1 he then pointed his finger at Langton.

'Good morning, I am Detective Superintendent Langton and the reason for this press conference is to appeal to the public for help in relation to a missing person Janet Crosby. Janet went missing from her boyfriend's house over a year ago now and hasn't been since. We would like anyone with any information to come forward. He then handed over to the parents; Mrs Crosby was so overcome with emotion she broke down in tears. Her husband took over saying 'please Janet if you're listening to this, please come home or just call to say you're alright please, or if anyone has any information let the police know.' Then he also broke down as they both left in tears holding each other for comfort as they were led out by a female officer.

Langton then introduced Sumner, who started off with a plea for Janet to come home or make contact, but the news hounds had already smelt a rat and began asking their own in-depth questions which was good. 'What time did she leave the house and what was she wearing? Did she walk or go by car? Had you argued before she left or fought beforehand? Was she dressed for work? Has she ever gone before?' The questions came thick and fast.

Even Jim could see he was lying he didn't need a psychologist to tell him that. The psychologist was out of sight watching from the wings and making notes on the questions asked and Sumner's reactions as he answered.

Jim could see by Sumner's hand movements and shuffling feet he was lying, his eyes were darting from place to place, his hand gestures making the subtle movements which coupled with the other movements showed he was lying; he had nowhere to hide, he was in the spotlight and he knew it.

He had tried as hard as he could to keep his composure, but he was on the point of losing it.

Sumner was getting more and more agitated as the interview went on; he started to lose his rag. Langton then interrupted the appeal before Sumner totally lost control and it became a circus, which would have lost the impact of the appeal to the public.

Sumner was really angry at Jim and Langton 'why did you let that go on like that? They're making out I have killed her well I haven't.' He then stormed off and went on the piss.

Langton the psychologist and Jim sat in Langton's office where they discussed the implications of the interview. The psychologist said 'well I don't think you need me to tell you that he is lying through his teeth.' Jim said 'he's guilty as sin; I just need something; a witness, something other than suspicion. I think we should tear his house apart.' Langton nodded, get a warrant and I'll organise the works including his garden to be dug.'

CHAPTER EIGHT

Jim arrived home to find Jackie lying on the floor; it looked as though she had fallen. He felt her pulse which was just about there, he tried to wake her, but she was out cold. He called an ambulance which arrived in minutes, she was rushed to hospital. Jim travelled behind in his car, but he couldn't keep up with the blue lights as the ambulance went through red lights as traffic pulled out of the way.

He arrived at A&E where he was shown to a side cubical where Jackie was lying looking as white as sheet with an oxygen mask on and a saline drip in the back of her hand.

The on duty doctor came in and shook Jims hand, he made enquires as to her general health and her eating habits; all he could say was, that they had been away on spa week-end and they had both eaten much the same during their stay. The consultant ordered an x-ray; Jackie was pushed down to the radiology dept. by a porter as Jim walked along-side her. She was still out like a light completely sparked out.

The radiologist was very attentive and before long she was heading back to the A&E. The consultant pushed the x-ray negatives into the holders and looked at the results, he then stated she had a broken leg as a result of her fall and had banged her head and was severely concussed; your partner needs an operation as the break is close to a major artery and she needs to go under now as matter of urgency. With that Jim signed the consent form for Jackie as she was rushed down to theatre.

Jim could do nothing as he paced up and down. He went outside where he called Langton informing him of the situation. 'Right Jim don't you dare come to work till this is sorted, I mean that, I don't want to hear about you working, look after Jackie. I'll sort matters out here, don't worry about your time I'll book you on and off. Right bugger off Jim, just update me when you can.' Jim thanked Langton as he was almost in tears as the emotion of the situation was hitting him.

Jim stayed the night just pacing up and down then sitting on a bench seat. He was just about to nod off when a drunken yobbo came in slurring his speech demanding to see a doctor now. One of the nurses told him to calm down. He grabbed hold of her and slapped her in the face. That was enough for Jim, he stood up and grabbed hold of the yobbo and took him outside by the scruff of the neck; on the way out he asked the nurse to call the police on 999.

Once outside Jim gave him a crunching blow to the guts which made yobbo curl up on the floor and spew up. Jim just stood beside him as he could hear the sound of police two tones in the distance. He knew the difference between the services sirens. Within a few minutes a police area car arrived; the driver acknowledged Jim, he informed him had taken the yob outside after he had slapped a nurse then he collapsed. The officer nodded he looked at the yobbo and indicated with spew and piss all over him he wasn't going to take him in his car so called for a police transit. When it arrived the yobbo was dragged inside and taken to the drunk cell.

Jim went back inside and saw the nurse who was grateful to Jim for intervening. He looked at her face which was glowing red having received a full-force slap. He said 'you're in the right placed to get that seen too,' as he laughed. The nurse nodded and tried to smile then went back to work holding a hand to her face.

The remainder of the night was uneventful as he drifted in and out of sleep. The nurse that had been slapped came to Jim and said 'Jackie is out of theatre she is doing fine and was in the recovery ward, I can sneak you in for five minutes then you better go home, she will be out of it for some time yet.' Jim nodded as he was sneaked into the ward; he looked at Jackie with all different tubes and devices coming out of her mouth and nose. She looked so peaceful. Jim held her hand for five minutes then his time was up.

Jim arrived home where he crashed setting his phone alarm for 4 hours. No sooner had he crashed when the alarm went off. He got up and called Jackie's D/I informing him of the emergency; stating he would update him later on her condition and visiting hours.

He grabbed a bite to eat then went back to the hospital; by this time Jackie had been moved to a normal ward. Jim took the lift to the top floor. He spoke with the ward sister who smiled and said 'ah Sir Galahad I heard how you helped out last night.' He smiled 'how's the patient?' 'She's fine she's in room number 5, just take as long as you want, but don't let her move too much she's had a big operation and needs all the rest she can get.' Jim thanked the ward sister and went into the room. Jackie looked so peaceful; there were fewer tubes than before so her face was more visible.

He sat on a chair next to her bed and held her hand then stroked her forehead. After about 20 minutes the tea trolley came around, he winked at the assistant and said 'I'd love a coffee sweetheart.' 'Shhh, I'm not supposed to; here you are my love and one for your wife.' That struck a chord with Jim as he looked at Jackie. Then thought; she could be my wife.

Jackie began to stir as she tried to lick her lips which were so dry, she tried to say something, but her tongue was so swollen from lack of moisture. Jim picked up one of the plastic cups with a bendy straw in; he placed the end in her mouth as she drew the moisture up. She only took in a little sip; it was just enough to enable her to put a couple of words together. As she looked at Jim; 'what am I doing here? Where am I Jim? Why am I in bed?' Jim stroked her head and said 'shhh babes you're in hospital, you've had an operation, but you're okay now, just rest.' Jackie smacked her lips together as she frowned; Jim knew she was trying to form some kind of questions, she continued to smack her lips which were still so dry from the lack of moisture. Jim held the plastic cup and placed the end of the straw in her mouth again as she took another sip.

Jackie's head was still fuzzy as she continued frowning; then said in a half awake husky voice 'the last thing I remember was being in the flat; what am I doing here?' As if saved by the bell one of the nursing staff came in to take her pulse and blood pressure and give Jackie her medication. Jim stepped outside for five minutes where he took in copious amounts of air breathing deeply. He rubbed his hands over his eyes feeling the tiredness creeping up on him. The nurse came out and said 'she needs to rest as she is tired.' Jim nodded as he went back in the room; Jackie by this time had drifted back to sleep he stroked her head then kissed her on the forehead and went home.

Once he arrived home he called Langton to update him; then rang Jackie's D/I who enquired when she could receive visitors. Jim stated in a day or so, but would let him know.

Jim then undressed and collapsed on the bed and slept for a few hours catching up on much needed sleep. When he woke up he quickly showered then went back to the hospital. When he entered the room the he saw a completely different Jackie; the anaesthetic had worn off and she had colour in her cheeks; this was a complete contrast to earlier. Although still tired she was not as groggy as she had been in the morning.

'Oh Jim what happened I can't seem to find out?' 'It appears you must have fallen awkwardly and broke you're leg.' Jackie smiled 'Oh Jim I was so tired I just wanted to get home I must have tripped over that bloody door mat, that's the last thing I remember.' 'Well you're okay now that'll teach you to get pissed' as he smiled. Jackie slapped his arm as she laughed.

The anaesthetic having worn off brought the pain on; as a result she was administered pain killers.

The doctor examined Jackie then confirmed she would be okay to go home in a day or so the plaster cast was fully set. It was all the way up above the knee; it was the concussion that was worrying them; they wanted to monitor her for another 24 hours.

Jim then let everyone know she was okay for visitors, but not all to arrive at once, suggesting that someone chart the numbers and times. Slowly the visitors arrived which cheered her up with flowers and chocolates.

CHAPTER NINE

The warrant obtained for Sumner's address the workforce went about a full house search but nothing was found. State of the art heat seeking and x-ray devices were used to walk the garden, but disappointingly it turned out to be a negative search.

The search of the common was the last resort. Langton nodded as he looked at Jim saying 'it's a massive area it will take weeks to search; okay let's do it.' Langton called the special unit which dealt with searching and asked the head to issue a press release for volunteers.

The day of the search came as hundreds of volunteer's turned up wearing an array of bright coloured clothing; most were ramblers; although there were others underdressed for the occasion, but nonetheless willing people.

The head of the search unit had been involved in many searches and knew that refreshments would be needed. He had arranged a tea wagon and enlisted the Women's Royal Volunteer Service (WRVS) to help. This group of women loved this kind of occasion, as it beat the cream cake competitions and jumble sales.

The teams were divided so volunteers were spaced between officers as some people could get over enthusiastic and race ahead; a straight line was necessary to achieve the best search pattern.

The multi-coloured line began the walk through the woods. The bracken was hard work as the thick stems were entwined with brambles causing unbreakable trip hazards; but slowly and methodically the search continued until midday when the tea wagon arrived; the WRVS served tea and coffee; on a separate table ready-made sandwiches were handed out. Once fed and foddered the search continued; in total it took 3 weeks to complete, but nothing was found. Jim was so disappointed; it had been a long shot which had to be completed; although he had hoped for a better result.

Jim continued to work half days until Jackie could get up and about, although then he never worked beyond his eight hours till she was strong enough. Slowly Jackie was getting sturdier on her feet aided by crutches. The concussion had left her with a few balance problems which was not ideal while trying to walk on crutches.

The physio treatment after the plaster came off was slowly helping, although that too came to an end after six weeks, so it was down to Jim to encourage her and then join in with the exercises, much to the laughter of Jackie. Slowly she was back to work, then back to full time.

CHAPTER TEN

Jim could do nothing else; albeit he was convinced Sumner was Janet's killer. His arrogance and the way he had reacted at the press conference made him think he was the one; he had nothing to go on other than his intuition. He had to leave it until something else came to light; as a result the incident inquiry was being scaled down.

Jim had suggested some kind of surveillance on Sumner to see who he was meeting, but that was knocked on the head. The force unit that conducted surveillance was under pressure and had to provide the top cases with their service. They used a graph of importance; all the jobs that didn't fit the criteria were not even considered; those that were then underwent another means test till finally the top 3 were chosen, so as soon as one was completed, they moved onto the next.

Jim decided now that Jackie was better he would do some observations on Sumner himself to try and establish some kind of intelligence against him. He would sit in his car just monitoring his movements and tried to undertake a one car follow, but that was near impossible without showing out.

He eventually had to give up it was too time consuming, plus Jackie was asking questions about his late nights out.

He just needed that one piece of information or evidence that would give him the ammunition to get Sumner to the interview room. He couldn't interview him as a suspect without something concrete; well not the hard type of questioning he wanted to put him through.

CHAPTER ELEVEN

Jim sat at his desk contemplating where and how to move the investigation forward. He opened his A4 book and began re-reading all his notes; no matter how much he read and re-read his notes nothing came to light no spark.

He sat back in his chair and put his hands behind his neck interlocking his fingers and closing his eyes just hoping that something, some spark of inspiration would spring from somewhere; but nothing did. He looked around the office seeing no one was in, said out loud 'fuck it, I know it's him,' then he slammed the desk.

That didn't make him feel any better he just needed the relief from the deep frustration he was feeling. He continued to sit at his desk still hoping for the spark to ignite from somewhere; when Langton called him into his office. 'Yes guv?' 'Close the door Jim.' Jim closed the door as Langton poured two fingers of scotch handing Jim one. 'How's Jackie?' 'She's fine thanks nearly back to full fitness.' 'That's good news, must have been a shock to find her that way.' 'Yeah it was; that bloody door mat, you know we had discussed changing it a number of times, but never got around to it.' Jim finished his scotch as he put his hand over his glass as Langton went to refill it. 'Need a clear head. This enquiry has got my senses going again, Sumner definitely is the murderer, we need a body or some other information; I know he is her killer.'

Jim thought he would re contact Sandra Rose to go over the places they went, and anything else that might give him a clue as to where Janet maybe.

Having made arrangements he knocked on Sandra's door, she opened it, he thought wow! As she stepped back so Jim could enter the hallway. She was wearing a short skirt and low cut top. 'Would you like coffee?' 'Yes please.' He watched her as she walked to the kettle and put coffee in the mugs making no effort to hide her figure as she over emphasized her motions. She could feel Jim's eyes on her and was relishing the attention.

She bought the cups to the table and leaned forward purposely as her top opened she put one cup down as she smiled and attempted to cover up her ample cleavage. Jim nodded and smiled.

Sandra sat down and cupped her hands around her mug and smiled at Jim. 'Okay Sandra I want you to think about the places you went to with Sumner, anywhere, lonely spots somewhere special, somewhere just you and him went?' 'That's quite difficult as he never took me anywhere nice. Oh just a minute we did go sometimes to a spot near some woods he liked playing games and pretending, you know play-acting, pretending he was the game keeper and me Lady Chatterley.' He saw her smile and colour up as she drank some more coffee. Her eyes were bright and glistening as she peered over her mug. 'Which woods were they?' 'Near that big estate, you know the big shooting estate.' 'Did you agree to those play acting games?' She smirked as she nodded and coloured up again. She changed the subject; 'more coffee?' Jim nodded as he smiled at her. She was inwardly enjoying his attention on her as she got up allowing her top to billow open again, but this time she made no attempt to cover up. Jim was fixated by the sight of her well-endowed breasts. She then went to the sink. She washed up the mugs; Jim got up and stood next to her as he dried the mugs.

33

He had to fight the thought of grabbing her but, instead he returned to the table. He picked his pen as he opened his A4 book. 'Could that be the Larches Estate?' 'Yes that's the one, now you've mentioned the name, I remember it.' 'Any chance of showing me the place you went? Was it always the same place each time?' 'No problem; finish our coffee and I'll show you.' 'Yes mam.' As Jim mocked her jokingly, she responded 'now Mellor's behave. Although I think I will have to change, on the other hand I won't.' They finished their coffee as Jim went to the toilet; then they set off.

Jim couldn't take his eyes off her long legs as she tried to pull down what little material there was of her skirt. Jim laughed 'perhaps you should have changed.' 'He used to like me in short skirts.' 'Well I Can see why, you have a lovely figure, very nice mam.' 'Well thank you Mellor's.' 'You better be careful I might turn into Mellor's.' 'I bet you could.' She was now openly flirting with him; as they sent comments back and forth laughing as they went. Jim thought, no I can't; but what gorgeous legs she has; no fuck off Jim, down boy.

As they approached the estate Sandra directed Jim to a narrow entrance, 'this is it, in there.' Jim carefully drove into the secluded entrance track. 'He would stop about here; then well you know.' Jim smiled 'yes Mrs Chatterley.' They laughed as Jim got out of the car and thought; could Janet be buried in here somewhere. He began walking a short way into woods, but couldn't see anything obvious. He needed to seek the help of the game keeper.

Sandra sat in the car as she watched Jim walk into the woods, as she thought he is so nice, and tall with it. She liked tall men and a nice bum. Her mind went to the games in the woods that she had played; then thought, it would be nice with Jim; she smiled to herself thinking of how she would like him to make a move on her. Then she thought of Sumner, as sadness came across her face.

34

Jim returned to the car to see Sandra smiling at him, he got into the car as he looked at her and said 'what?' 'Oh just imagining you as Mellor's.' 'Now, now behave.' 'I suppose I must you being a copper.' 'Mmm; perhaps another time.' 'You promise.' 'When this is over, I'll pop around for a coffee.' 'That would be very nice.' Jim started the car as he drove back to Sandra's house dropping her off. He thought fuck me she's a right little raver, what a body.

The following morning Jim went to the game keeper's cottage as he drove along the lengthy drive negotiating the speed bumps and potholes, he noticed the pheasants on the edge of the woods; he also saw a herd of fallow deer grazing in the field. He then thought how much he missed the country scene.

He knocked the door of the keeper's cottage; June the keeper's wife answered it wiping her hands on her apron. Jim introduced himself asking if Brian was about. June invited him and called Brian on the 2 way radio. June came back 'he'll be 10 minutes or so, would you like a coffee while you wait? Jim nodded 'white no sugar please.'

Jim admired the décor with an array of shooting paraphernalia. He had noticed the kennels when he entered which were empty so presumed the dogs were out with Brian. Jim made small talk with June about the idyllic way of life that she and Brian lived. June smiled 'it looks good from the outside, it's not the best paid job, but Brian loves it.'

June looked out of the window as she saw Brian's Land Rover coming down the long drive, 'here's Brian now.' Jim finished his coffee as he heard the rattling diesel engine of the Land Rover pull up outside. Brian entered as Jim introduced himself. June made more coffee asking if she should go. Jim shook his head 'you're fine no problem.'

Jim then explained his reason for being there as he spoke of the missing girl and the suggestion the suspect had visited the estate at night with another woman. Brian took out a reduced sized map of the estate asking if he knew where. Brian spread the map on the table. Brian pointed to the location of the cottage as Jim tried to get his bearings of where he had been with Sandra. He backtracked to the main road re-tracing as best he could the route he had taken to the cottage; after a while he was sure he had found it. 'Right just here, I'm sure that's' it, as he pointed to the track he had driven into. 'How often do you go there?' 'Not very often, it's part of the estate, but is not used for shooting, apart from deer stalking. Jim's ears pricked up 'is that high seat or stalking?' 'High seat only, why do you shoot?' 'I used to, but what with work and failed a marriage I had to give it up.' 'If you fancy sitting in a high seat sometime then give me a call, you can borrow one of my rifles.' 'I might just take you up on that.' 'Please do, as the deer herds are growing and need to be thinned out.'

'Right come on then I'll take you to the place you pointed out; we can drive through the woods it will give you a chance to see the size of the place.' Jim climbed into the Land Rover as Brian was putting his Spaniels in the kennels; he smelt all kinds of odours. 'Excuse the mess but, it's a working vehicle.' Jim smiled as he nodded. The hard springs of the Land Rover jostled Jim from side to side as Brian went across the rough edges of the fields till he reached an entrance to the woods; the mown grass rides were less rough. It wasn't long before they reached the area Jim had pointed out on the map; Jim confirmed it was the place.

Brian stopped and got out. He looked at the tyre marks on the grass 'were you here before?' 'Yeah I popped in yesterday to confirm it was the place.' 'Oh that's okay; I thought it may have been poachers.' 'Is it a big problem?' 'Sometimes; it varies, I just have to watch for signs then try and get the police involved.'

Brian walked the area as he kicked over the leaves from the fall he then stood and looked at a patch he had just kicked over. He pondered then moved on kicking over more leaves, he then returned to the spot he had been to earlier. Jim said 'what you looking at?' 'How long has this girl been missing?' 'About 15-16 months; why?' 'This patch here looks disturbed; it's not as firm as the rest.' Jim looked at the ground and bent down as he pressed the soil with his hand. 'Okay thanks I need to get this looked at by a search team.'

Jim went back to HQ where he liaised with Langton who arranged for a search team and SOCO to meet Jim there the following morning.

CHAPTER TWELVE

The search team arrived at the woods together with SOCO. Brian and Jim showed them the suspect site; then the long careful process began as the earth was moved. The excavation was painstakingly slow; it had to be to ensure potential evidence wasn't missed. Slowly the earth began to reveal an odour in keeping with rotting flesh. The earth was moved more slowly with trowels rather than shovels. The smell was becoming ranker the closer the unearthing got. The suspense was growing with Jim hoping it was the body of Janet.

Then one of the team shouted it's a fucking dog, a dead dog. Jim thought 'fuck it.' As much as he was relieved for the Crosby's, he so wanted it to be Janet so, he could try and gain evidence to convict Sumner.

Jim called Langton telling him to stand down, as it was a dog buried and not the victim. Langton was also disappointed as he wanted the grave to be the site of Janet Crosby.

Jim thanked the team then went to the keeper's cottage to find Brian. June met him at the door looking worried. She invited him in as she took the kettle off the Aga and made coffee. 'Brian is just on his way back. Is it bad news?' 'No it's a dog; someone's buried a dog in the woods.' 'Oh that's a relief; the thought of a dead body in the woods frightened me.' 'You can relax now.' June looked out of the window, 'oh here we go; Brian's just coming down the drive.'

Brian arrived kicking his boots off at the door, he shook Jim's hand as he looked enquiringly at Jim 'you can relax it was a dog, someone's buried a dog in the woods.' 'Phew that's a relief; that'll please the boss he was getting worried; so was June.' June smiled as she poured water into Brian's coffee cup. They continued their small talk for an hour then Jim got up to leave. Brian said 'have you got a few minutes?' 'Yeah, why?' 'I just want you to check my rifle is zeroed in for you; then I will leave that one for you. I can use one of my others.' 'What calibre is it?' 'It's a Steyr .243 with a Zeiss scope; it's a nice set up.' Brian opened his big gun cabinet and handed Jim the rifle, he had a peak into the cabinet and said 'you starting a war?' As they both laughed at the number of guns he had. Jim racked open the bolt confirming it was unloaded. Brian said 'that's what I like to see good safety procedure.' 'That's how I was trained.'

They went out into the yard where Brian had a target already set out at 100yds. Jim rested over the Land Rover bonnet and got the feel of the rifle; he tested the trigger pull with a dry fire. It was a light pull, which he hadn't been used to.

Jim operated the bolt then slid one round into the chamber as he actioned the bolt forward. Even this felt good as he recalled the days gone by. He softened his breathing then steadied his hands as he took a deep breath then released it then took a half breath, as he settled the crossed hairs, then squeezed back the trigger, then bang. The muzzle flip sent the rifle barrel up, when it settled he was only an inch to the left of the bull; with an adjustment he was spot on.

Jim thanked Brian as he proofed the rifle then handed it back, 'I will be in touch when I get some free time, I would love to sit in a high seat for an hour or so.' 'Any time Jim your more than welcome.'

Jim headed back to HQ's where he sat with Langton discussing the way forward; but other than arresting

Sumner   with the anticipated no comment reply he had no other lines of enquiry to complete.

Langton wanted Jim to get Sumner interviewed to at least let him know he was a suspect.

Jim agreed; the following morning he would invite him into the police station, if he failed to attend voluntarily he would arrest him.

Sumner arrived at the police station the following day with a brief. At that point there was no point in playing the voluntary side of things, so formally arrested him on suspicion of murder. The interview went as expected with no comments being made. Sumner was smirking at Jim, not taunting him just enough to let him know that Jim had nothing on him. This pissed Jim off as he liked to interview from a position of strength, not weakness. He had no alternative, other than to release Sumner.

CHAPTER THIRTEEN

Janet's parents were still hoping their daughter was alive, but the not knowing was painful as they had no closure. They had been preparing themselves for the worst, knowing that one day her body would be found. If she turned up alive it would be a joyous celebration, but in the back of their minds it was her being found dead which was so hurtful to them.

The months went by with nothing coming forward, no sign of Janet; she had completely disappeared without any trace.

Jim still had Sumner in his sights, but he had nothing to challenge him on, the house and garden search proved negative. Janet's mobile phone was switched off; not a trace of her was found, no clothing or belongings, nothing.

He then thought of trying to get Sandra involved by getting her back with Sumner, then thought better of it; anyway she was so scared of him she wouldn't agree to it.

Jim sat in with Langton discussing scenarios of how to move it forward and get evidence on Sumner, but with no body, they were struggling to come up with something to move the investigation forward.

They even considered an undercover female officer who would show a liking for him and try to get close to him and get him to spill the beans; but he knew it would be inadmissible.

They continued to discuss ways of getting to Sumner but everything fell by the wayside, they were just about to put it to bed, when Jim said out of the blue 'I've got it, yes I've fucking got it!' This has been in the back of my mind ever since I first saw him; 'I knew I knew him from somewhere.' Langton just looked at him waiting for the punch line; then saw the knowing smile across his face. 'Come on then spit it out.' 'Some years ago I dealt with a nasty assault on a young girl she had been left for dead, but she survived, although she knew who the assailant was she wouldn't name him. It was when I was looking at her pictures in her bedroom in her parent's house, that I saw the picture of her in the arms of a man, but she refused to name him, or say if he was the assailant. That picture was Sumner, I'm sure of it. If I can retrace the steps and find her, then see after all this time if she would be prepared to name him; perhaps I can get him that way.'

Langton nodded 'it's a long shot, but give it a go, we have nothing else.'

Jim had to try and remember out of all the cases he had dealt with over the years, the name of the girl; it was so long ago. He was sure it was Debbie, although her last name was evading him.

Jim arrived at Central, although the number of people he needed to talk too had either moved-on; some had retired and taken all the knowledge they had with them.

He went to the archive section, but without a last name he was buggered. There was no way he could search the index with just a Christian name. He was on the verge of calling it a day when he saw Trevor. Trevor had been in the intelligence section about the time he had been dealing with the case. 'Hey Trevor, you got a moment mate?' 'Yes Jim,' 'you fancy a coffee Trev?' 'Sounds good to me; you buying?' Jim smiled 'yes mate it's on me.'

They sat in the canteen discussing old times and the way things were today, compared to days gone by. Jim then asked him to cast his mind back to the case of Debbie he was sure that was here name. Trevor sat and listened; he

42

bowed his head and put his head in his hands 'I do remember it, poor girl she only just made it; yes hold on a minute, don't say a word.' He sat with his head in his hands; Jim could hear the cogs whizzing around in his head.

Jim went to get more coffee and came back with a couple of pre packed ham sandwiches. 'I'm nearly there Jim, it's on the tip of my tongue; come on, come on.' Trevor opened his pre-packed sandwich, then took a big bite and slurped his coffee. 'Sorry Jim, it's there mate not far away, I just need a little bit more time, it'll come to me just talk about something else for a minute.'

They sat chatting and mulling over the good times, and how close Trevor was to his final retirement date. Jim then thought once he was gone all his information would be gone as well. 'It's no good Jim, give me your number I will call you when it comes to me.' They shook hands and parted. They got to the door and about to go in different directions, when Trevor said 'Anderson, Debbie Anderson that's her name, bloody hell mate that took some dragging up from depths of beyond.' 'That's it Trev, as soon as you said the name, it came back, thanks mate, you're a star.' They shook hands again as they smiled and went their different ways.

Jim then went back to the intelligence section and punched in the name Debbie Anderson, but nothing came up, he sat pondering; he was sure it was Anderson he then had a flash of inspiration as he tried Andersen. He punched that in and up came the file; Jim read it as the case came flooding back. He found the archive number and retrieved the hard copy file.

The big manila folder was overflowing with statements and other documents including his final report. He signed the file out and took it home. He opened it on the table and read his closing report. He sat back as he put his hands behind his head, then closed his eyes as he went back to when he interviewed Debbie; it was some 7 years ago, she was a young girl only about 17 very pretty. But her face had been bruised and battered from the assault and her neck swollen from being strangled and left for dead.

He re-read her statement which described how she received her injuries, but had refused to name the person involved she was so frightened of him, he recalled interviewing her at her parent's home and looking at the photograph of her and Sumner, but she refused to name him as the assailant.

Then he thought if he could get her to name him now and then get Sandra Rose to name him as well regarding his assaults on her, he could start to build up a pattern and at least get something to interview him on.

Jim checked the address of Debbie, but there was no phone number. The next morning he arrived at her parents address. He knocked the door there was no reply, so knocked on the neighbour's door, the occupant an elderly woman informed him that occupants had moved somewhere a couple of years ago. The current occupant worked all different hours so it would be a hard job to catch them in. 'Do you know the new occupants names?' 'There's only one, I think he's called Martin, but we hardly ever see each other, even when we do it's just a nod or a wave.' Jim thanked her then wrote a brief note with his phone number on, then posted in his letter box.

Jim called Sandra and requested another visit as he had a proposition. 'Now, now Mellor's.' Jim laughed as he said 'I think I may need a chaperone.' 'You might do' as she laughed, 'look I'm about to finish early as I was going to have my hair done, but my appointment has been cancelled.' 'Okay say half an hour.' 'Yes that's fine I'll be home by then, if not, just wait outside I won't be far away.'

Jim left it a bit longer than the half hour; as he was driving he thought fuck me if she gave a statement, as well as Debbie he could be on a winner. He arrived and rang the doorbell. The door opened as he saw Sandra stood in a tight low cut sweater and track suit bottoms. She beamed a welcoming smile as she stepped back allowing Jim inside. 'You don't need your hair done it looks very nice as it is.' 'Oh very smooth Detective Sergeant Broadbent.' Jim smiled as she showed him to the kitchen. 'Coffee, Jim?' 'Please you probably remember white no sugar.' Sandra nodded.

Jim admired her bum as she filled the kettle; she made sure she was expressing her sexuality. She had been without a man for so long, although not looking for anyone, Jim seemed like a nice man, probably married, but she didn't care as she continued to flirt with him.

'Now what is this proposal, is it a ring?' As she laughed; 'now, now you; no it's more serious than that.' Sandra's face then changed as she looked worried 'Oh my god he knows where I live?' 'No not that, I told you all this is confidential.' 'Okay what then?' 'Look Sandra I'm looking for someone called Debbie, she was a previous girlfriend of Sumner before you; if I find her and she is willing to make a statement against Sumner for the injuries he inflicted on her, would you make a statement against him as well? If we got two previous statements regarding his demeanour to women and his loss of temper and violence we could stand a chance of getting a conviction against him.'

Sandy brought the coffee over to the table, then said 'look Jim I'm so scared of him he was so violent towards me and his temper is really vicious; when he loses it, he goes berserk he goes into a red mist, and just lashes out. I will have to think about this, it has all sorts of connotations; what if he doesn't get convicted; even if he did and wasn't sent to prison where does that leave me?' 'That's the reason why I needed to talk to you face to face.' 'Look if the other girl Debbie makes a statement I will think about it, but I won't promise anything because my life is back on track now and I'm doing fine, I don't want to be looking over my shoulder every five minutes wondering if he has sent someone to keep me quiet.' Jim nodded 'okay I understand I will let you know how it goes with Debbie.'

45

Sandra cupped her hands around her coffee mug then looked at Jim and said out of the blue 'are you married Jim?' 'No divorced for a while now; why?' 'She smiled at him 'oh just wondering; more coffee?' 'Please.' Sandra leaned forward as she stood up pushing the twins forward on purpose as she made no attempt to hide her cleavage. Jim smiled as he half closed his eyes looking longingly at her body. Sandra accepted the attention having lustful thoughts. He watched as she washed up the cups and saw her wiggling her bum on purpose for him.

Another mug of coffee was bought to the table where they sat and chattered about various topics. Jim looked around the kitchen admiring how clean it looked, then commented on the décor and cleanliness. Jim then thanked Sandra for the coffee and stood to leave as Sandra stood up and stretched on purpose pushing her ample breasts towards him. He couldn't avert his eyes as he nodded knowingly. She smiled as she showed him to the door, she turned and said 'thanks for calling around Jim; you must come around for a spot of dinner sometime?' 'That would be nice.' Then she reached up and kissed him on the cheek then squeezed his arm. Jim smiled as he left the house.

Once in his car he thought fucking hell Broadbent what body she's got you must be slipping, but then thought of Jackie and came back down to earth.

The occupant who Jim left the note for contacted him and gave him a forwarding address for Debbie, but no phone number.

Jim went back to see Langton to update him on the progress or in this case the lack of it. 'I've just got Debbie to see and try to persuade her to make a statement, if that fails Sandra won't make one, she's shit scared of him.' Langton opened his bottom drawer and poured two fingers of scotch in each glass they chinked glasses as they toasted the hopeful conclusion to the case.

'Jim, you just need to be aware the spooks are making more noises about another job for you.' 'What now; where, who, when?' 'I don't know any more than that; Yvonne called this morning to say another important issue has arisen and your talents may be needed. Are you sure you're not giving her one?' 'No guv, I've told you she's 'M' she's way out of my league.' Langton looked suspiciously at him through half closed eyes. Jim smiled at him as he drank his scotch, then nodded to him as he got up and opened the door; leaving Langton wondering if he was, or wasn't.

Jim thought as he walked out 'what do the spooks want now?' He wracked his brain for scenarios, but no point; it could be anything, so no good in trying to second guess.

Jim checked the phone book for Debbie's number; she could have married and changed her surname by now. He couldn't find anything under Andersen, he then checked directory inquiry's, still nothing. Although it was getting common for people to just use mobile phones these days.

Jim got up early the next day and drove the twenty or so miles to Debbie's address; he sat outside of the house in Brompton village, number 32, Brompton cottages, which was in amongst a long row of cottages all constructed the same; they looked as if they had at one time been tied cottages probably attached to the village farm. The whole row as in darkness, but then as if there was a communal alarm all the lights of the cottages virtually came on at once.

Jim watched as the activity in 32 came alive, he gave it a few minutes, and then knocked the door. It was opened sheepishly as he saw a young woman striking in appearance and instantly recognisable as Debbie answered, then he heard the sound of a male voice in the background inquiring who it was.

Jim introduced himself to Debbie as she nodded and smiled in recognition of him. Jim asked if he could make an appointment to come back when more convenient. Then the male person appeared at the door, a big muscular guy, who looked like he could handle himself. Jim was expecting a confrontation, but the guy asked him in.

Jim then outlined the reason why he was there and understood if they wanted him to come back. Debbie looked at her husband who just nodded then said 'no carry on we can make time for this.' Jim went into the reason for his visit including and most importantly Janet Crosby, who had been a girlfriend of Sumner's after Debbie; she had been missing for some 15 months. He then discussed the issues of her assault and asked if Sumner was the assailant when he investigated the assault against her. Her husband Craig looked a Jim, then said 'I know all about him, Debbie told me how he used to beat her up, it was all I could do not to go round and give him a good hiding, a taste of his own medicine, but Debbie stopped me.' 'I must say you look like you can handle yourself?' 'Yes I train as often as I can, and I'm a black belt in Karate.' Jim nodded 'The crunch is Debbie we need to get something on Sumner for his violence against women. If we could get enough women to come forward it would be enough to place him before the court on a suspected murder charge, as the coincidence of Janet missing, and him having such a violent temper which he inflicted on you, and nearly killed you, would be enough to throw suspicion on him for the murder of Janet. When you were assaulted battered and bruised you refused to say who your assailant was, was it Sumner?'

Debbie looked at Craig who shrugged his shoulders and said 'Debbie, this is your call, I know how sacred you were before we met, but he won't hurt you now, he won't get through me. This would also be the way of paying him back for what he did to you.' Debbie looked at her husband Craig then looked at Jim then said. 'Give me your number let me have a think about it, I will let you know.' Jim handed Debbie his card then said 'was it him who hurt you; she welled up as she hugged Craig and nodded; then started crying. 'Look Debbie I know this is a cliché, but we need to prevent him from doing this again.' Debbie nodded then said 'I'll call you.'

Jim got to HQ's where he saw Langton and updated him. Langton nodded then said 'you need to be here later this afternoon about 2.30 as Yvonne will be here with your next assignment.' 'Any idea what or where it is?' 'Not a clue.' Jim nodded then went back to his desk and began looking at the paperwork; he went over and over the same old ground looking for inspiration seeking something he may have missed, but nothing came to light.

He sat and pondered thinking if he got Debbie and Sandra to make statements against Sumner for ABH or GBH then, if CPS would agree to similar fact evidence being used to show how he was a controlling person, who had used violence on women before, then using Sandra and Debbie as his previous victims he could, if they agreed charge him with Janet's murder. He rubbed his hands together then made a loud noise as he clapped them together. Then smiled to himself saying 'Sumner, your mine my old son.'

Debbie hugged Craig and sobbed for a couple of minutes then Craig said 'this is up to you Deb's I will stand by you either way.' 'Thanks, you are my rock Craig, I feel so safe in your arms.' They then began to rush around getting ready for work.

Debbie spent the day thinking and mulling over the issues involved in making a statement. Her mind was on nothing else, she just kept welling up each time she felt his hands around her throat. She had seen a film the night before it happened when a woman was strangled and played dead by flopping her arms and going limp which made the assailant believe she was dead, and then he let her go. This had saved her as she did the same and it worked; Sumner had left her lying in the street, he ran off when he heard noises. She had been found by a passer-by who called the police and an ambulance.

The tears continued to fall as she thought of that time and how she nearly died at the hands of Sumner. She had met Craig about a year later. They met in the gym where he trained on weights; she did aerobics and used the running machine. She had seen his physique he was muscular and tall. She had anticipated him being arrogant, but he was gentle and kind. They started dating then after a whirlwind romance they married. She told Craig about Sumner, he was fuming and wanted to go and sort him out, but she had persuaded him not to. It was about the time that Craig was training for his black belt in karate. He used to train so hard and she saw the power in him as he practiced at home. He was so pleased when he obtained it after the long hours of dedication.

Debbie never told Craig the full truth about Sumner; it would have ripped him apart to know what he had done to her.

CHAPTER FOVRTEEN

Jim sat in with Langton as Yvonne was shown into his office; they both stood as Yvonne shook both their hands and smiled greeting them both as she gently squeezed Jim's hand.

She looked ravishing; her business suit was pristine, she unbuttoned her jacket as she sat down showing offer her brilliant white blouse which was being pushed forward by her ample assets. Yvonne relished the attention she was getting from both Langton, but more so from Jim; she crossed her legs then tugged at the hem line, but it was fixed with no material left to cover her exposed knee.

The pleasantries were exchanged, as Langton looked at Jim then Yvonne; as he sat wondering is he giving her one or not? Jim sat poker faced as did Yvonne, not giving anything away.

Yvonne opened her briefcase taking out a manila folder with top secret stencilled in red across the top. Jim thought why put that on it, as it only makes people more nosey as to what's inside.

Yvonne opened the folder, clearing her throat 'okay guy's this is another issue that has arisen and involves our American cousins again. They have uncovered a plot by a terrorist group to assassinate someone from the UN council. Which member we don't know yet? That is your job Jim, working with Barney, he is our trusted CIA operative.' Jim interrupted 'when?' 'We don't know; there are background checks going on at this time and operatives all over the world are listening into radio and phone messages. It maybe we will pick something up, then we won't need you, but on the other hand if we don't; it will be down to us and the Americans to protect all the UN council members as the meeting is in 2 months-time in New York, so we are on a short fuse.' Langton said 'But surely you must have agents all over the world, including undercover operatives involved with all kinds of terror organisations who could handle this?' 'Yes we do, but there are break-away cells being started up all the time, so we need to try and infiltrate the newest ones. The one making this threat is from one of those new terror groups.' 'Where do I come in I can't infiltrate any organisation?' 'Quite so Jim, nor would we expect you to do that; what we want you to do is get back in the good books of Carol-Anne, she is now working on the desk where new terror groups are looked at. We believe one of her colleagues has gone rogue, we may want you to work with her.' 'She was under the control of Barney surely he can do that, can't he?' 'Yes she was, but a big re-shuffle was made, and now she can't openly mix with him due to different areas of work, it would not be seen as protocol.' 'But she can mix with a Brit cop?' 'Yes she can, you won't be seen as an internal threat; just an across the pond love affair.' 'Okay when; and how long for?' 'Probably next week, I'll let you know; we will top up your credit card account again, is it the same number?' Jim confirmed it was. The meeting finished Jim showed Yvonne out, they got in the lift as he put his hand on her bum and squeezed her, she looked at Jim as she said 'not here Jim, god I've missed you, I'll book a room in Birmingham next week, I need you inside me again.' They alighted at the ground floor as Jim took her visitors pass; he shook her hand as he tickled her palm. She coyly smiled as she slowly removed her hand then walked to the carpark as she waved to her driver who picked her up.

Jim returned to Langton's office where he said 'you are, aren't you?' Jim said 'what you on about now?' 'You know what I mean; you're giving her one aren't you?' 'I told you she's beyond my station.' Langton smiled as he opened the bottom drawer and poured two fingers of scotch in two glasses, as he handed one to Jim, they chinked the glasses, then Langton said 'You'll be gone for a while in the states so get me all the information on Sumner and how far you've got with it?' 'No problems, but I want if possible to be the one that interviews Sumner.' Langton nodded as he tipped his glass taking a mouthful of the golden liquid. 'Anyway next time you see Yvonne, give her one for me.' Jim smiled and said 'you just won't let it go will you?' 'I just know you are?' Jim smiled swallowed the last dregs from the glass, then got up and went back to his desk.

He reopened the file when his phone went, it was Debbie 'I've decided to help you, I never thought I would because I was so afraid of him, but now I have Craig to protect me I feel better and more secure.' 'Okay when can I pop around?' 'This afternoon if you like I finish at 4.30.' 'Okay see you then.' Jim called Jackie 'Hi babes I will be late tonight, I'll grab something on the hoof; speak later.'

Jim collected his brief case and checked for the forms he would need and topped them up. Then drove to Debbie's house; he knocked the door and was let in by Debbie. They sat in the kitchen as Debbie made coffee.

'Thanks Debbie, I needed this. Okay let me tell you what I need; then I will talk you through it.' Debbie smiled and nodded. 'Right Debbie, I want to know your relationship with Sumner? Where you lived? Where you went? Who you went with and whether you knew or were aware of any other girlfriends he had?'

'Okay; when I was sixteen, I didn't get on with my mum and dad at that time, I drifted from boyfriend to boyfriend then bumped into Sumner at a party; I'm not sure if I was invited or gate crashed; anyway we got talking and one thing led to another and I ended up at his place. Then a couple of days went by and we ended up in bed.' 'Did you consent to sex with him?' 'Sort of.' 'What does that mean?' 'He said I could stay with him now and then' 'Okay go on?' 'It was okay to start with then he started to get rough with me and wanted to do all sorts of weird things to me; then wanted to get other people involved, when I said no and ran away from him, he caught me and hit me, he hit me so hard he broke my jaw and tried to strangle me if it hadn't have been for someone coming along, he would have finished me off, I'm sure he would. I was so afraid of him after I was released from hospital I went home to mum and dads where they looked after me, that's when you interviewed me.' 'Are you okay now?' 'Oh yeah Craig is so good to me, he is my protector. Even my mum and dad like him, so he must be okay.' Debbie laughed as she cupped her hands around her mug and sipped the hot coffee.

'Did you ever get involved with any other people he suggested to you?' Debbie nodded 'Yeah he made me.' 'Did you get their names?' 'Yeah one couple were called Stuart and Lynda.' 'Do you know where they live?' 'Yes, but don't tell Craig any of this will you?' 'I won't, but I need you to make a statement, that's the only way I can get Sumner, so I suggest you talk with Craig, you needn't tell him everything, just prepare the ground for him.'

'Okay they live at 76, Tall Pines Road.' 'Are they still there?' 'I don't know that was a long time ago now, it's a big house.' 'Have you been there?' 'Yes, I think Sumner took all his girls there, they held parties there and I was forced to do all sorts of things, sorry I can't talk anymore today, I'll call you next week after I have talked with Craig.' Debbie burst into tears. 'Sorry Debbie, I know this is painful so, let's leave it for the moment, if you want one of my female colleagues to talk to you, I can arrange it?' 'No you're fine, just give me a couple of days, I'll be alright; it's just bought it all back to me.' Jim finished his coffee then said his goodbyes.

Jim grabbed a sandwich from a corner shop and ate it on the way home. Jackie was laid on the sofa fast asleep. He poured a scotch and sat reading his notes.

He spent an hour or so then lifted Jackie's head as he slid underneath so she rested on his lap the stroked her head. He watched a bit of TV for another hour then lifted Jackie up and carried her to the bedroom he undressed her and put her under the duvet, he spooned her as he tried to sleep. He couldn't get Sumner and those parties out of his head.

Craig came home to find Debbie in tears 'what's a wrong babe?' 'Oh Craig, look this police thing has brought back all kinds of bad memories, I'm churning up inside.' 'Hey; look if you don't want to do it then tell that copper you don't want too.' 'No Craig I need to do this, but it's bought some things up; I need to tell you about that I kept back, so it won't surprise you okay?'

'Go on?' 'Look Craig when I told you I had been beaten up, yes I was and yes it was Sumner, but he not only beat me up but also raped me.' 'I'll fucking kill him, the bastard.' 'No Craig let the police do it, I don't want you locked up I need you, you're my life; so strong for me please don't.' 'Okay but, if the police don't do him I will I promise you that.'

Debbie hugged Craig as he cuddled her close, he could feel her pain and wanted to protect her and keep her safe from any harm. They weren't hungry so they had a glass of wine and cuddled up in front of if the TV. Debbie felt so good and so safe wrapped in Craig's arms.

Craig would normally have been at the gym training, but this moment was far too important for Debbie, so he stayed in to keep her company.

The following day Debbie called Jim and said 'yes she would do it' Jim made an appointment to suit Debbie a couple days later.

Jim Called Sandra and explained the situation asking to pop around. 'Pop round any time today I'm off for a couple of days.' 'Half an hour okay?' 'No make it an hour?' 'Okay.'

Jim arrived, he was just about to ring the bell when the door opened and there stood Sandra, he thought wow. She looked ravishing, 'well don't just stand come in.' Jim thought 'as the spider said to the fly.'

Sandra was wearing tight pink knee length leggings, with a loose black V necked jumper; with matching pink lipstick. He immediately thought of Sandy out of Grease.

'You look a picture, very nice.' 'Well thank you Jim; you want a coffee?' As she poured the water into the cups; she sat down and leaned forward not attempting to correct her billowing jumper from opening. It was then she noticed that she was bra-less and the twins were free flowing. She smiled as she straightened up accepting his eyes on her, relishing his attention.

He could have grabbed her and planted a kiss on her; he had to control his eagerness although the temptation was there. Then she leaned over again displaying the twins, it was then he caught her perfume. That sent all kinds of images through his mind.

'Okay Jim how can I help you?' As she smiled, flirting with him. Jim thought 'fuck me Jim what a body she has got, fucking hell, she really could help me.' But he snapped out of lust mode.

'Okay Sandy; remember I told you about the other woman who had been assaulted by Sumner, and if she made a statement, would you also make one?' 'Yes I do; has she given you one then?' Jim smiled at her loaded comment. 'Not yet, but she is going too soon, although she gave me certain pointers to other things that happened when she was with him.' 'Like what?'

'I'm not disclosing those at this time; I will give you indications, and see if you come up with the same information.' 'Like what?' Sandra was getting less provocative and more inquisitive.

'Okay, when you were with him did he introduce anyone else to you?' He watched as Sandra's eyes lowered and the sexy smile dropped from her face as she nodded. 'Did you know their names?' She nodded 'they were called Stuart and Lynda,' 'why were they introduced to you?' 'He made me have sex with them, he made me; they raped me.' That was it Sandra just went to pieces with tears streaming down her face. 'He raped me and let them rape me too, the fucking bastard.' Jim went around and hugged her. 'This is going to be your healing process, bottling this kind of emotion inside only supresses it for a while; it has to come to the surface and be shown the light of day, so you can let it go, and proudly move on. You're a beautiful woman so come on, let's finish this and get it out in the open, there's a good girl.'

Sandra smiled 'he used to take me to their house as well, I can't remember the full address something Pines Road or something like that.' 'Hey you're doing fine well done.' 'What happened there?' 'They held parties, sex parties I would be held down whilst anyone who wanted to, could have me. Oh god it was awful.' Sandra flooded again then said 'yes that bastard ruined my life, yes, I'll make a statement yes, and I'll fucking do him.' The pretty face was now showing fits of rage as she narrowed her lips, her eyes full of anger; this was now a woman scorned a woman seeking revenge. Jim was going for it; he wanted this down on paper now.

He reached for his briefcase, but before he could pick it up she said 'I have something to show you upstairs.' 'What's that; am I safe?' 'Maybe I haven't decided yet.' She led the way as he watched her negotiate the stairs watching her pert bum. She went into her bedroom then sat on the bed lent over and pulled a case from underneath, then placed it on the bed as she opened it, then took out an A4 lined note pad.

'This is my diary, everything that happened is in here, I was going to throw it away, but something made me keep it.' She handed it to Jim; he opened it and began to read it as tears started to well up in her eyes. Jim sat down on the bed as she instinctively lent her head on his shoulder. It was all there, every blow she received every forced sex act with him and others.

Jim looked at it, this was dynamite 'wow, Sandra, this is powerful stuff, I need to take this and read it, as it might throw some light onto the whereabouts of Janet.' Sandra looked up from his shoulder as her tears were rolling down her cheeks, then said 'thank you for your kindness and understanding.' Then she leant over and kissed him on the cheek she lingered a moment hoping he would turn to her, her heart was now pounding as she looked at him, she smiled then kissed him fully on the lips as she put her hand behind his head running her fingers through his hair. Jim was nearly at the point of no return, he just managed to pull away from Sandra saying 'that was really nice Sandra, on any other occasion I would have taken it further; but you are a potential crown court witness, it would be totally wrong and could have serious repercussions if it got out that we had been intimate. But, I promise when this is over, I will ravish you big style.' Jim stood up Sandra stood on tiptoe and kissed him again. 'You promise Jim?' 'Oh yes mam I do.' As his hand patted her bum, he smiled, thinking fuck me what a body.

Jim collected his brief case, and placed the A4 diarised account inside. He smiled at Sandra and said 'after I have read this I will come back and take a statement?' 'That will be nice I'll be waiting.'

Jim sat in the car and thought fuck me Broadbent I bet she would be good, as he smiled to himself. He then drove to HQ's where he sat at his desk and began reading the diary.

He jotted down the dates recording the sexual acts performed on her and by whom.

It was clear from her diary as the time had gone on, Sumner had become more violent towards Sandra; he had become more deviant in his demeanour towards her as well. The diarised accounts of the forced sex on Sandra were graphic in detail. The only names recorded were Stuart and

58

Lynda's, although according to her account there had been many others at the parties.

He thought, there are some sick bastards out there; those poor girls, being raped and buggered then being tied up and beaten to satisfy some sexual kick of Sumner and others.

His thoughts took him back to all the other cases he had dealt with, including the kids, realising how sick some people were. He also wondered how many more influential people were going to be involved.

Then he thought, had this been the plight of Janet; had she suffered at Sumner's hands and others, had he gone too far and killed her? Then he thought; was she being kept prisoner in the Pines. 'Yes, let's up the ante' as he spoke out loud to himself. He spoke with Langton and got a warrant and arranged for a couple of officers to be available the next morning at 6am.

Jim went home where he found Jackie asleep again on the sofa, she was absolutely whacked out; the pressures on her were so intense, with staff cutbacks with more and more cases to deal with.

She was no longer the sexual animal she used to be, well not as often anyhow. Jim sat on the edge of the sofa and stroked her head. He saw a faint smile appear across her face as she said 'that's nice Jim' then she drifted off again then came back 'oh sorry Jim, dinner, oh no.' 'Hey don't worry, you stay there what would you like?' 'Nothing I ate at work.' Jim looked at her and knew she was lying.' He stood her up with great protestations and took her to the bedroom undressed her then walked her to the shower; he turned on the water then shoved her inside and closed the door. Jackie was shouting obscenities as Jim laughed. He left her shouting and cursing at him; then ordered a curry from the local takeaway.

Jackie came out of the bedroom in her dressing gown with her hair all over the place dripping wet as she put on a towel in a turban fashion. 'That's ironic' as he looked at her.

'What is?' I just ordered a curry' as they both laughed. Jackie then said 'Broadbent you're an arsehole' as she dried her face and laughed.

'Oh Jim I've been so tired and eaten up inside by the cases I've been dealing with; there are some sick bastards out there.' 'Tell me about it babes; I'm dealing with another one. I've got an early start as well.' Jackie looked at him, she saw that look again in his eyes; she knew he would be totally wrapped up again. He looked at Jackie 'look, promise me you will eat properly when I'm not here?' 'Why? Where you going? You're not going away are you, not again?' 'Look the spooks have another case in the states so, yes I maybe going away again.' 'Oh Jim, I miss you when you're away.' 'I know babes but, the money is good, it will clear my credit card, with a bit extra for a nice present for you.' 'I still don't like you working for the spooks Jim, it scares me.' Then the doorbell rang; Jim released the entrance door and received the curry.

The dinner dished up they sat, as they ate and drank wine. After dinner was over, Jackie dried her hair with a hair dryer and brushed it out then they both crashed to bed, Jim set his alarm for 4.30 am. He hadn't been asleep for a moment or so it seemed, when the alarm went off. He threw himself out of bed as Jackie rolled over onto the warm spot he had just vacated. The shower did its work as he felt the water hit his face. He just stood there in the warmth absorbing the feeling. He got out shaved then made some toast and dressed on the move, he put his coat on and grabbed his case; he looked at Jackie snuggled in the foetal position with the duvet wrapped around her, wishing he was still there next to her.

CHAPTER FIFTEEN

Jim stood in the briefing room as he gave the morning's task; he highlighted the issues of a suspected sex house so he wanted SOCO on standby to come in, if the information was found to be correct. He also wanted anything which highlighted names, including diaries and address books; he also wanted photographs and videos seized.

The journey to Tall Pines Road was short; the cars were quietly parked a little way away. Jim looked at the house it was big; it looked like an old Victorian place. Jim eased the front door top and bottom and felt no resistance so stepped back and kicked it in. The lock gave way easily as the hasp was sent tumbling across the hallway. The allocated officers went to their nominated rooms; those who were allocated the upstairs went first. This was always a heart thumping time. What was waiting behind closed doors, guns, knives resistance or compliance? The adrenalin was high as the officers entered with shouts of police.

Jim heard a noise from the upstairs then screams and shouts and crying from one of the bedrooms, he then heard one of the officers call 'Jim come here quick.' Jim ran up the stairs he went into the room where the noise was coming from 'in here Jim.' He entered and has he did so he saw the room was bloodstained with bloody a handprint on the wall, smeared as if someone had slid down the painted walls leaving streaks of blood. 'Right everyone out and get SOCO here now.' Jim closed the door and went out into the hallway. 'Where are they?' 'In there' as one of the officers pointed to another bedroom. Jim went in and saw a man and a woman in dressing gowns sat on the bed.

Jim looked around the room then went to another room which was empty, he then took the male person into the empty room the closed the door. The figure in front of him looked petrified and sullen. Jim said very quietly but, menacingly as his lips tightened over his teeth 'right my old son you have got this one chance only, so start talking because, you could be looking at the rest of your life behind bars; your name is?' 'Stuart.' 'Good boy, now just to let you know, I know lots so don't fuck me about you understand, you fucking understand?' Jim clenched Stuart's dressing gown at the throat as he looked menacingly into his eyes. Stuart's eyes were wide open with fear and he was physically shaking.

'Right what happened in that room and when?' 'I can't say.' 'Right my old son, can't or won't?' 'He will kill me' 'who?' 'Not saying.' 'Let me help you, so you know I'm not fucking about; Sumner.' 'You know?' 'Look I told you, don't fuck me about son, right?' 'Yes he was here,' 'when?' 'Yesterday.' 'Who else?' 'I can't say.' 'Fuck me mate you're doing my fucking head in. I know about the higher ups as well.' Jim was trying to get him to name someone, a VIP, so he could go to town on Sumner. 'You know about them?' 'Of course, I fucking do; I just want to know if you're telling me the truth.' Stuart then reeled off a couple of names. Jim thought not again. He recognised one as a solicitor and another as an MP, a back bencher.

'Okay Stuart who was in that room last night and what happened?' 'Look I like sex games and so does Lynda, but Sumner was getting more and more violent, then last night he brought this woman in they tied her up and raped her.' 'You rape her as well?' He nodded, 'then what?' 'They got a video camera and filmed them taking it turns then Lynda got involved.' 'Then what happened?' 'They let her go and she attacked Sumner scratching his face deeply with her nails. Then he hit her hard causing her nose to bleed, she held her face, blood was everywhere, he hit her again and she slid down the wall, there was blood on her hands.' 'There you go my old son, you're only way now is up. So I suggest you get dressed, oh before you go, what was the woman's name?' 'I don't know he never said.' 'Where's the video camera.' 'I'm not saying.' 'Where's the fucking video camera!' Jim grabbed him by the dressing gown as he thrust him up against the wall banging his head as he did so. 'One more time son where's the fucking video camera!' Jim brought back his fist ready to unleash a punch. 'Okay, Okay, under the floorboards in my bedroom, please don't hurt me.'

Jim then dragged him back to the bedroom then said 'where show me?' Stuart lifted the bedside rug. 'In there.' 'Okay get dressed.'

Jim then heard SOCO arrive. Jim said to the other officers, 'Okay take them to the nick I will be there soon.'

Jim took SOCO to the bedroom with the blood in as he explained the activity in the room, so wanted a full fingerprint and sexual search as well. He then took him to the main bedroom and showed him the floor boards requesting a full photographic sequence as the floorboards were removed and the recovery of the camera and tapes was made. Once that was undertaken he would take them to the technical department to get the tapes copied for interviewing.

Jeremy the SOCO got changed into his white suit then brought his box of tricks and cameras upstairs to the bedroom. He photographed the floorboards as they were; then removed the loose one and took out a small case, he photographed each procedure then opened it, where he found a video camera and mini cassettes, he bagged the items, removing the tape already in the camera, then handed them to Jim who hot footed it to the technical lab where he pleaded for a quick turnaround of the tape taken from the camera. The engineer loaded the tape machine then inserted the mini cassette and began to record. Jim managed to view the images as it was being copied; there was a woman being raped by Sumner and others. Jim punched the air as he shouted 'yes you bastard, I've fucking got you, yes, I've fucking got you, you're mine, I've fucking got you my old son, got you!' Jim sat and waited for the tape to be completed then shook the operators hand and requested a quick turnaround of the others for interview; then went back to HQ's where he went to a room with a TV and video player then sat and watched the sequence from the start to finish.

The opening scene was of a room, it was empty then in walked three men and two women, then started to undress as the women engaged in various sexual acts on each other and the men. This included Lynda and Stuart. This scene went on for a few moments when the camera panned to the door, it opened as Sumner entered leading a woman in who was blindfolded and hands tied, as soon as she was in, the two women started to undress her. The woman began to struggle, but she was held by Sumner, then the blindfold was removed as she began to really struggle then one of the men slapped her then she was tied down and raped continuously. Then the two women joined in using vibrators on the woman and each other.

It was shortly after she was allowed to get up, then she started to fight with Sumner who punched her in the face causing a severe nose bleed. She put her hand to her nose as he hit her again she looked unsteady on her feet as she put her hand on the wall for support then lost her balance as she slid down causing a hand print and smear of blood down the wall. Sumner then picked her up; he handed her clothes to her then pulled her out of the room as she cried shaking her head; she was in hysterics.

The occupants of the room then started to get dressed then left. Jim smiled as he thought to himself, I recognise a couple of the men; as his mind went into overdrive although he couldn't think of their names at the moment.

Jim called the local police station and spoke to Sam one of the detectives present at the search asking him to prepare an interview room with a video player and TV in it; he would be there shortly to conduct the interview and wanted him present, Sam said 'great it sounds like a good job.

CHAPTER SIXTEEN

Jim inserted the video cassette into the player as Sam brought Stuart Small to the interview room.

'Right Stuart your full name before we begin?'

'Stuart Small.'

Okay you know me Detective Sergeant Jim Broadbent and this Detective Constable Sam Ash.'

'You're under arrest for rape, kidnapping and sexual assault, and for those offences you have been cautioned you understand?'

'Small nodded.'

'You want a brief?'

'No I'm fine.'

'Right Stuart when we arrested you this morning in your house we found a video camera, who does that belong to?'

'It's Sumner's.'

'Why do you keep it at your house?'

'Because he asked me too.'

'There was a cassette in the recorder when we took it; who was operating it when the recording was made?

'I'm not saying.'

'Not saying or won't?'

'Means the same.'

'Okay I have watched it, so let me remind you of the events of that day.'

Jim nodded to Sam who operated the play button.

'Just watch this; then I will talk you through certain sequences.'

66

Jim watched Small as he winced at the scenes.

Jim nodded to Sam who stopped the sequence.

'Okay Stuart I want to know the names of the others present please?'

'I'm not saying they have a lot of contacts.'

'The problem is mate when this goes live in the court room, not only will you be on the charges I spoke of, you will also be charged with conspiracy to rape and kidnap with those on the video, so it would be better to name them and be seen as helpful rather than not, because my old son when they are nicked and they will be, they will sing like canaries especially to save their own skin and not worry about yours.'

Small sat there his head in his hands. Then he looked and nodded, as Jim picked up his pen and began writing down the names of the men and the women in the sequence.

'Well done Stuart that will go a long way towards showing how cooperative you have been.'

'Right in this sequence you are seen holding the woman whilst she is being raped by others then you raped her. You agree with the video sequence?'

Small nodded.

'I take that nod as a yes?'

'Yes it is.'

'Okay Stuart, I have other tapes for you to watch but, that won't be today. So before we wrap this up; who decided it was your house to be used?'

'Sumner, he said, we could use one of the rooms as it was a big house.'

'Okay mate that's good, now we need to know where's the woman who was raped?'

'She was Sumner's girlfriend I don't know where she is.'

'After this video sequence Sumner punches her in the face that puts a more sinister overtone on the investigation?'

'I don't know where she is.'

'I can't say I believe you; we will be interviewing those on the video, so it will all come out in the wash?'

'Look all I know is he never spoke of her after he left, he never mentioned her again.'

'Okay, before we wrap this up, how many other different women are on the other videos and who are they; and more importantly, where are they now?'

Small sat in silence as Jim let him stew in his situation, he put his finger to his lips indicating to Sam not to speak.

Small just sat with his eyes closed as he began to shuffle his feet, then after ten minutes of silence.

'You know she's dead don't you?'

'I guessed as much.'

'Look, I never killed her or the others.'

Jim's ears pricked up, as he thought, the others? His mind went into overdrive.

'How many Stuart, you're doing really well?'

'I think about 4 or five; look he killed them not me, I just helped dispose of the bodies.'

'Well done Stuart, how did he kill them?'

'Strangled them; that's what he said; I was never there when he did it.'

'Where did he do it?'

'In his car I think then I helped him bury the bodies.'

'Where are they buried?'

Jim then thought conspiracy to murder, he had to arrest him for that as well or all this evidence would be thrown out.

'Okay Stuart, let me just stop you there for a moment I need to inform you that that you are also being arrested for conspiracy to murder and the same caution applies you understand?'

'I never killed anyone why am I being arrested for that; I just helped him bury the bodies?'

'If it had been only one, then yes I would agree, but with more than one you must have known what he was going to do, whether you agreed with it or not, you went ahead with it, you were complicit in raping women and used your house

68

as the place where they were raped, knowing they were going to be killed by Sumner; that Stuart is conspiracy to murder.'

Jim looked at the sad looking excuse for a man sat opposite him, who was now full of remorse, but he hadn't looked like that when he was involved in raping the women as seen on the video sequences.

'Fuck me this is heavy duty stuff.'

'Yes it is mate, I need to know where the bodies are so we can close this, and recover them so the parents can officially bury them properly, so where are they?'

'Look he's a sick bastard really sick; they are in some woodland, out of town on the edge of some farmers fields.'

'Okay can you take me there?'

'Yeah, it will get me out of here.'

'Okay we'll wrap this up, but just tell me, are all the bodies there?'

'Yes, all close to each other.'

'How many Stuart?'

'God this is really bad isn't it?'

'That's an understatement.'

'I think 4 maybe five.'

'In that number is one of them called Janet?'

'Yes she was a long standing girlfriend of his.'

'Did you know the names of the others?'

'No they were just brought in by him.'

'Besides the women on the tapes and the ones buried in the woods were there any other women that were raped in your house?'

'Yes.'

'How many and can you name them?'

'Not really I think there were three, I think one might have been called Debbie she was a young girl I don't know the others.'

'What happened to Debbie?'

'I think he said she'd run away, but she wouldn't have talked anyway she was too scared he had really hurt her.'

'You sure she ran away or was she killed by him as well?'

'No I'm sure, I think if he had killed her, he would have told me if he had, he just said she was in hiding somewhere.'

'Okay we'll wrap this up and go for a drive, but before we do, is it muddy or easy going?'

'Easy going we drove right up to the spot.'

'Okay let me get a car and then we'll head on out; are you sure you know the way?'

'Yes, I know where it is.'

Jim left Sam Talking with Stuart. He got outside and called Langton as he punched the air. 'Yes guv, he say's four maybe five bodies in woods, one of them is Janet Crosby; we are just going to try and find the site, can you put the circus on standby and some uniform officers to protect the site if we find it. I will call you from the location.'

Jim drove according to Stuart's directions; they drove past the entrance to the Larches estate as he directed Jim into a narrow track that ran alongside some agricultural land.

'Okay not far now; easy; this is it, just hear.'

'Right Stuart out of the car, I need to cuff you to Sam; rules and regulations okay?'

'I won't run promise.'

'Sorry mate it's regulations.'

Sam slipped on the cuffs Stuart; he then directed them a short distance to the edge of the woods.

'Just here, that's where the last one is.'

Jim saw fresh dig signs with undergrowth placed on top to hide the grave. Jim called Langton

'We have one grave, with fresh signs of digging. The location is approximately 2 miles past the Larches estate entrance on the A road heading towards Cinder town. Then take a track on the left hand side and drive down a couple of hundred yards; I will place a sign on the side of the road till uniform get here with a cordon tape.'

Jim left Sam looking for the other sites. He drove back to the main road. He opened the boot, but couldn't find anything to use as a marker; he then saw a plastic fertilizer bag in the hedgerow. He was just about to hunt for something to use as a peg when a Land Rover turned up, it was Brian the gamekeeper from the Larches estate. They greeted each other, as Brian stated he had been called as someone thought they had seen poachers. Jim explained the reason for being there. Brian's face went ashen as he was told of the potential graves.

Brian went to the back of the Land Rover and took out a peg then used his hunting knife to fashion an arrow from the fertilizer bag. He then attached a cross piece to keep it erect. Jim asked Brian for five more stakes so he could mark the graves.

Brian followed Jim where he met Sam. Sam nodded to Jim, 'he's pointed out 5 potential grave sites.' Jim nodded then said to Brian 'is this all part of your estate?' 'Yes it's just a small wooded area sometimes we shoot it, but not that often.' Jim took Brian to one side. 'Look Brian you better tell your boss that we will be looking for bodies in this area so will be digging and there will be a lot of activity for a week or so.' Brian acknowledged Jim. Brian then left and drove back along the track, as he reached the main road he saw a police patrol car and directed them to where Jim was.

Jim directed the uniform crew to tape off the area then await the arrival of SOCO and under no circumstances to let anyone go tramping over the area.

Jim then called Langton confirming 5 grave sites identified. He also confirmed that a uniformed presence was there protecting the scene.

Jim got back to Central with Small. Sam bought some coffee and some sandwiches into the interview room.

'Okay Stuart, you took us to the woods where you identified 5 separate locations close to each other where you say there are 5 bodies of women who had been brought to your house then raped by those present including you; then they were murdered by Sumner, is that correct?'

'Yes, but, I didn't have anything to do with their deaths.'

'But you did help bury them; yes?'

Small looked down and began sobbing, more a sympathy sob than a real cry.

'I say again, did you help to bury the bodies?'

'Yes.'

'Okay Stuart I will arrange a charge then you will be in court in the morning.'

Jim prepared the charges; Small said nothing in reply to the rape allegations. He was then placed into the cells to await the morning's court.

CHAPTER SEVENTEEN

Jim had nominated Vicky as the interviewer of Lynda Small; he had made sure a video player was in the interview room and given her a copy tape for the interview.

Vicky brought in a junior detective Chris, to sit in and scribe the notes of the interview.

'Okay Lynda your full name please?'

'Lynda Small.'

'Okay you have been arrested for indecent assault, kidnaping and rape you understand.'

'I don't know what you're talking about.'

'Do you want a brief?'

'No don't need one I haven't done anything.'

'Okay; you know your husband has been spoken to and he has been interviewed by other detectives; you understand?'

'Yes.'

'You enjoy sex Lynda?'

'What?'

'Do you enjoy sex?'

Lynda looked down and shrugged her shoulders.

'I suppose, doesn't everyone.'

'Who do you have sex with?'

'What?'

'Simple question, who do you have sex with?'

'My husband.'

'Anyone else?'

'No, what are you saying?'

'Just asking a question; have you ever had sex with anyone else other than your husband in your house?'

'Are you getting some kind of kick out of this?'

'Just asking a question which is relevant to the enquiry?'

'Well then, no I haven't.'

'Do you want to think about that answer?'

'No I don't need to, the answer is no.'

'Okay have you ever had sex with a woman?'

'What?'

'Another simple question; yes or no?'

'No.'

'That is all I wanted to know?'

'Why?'

'Because I'm about to prove you're an outright liar?'

'What I've told you is the truth?'

'Well I'm about to blow a hole right through your truth.'

'What do you mean?'

'Remember we searched your house?'

'Yes.'

'Tell me how long have you known Charles Sumner?'

'Oh ages a long time.'

'Has he ever bought women to your house?'

'Like who?'

'You tell me?'

Vicky wanted her to deny everything then bang, hit her with the video, as that would crucify her.

'He had a couple of girlfriends.'

'What were their names?'

'I don't know just girls he went out with.'

'Why did he bring them to your house?'

'Just for a drink.'

'Okay did he ever have sex with them at your house?'

'Not that I know of.'

'Do you remember woman called Janet?'

'I think so.'

'Well she's missing do you know where she is?'

74

'No idea.'

'Okay, I'll go back to what I just said, we searched your house, have a guess what we found?'

'No idea; what?'

'A video camera and cassettes.'

'Oh my god.'

'Sorry, he won't help you; on the tape in the video is some quite interesting footage, would you like to be reminded of what's on it?'

'Oh god no please you can't show that, can you?'

'It will be interesting for the jury to watch, you naked holding down women while they are being raped by men including your husband, then you using them for your pleasure as well?'

'Oh I don't know what to say?'

'Well let me help you, I'll ask again have you ever had sex with anyone else in your house?'

'Yes.'

'Who?'

'Lots of men and women.'

'Did the women consent?'

'Some did.'

'Which ones didn't?'

'The ones bought by Charles.'

'How did you know they didn't consent?'

'Because they struggled and had to be held down.'

'Who held them down?'

'Sometimes I did and sometimes others did.'

'What happened to the women afterwards?'

'What do you mean?'

'Oh come on Lynda, women raped, the fear of them reporting it to the police; what happened to them?'

'I don't know Charles would take them out after, then he and Stuart would go.'

'Go where?'

'I don't know.'

'Let me tell you, Stuart led officers to grave sites pointing out where the women had been buried after being raped and strangled. So what did you know about that?'

'I had heard they had done it.'

'Done what?'

'Killed them.'

'Right you are also being arrested for conspiracy to murder as you said you were aware the women brought by Charles to your house were going to be killed?'

Vicky watched the confident woman in front of her now looking broken.

'Did you talk to Stuart about it?'

'Sort of.'

'What does that mean?'

'He just said they had buried the bodies.'

'Okay so you knew that each woman who was bought to the house where you lived was going to be raped then killed? Then you took part in the rape and sexual assault, is that what you are saying?'

Small just sat there crying into a tissue and shaking her head.

Vicky thought; you weren't shaking your head when you were holding the women down as you were being taken from behind on the video sequences.

'Yes when you say it like that; well yes I did.'

'And you did nothing to stop it?'

'No how could I?'

'Reported it to the police?'

'No I couldn't; they would have killed me as well.'

'Okay we will leave it there for now, have you anything else to say?'

'No just I'm so sorry, I should have said something.'

'Yes you should of. What I want now, is the names of the other women who were present?'

'I don't know their last names, they were friends of Charles, I didn't know them.'

76

Vicky then nodded to Chris, who pressed play on the video. Lynda turned her head away, she was there standing naked being groped and performing oral sex on the men whilst holding down the victims.

'Okay Lynda those two women, their names please?'

'I only know their first names; the dark haired one is Julie, the blonde was Maria, I don't know if that was their real names, that's all I knew them by.'

'Addresses as well Lynda?'

'I don't know that; not even sure if that was their real names.'

'Phone numbers?'

'No, Charles had those; he did all the arranging for the parties.'

The interview continued for a while longer then she was charged with rape and sexual assault.

Vicky found Jim where she let him know the result of the interview; he congratulated her on the interview, as she started to compile the remand in custody papers.

Jim had sent a team to Sumner's house for him to be arrested and his house searched. But the jungle drums had beaten loudly; he together with some of the others on the video had done a runner.

Jim hearing the news was somewhat disappointed to say the least, he wished he had nicked him earlier, but he couldn't be in two places at the same time.

Jim knew he had to view the other tapes as well to try and identify the other victims; he hoped Janet was in one of the sequences

He applied at court for remand to police cells for 3 days to allow time to view the tapes.

The court application was made; the CPS lawyer gave a good speech and although the defence lawyer's tried to have the application refused; Jim knew the magistrates would be sympathetic to the police investigation; the Small's were remanded as per the application.

Jim received the remaining tapes the same afternoon. He worked through them making notes; there were four more women being raped who he hoped would match the identities of the four victims in the graves. Then he came across the tape, the one he hoped would be there. He watched the woman being led in blindfolded with her hands tied, as soon as she was in the room, hands were all over her removing her clothes, some were unceremoniously torn from her. He instantly recognised her face as the blindfold was removed; from the pictures he had seen, it was Janet. She was struggling, but was overpowered by those present. The women held her down then, one by one the men raped her. The scene was graphic as Sumner jeered at her as she was being raped and defiled.

Once over she was led from the room by Sumner; she was in hysterics carrying her clothes in her arms; shortly after Stuart Small left as well. This confirmed his version of what happened. That video clip would have been the last time that Janet was seen alive.

Jim made notes for the further interviews of the Small's as they featured in the rapes and sexual assaults on the other nameless victims. He saw that Sumner was the only person bringing each of the victims into the room blindfolded with hands tied, then stripped and raped by the men present with the other women joining in by holding the victims down as they too were engaging in sexual activity with each other and the men present.

He also noticed that it was the same people in the video sequences. Jim just sat and watched knowing that the sick bastards were aware or must have been aware that the unwilling women were going to be killed after being raped.

CHAPTER EIGHTEEN

Jim got home as he opened the door Jackie was standing at the sink dressed in one of his shirts again. She heard him come in but, loved to play the game of letting him creep up on her pretending she hadn't heard him.

Jim crept up behind her and patted her bum then cradled his arms around her as he cupped her breasts in each hand, then kissed her neck. Jackie loved this attention as she lifted her head allowing his lips access to her throat and her ears, which she adored; the feeling of his warm breath tumbling inside her ear sent sensual shivers down her spine exciting her, sending instant moistening signals to her vagina which responded instantly, knowing the excitement to be relished soon.

Jim breathed softly into her ear causing Jackie to scrunch her shoulder up at the pleasurable sensation as she giggled and moaned softly. She turned around then kissed him deeply and passionately. He was getting aroused as was Jackie, she turned the oven down low then turned off the veg and dragged him by the tie to the bedroom, where she undressed him then sat on the edge of the bed dragging his head between her thighs where he engaged in her favourite sexual activity, Jim feasted on her, absorbing her juices. 'Oh Jim please don't ever stop liking this will you, oh my god yes, yes, oh fucking hell Jim.' Jackie loved Jim performing on her, it was her favourite by far, it felt so good; she would hold his head keeping him there whilst she climaxed again and again. Then they engaged in making love for an hour.

Jackie hugged Jim and laid her head on his chest listening to his heart beat. After a while she got up and started dishing up the dinner. Jim could have slept all night, but he dragged himself to the kitchen where he helped dish up.

They sat eating in front of the television as they discussed their days work; Jackie was riveted by the investigation that Jim unfolded.

They finished dinner and went to bed both tired from their day and physical exertion with each other. Jim crashed till his alarm went off. Jackie had slept passed her normal time, then got up and started to rush about getting ready then they were gone.

CHAPTER NINETEEN

Jim arrived at HQ's where he debriefed Langton on his previous day; Langton had already begun to write his policy log and filled in the blanks from Jim's information. Jim had already sent a message to PNC for the arrest of Sumner for murder if he was stopped.

Jim and Langton then went to the scene where the tents had been erected over the graves. The teams were slowly beginning unearth each grave in sequence. The pathologist began to work on the uncovered bodies. All the officers were wearing face masks to try and reduce the smell of the decaying bodies. The stench got stronger the deeper the officers and the pathologist dug.

Jim knew so well the acrid smell that hit the back of the throat, the smell that one never forgets; there is no other smell that comes close to it. The smell just hangs in the air attaching to clothes; the smell of decaying bodies clings to the skin and hair.

Jim watched as the teams unearthed the last grave, none of the bodies could be identified by facial features, as all the flesh had been eaten by worms and bacteria; the normal decaying processes had well and truly kicked in. The only recognisable one was the latest victim although her face was so badly bruised from the punches inflicted on her by Sumner; she was not a pretty sight, but just about identifiable as having been the girl on the last video.

It was only dental records and perhaps the jewellery which was worn by some of the victims that would hopefully be identified, and confirm their identities.

The pathologist confirmed the post mortem dates, although his initial examination confirmed each body had indications of strangulation as the hyoid bone in each of throats had been broken. The bodies were removed to the mortuary in body bags by the undertakers.

Langton and Jim returned to HQ's in their own cars with windows wide open trying to rid themselves of the smell of decaying bodies. Once in Langton's office he poured three fingers of scotch which in some way aided the reduction of the smell. But as with all smells, the longer you remain in the vicinity the more the nose gets used to it. But to others who come in contact with it, they can instantly detect the distinct odour.

Jim drank the scotch then went to make more notes and prepare for the eventual interview of Sumner. He needed to have an interview package available just in case he was working for the spooks when Sumner was finally arrested.

Jim had removed the jewellery from the victims and placed them into separate bags and numbered them 1-5. He went to see Mr and Mrs Crosby where he prepared them for the worst. He opened the envelope which, from the description was probably Janet's; he couldn't show them the physical remains, it would have been too much for them and from what was left they couldn't have identified Janet anyway.

Jim carefully emptied the contents of the envelope onto the dining room table. There was a necklace with a heart shaped pendant and gold ring with a diamond in the band. Mrs Cosby on seeing the jewellery covered her face and burst into tears as she grabbed her husband and sobbed heavily into his shoulder. Mr Crosby looked at the jewellery as he welled up with a brick sized lump in his throat. He tried to speak, but all that came out was mutterings. Jim let them cry out; when they had settled; Mr Crosby said 'the ring was an 18th birthday present and the necklace a 21st. Where did you find them?' Jim thought oh my god this is going to kill them hearing the truth; so decided to lessen the impact by saying she had been found in the woods and he was waiting for the post mortem to establish the cause of death.

Mrs Crosby then said 'can we see her?' 'Sorry, the reason I bought the jewellery, is because well you know; it would be difficult after all the time she had been in the woods to establish the identity. Mrs Crosby brought her hand to her mouth again as she burst into more tears. 'Oh my Sandra, oh my god my poor baby, oh please it can't be, please god oh please.' She collapsed into her husband's shoulder again as the tears flowed, she could hardly breathe as the emotion overtook her. There was nothing more Jim could do; he took a short statement of jewellery identification from Mr Crosby; then left stating he would keep them informed as the investigation progressed.

Jim got outside, he took a sharp intake of breath as he thought, no matter how many times he delivered a message like this it was always difficult, especially knowing the truth, but having to hold back out of sympathy for the relatives. Albeit the truth would eventually come out, they would have had time to become stronger and be able to cope a little better when it did.

Jim got back to HQ's where he called the coroner's office to confirm the identity of body number 3, was that of Janet Crosby.

He then wrote on the dry white board 1-5, writing Janet's details; confirming the identity by the Jewellery as number 3. The other numbers would eventually, have their identities confirmed.

The next thing to do was get the remaining jewellery photographed by SOCO then use the media to circulate it through local papers and national news so it reached as wider audience as possible. The internal circulation would be made first to all surrounding forces to check against missing persons reports.

Jim prepared a charge for the next remand hearing for the Small's. Conspiracy to murder Janet Crosby on or about the date she went missing. If the identities of the others could not be confirmed then they would be charged with the murder of persons unknown on a date unknown.

Jim contacted Special Branch to trawl the airline and ferry crossings for Sumner; he was convinced he would have done a runner to Spain or Portugal by now. He then had a flash of inspiration and called Yvonne requesting a search of their system to ensure he wasn't one of theirs. Yvonne confirmed he wasn't, but would use their sources to place an alert on him. Then she said 'get ready Jim, don't pack yet, but get ready.' 'Is it still the states?' Yvonne confirmed the states, adding I need to brief you as well.' 'You mean debrief?' 'Behave Jim, but yes perhaps.'

Jim collected the photos from SOCO then met with the force press officer requesting him to call for a briefing and arrange for a press release, in order to give the jewellery as much coverage as they could.

The day came as the room where the showing was to be made was jam packed full of TV crews and photographers. Langton was chairing the conference as the press officer called for silence, the room slowly descended into a hush. The press officer opened the meeting then handed over to Langton, who then gave an impassioned plea for anyone who recognised the jewellery to come forward by getting in touch on the following numbers, or by calling their local police station. The room then erupted into a barrage of questions with the press officer conducting the reporters like an orchestra by pointing to the next one to ask a question; then the next and so on. Langton then nodded to the press officer, who then called a halt to the proceedings as Langton and Jim left the room. Langton then said to Jim 'fucking news hounds they can be a right pain in the arse sometimes, but on occasions like this we need them.' Jim nodded as he smiled walking into Langton's office where he opened his bottle of Islay and poured two fingers into two glasses they chinked them and toasted the success so far.

Langton looked seriously at Jim, as Jim cocked his head in a questioning manner, Langton then said 'they have found the back bencher in his holiday flat in Greece, it looks like a suicide, his wrists had been cut and he bled to death in the bath.' 'Was there a note?' 'Sort of; very sketchy, it just said, I'm sorry.' 'He's being brought back by plane, we will have to wait for the results of the post mortem, maybe the pathologist can ascertain if the cuts were self-inflicted or if they could have been caused by another, it's a long shot, but worth a try.' Jim nodded as he sipped his scotch.

Jim said 'I don't suppose the Greeks want a murder on their hands so will not push too hard at their end.' Langton nodded as he agreed.

The media circus had done their bit; the newspapers locally had front page coverage of the jewellery; whilst broadsheet papers had a small reference on the inside pages. The local TV stations gave a big coverage, but the national news hardly touched on it, as there were bigger headline issues to cover, including the death of the backbencher in Greece, which took primacy over other news of the day. Jim thought if only they knew the connection between the two they would have a field day.

Jim reviewed the tapes again making sure he could identify the other persons in the sequences. He was sure he had all the identities correct. He went back to see Langton confirming the names which now included a top ranking solicitor in one of the practices that the police used for advice on civil matters. Langton nodded at Jim and said 'I will notify the Chief as there will be a lot of press interest in this. Also Police matters already in the hands of that practice may have to be recovered and given to another firm.

But don't worry there will be no whitewash. Give me a day to sort it, then I will give you the nod.' Jim smiled as he left the office.

The okay was given after the Chief had been informed. Jim didn't need a second telling, he went to the solicitors offices where he requested to see Reginald Prentice. He was fobbed off initially by the smiling receptionist. He then informed her if she didn't notify Prentice he was here to see him, he would arrest her for obstructing him.

The receptionist quickly buzzed Prentice to come to reception immediately. Shortly after an interconnecting door opened, as out walked a smartly dressed pin striped suited man with greying hair at the temples. 'Yes how can I help you, what's the urgency, why can't this wait?' Jim saw the face and immediately recognised him from the video sequence. 'Can I have a moment of your time in your office please?' 'No I'm too busy now, make an appointment.' Jim could hear the arrogance in his voice which really pissed him off, so said 'In that case Mr Prentice I am arresting you for rape and conspiracy to murder.' Jim then gave him the text book caution, knowing everything had to be by the book. Jim saw his face drop and the jaw of the receptionist drop open even wider having heard the statement of Jim.

Jim then thought fuck him, as he took out his handcuffs, 'that won't be necessary.' 'Sorry rules and regulations, you know all about those don't you?' Prentice had no option but to hold his hands out as Jim placed the cuffs on ensuring they were loose not tight.

Jim placed Prentice in the back of the car as he sat in the front passenger seat; his colleague drove them to Central. There was an eerie silence in the car; Jim wanted him to stew in his own juices.

Once back at the police station he was booked-in. Jim wanted him to be humiliated so had him banged up in a cell.

Jim then prepared the interview room with video playing facility. Then after an hour he brought Prentice to the interview room, he got Vicky to accompany him. Prentice was brought in; Jim saw the man who looked so smart when arrested, he was now looking dishevelled, his tie and belt removed, his shirt collar undone and creased.

'Okay Mr Prentice; my name is Detective Sgt Jim Broadbent, my colleague is here making notes. I just want you to understand why you are here; you have been arrested for an allegation of rape and conspiracy to murder. Earlier you were cautioned. I will ask you, do you understand the reason you are here?'

Prentice just nodded as he looked down then said

'Yes I do.'

'You understand the caution?'

'Yes.'

'Do you want a solicitor?'

'No.'

'Right then; tell me how do you know Charles Sumner?'

'Who is he?'

'Now come on Mr Prentice you're an intelligent man, how do you know Charles Sumner?'

'No comment.'

'How do you know Stuart and Lynda Small?'

Prentice looked at Jim, trying to weigh him up. He had heard through the grapevine the police were on the hunt but, thought he was so far removed he wouldn't be connected.

'No comment.'

'Okay, do you read the papers?'

This threw Prentice for a moment as he struggled to come up with an answer.

'Yes why?'

'That's good; did you read about the backbencher found dead in Greece?'

'Yes; but what's that to do with me?'

'You will see as the interview goes on.'

'Did you see the news in the local papers regarding the jewellery found, and the police requesting for information as to who it may have belonged too?'

'Yes I did; look where is this leading?'

'Now now Mr prentice, be patient, all will be revealed very shortly. So you did see it in the papers?'

'No comment.'

'Have you ever been to the house of the Small's Stuart and Lynda?'

'No comment.'

'I think you have; no I'll rephrase that, I know you have.'

'No comment.'

'Did you know Janet Crosby?'

'Who?'

'Janet Crosby?'

'No, who is she?'

'Remember I spoke of the jewellery?'

'No comment.'

'Well her body was found in woodland near here and the jewellery she was wearing has been identified as being hers. You see she had rotted away in the ground and couldn't have been identified by facial features; so her parents were shown the items discovered on her remains, which they confirmed as identical to the gifts they bought for their daughter Janet.'

'Look what has this got to do with me?'

'We are getting there; who do you think showed us the grave?'

'No comment.'

'Shall I tell you, go on shall I?'

Jim was nearing the crunch time and was enjoying the squirming of Prentice. This high flying moneyed man had nowhere to go now. He so enjoyed the interviews when he was on the front foot watching the twitching and feet shuffling of those on the end of the questions.

'It was Stuart Small, and before you say no comment; I know you know the Small's. Now just think, go on think, how do I know you know him; just think?'

'No comment.'

'Oh yes, just so you know, next to the grave of Janet there were 4 other graves, and by the time we have identified those, we will prove you knew those as well.'

Prentice was now shaking, his hands were trembling, he was trying to look calm. although underneath he was in turmoil with the unknowing; how much did the police know?

'What have I got that makes me so sure you knew them, have a guess go on, have a guess?'

'No comment.'

Jim smiled at him it was now crunch time, he loved it. Prentice lowered his gaze as Jim stared into his eyes.

'Now you may be wondering why the television is here; well it has a video in it; in my brief case are four others, but let me concentrate on this one first. Don't worry about Vicky; she has seen it all before.'

Jim nodded to Vicky who operated the on-button, the white noise gave way to the scene where Janet was bought into the room and stripped then held down as the men gathered raped her as the women jeered and egged them on. Then the camera operator zoomed in on each of them showing clearly the faces of all who gathered. There as clear as day there was Prentice raping Janet and smiling at the camera as he did so. After raping Janet, Lynda Small engaged him in oral sex as he is seen laughing.

Jim nodded at Vicky who pressed the stop button. Prentice now had his head in his hands and started to cry. His big world of money that buys everything was gone, he had nowhere to hide.

'Now then Mr Prentice, this is where this interview is leading you have been seen raping a woman on camera, that woman was Janet Crosby who was later murdered and buried in the woods.'

89

'No comment.'

'Okay, you see the other four tapes also include you raping women, and no doubt when their identities are known it will match those on the video sequences. So, I think you either give an explanation or we watch the other tapes showing you and others raping the other four women, including the backbencher found dead in Greece. I presumed you knew him as he is in all the video scenes raping the women as well as you?'

Jim nodded to Vicky who ejected the video then started to load the second tape when Prentice said.

'Okay, what do you want to know?'

'Okay how do you know Sumner?'

'He was a client of a friend and was invited to a party where we met, then one thing led to another and then I became hooked up in sex parties.'

'Where were they held?'

'Oh, all over the place at different people's houses.'

'Then what?'

'I was introduced to Lynda and Stuart, they had a big house; I would go there with a select few where women would attend and have sex them.'

'Then what?'

'Sumner started to bring women who were less than willing, but we all engaged in sex with them.'

'By less than willing; you mean raped them?'

Prentice looked down and as he nodded.

'Does that nod mean yes?'

'Yes, okay, nod means yes.'

'So you knew they were not willing, but still had sex with them, is that what you're saying?'

'I've said that yes I did.'

'Then what happened to the women afterwards?'

'I don't know they were led away by Charles.'

'Why do you think the women never complained to the police about being raped?'

90

'I don't know.'

'If the women had been willing, why weren't they brought back?'

'I don't know.'

'They couldn't come back because they had been killed and buried in the woods. So each new party had another woman bought in and raped.'

'I didn't know they had been killed I didn't.'

'Okay I want you to watch the end of the first tape; just as Janet is being pulled out of the room.'

Jim nodded to Vicky who replaced video 1 inside the machine. Vicky pressed play, the scene showed Janet being led out of the room naked and crying, carrying her clothes. Then Prentice could be heard saying 'who is going to do this one, it must be exciting hearing someone die?'

'I think you may have thought the tape had been switched off. That comment Mr Prentice makes you a conspirator in the murder of the five women. So let me recap, and remind you again, you have been arrested for murder, conspiracy to murder, rape, conspiracy to rape, sexual assault and conspiracy to commit sexual assault. I will just remind you that you are still under caution.'

Prentice just sat there looking dejected and watching his whole world now going down the pan, his kids in private school, his big 5 bed house, his country retreat and wife would be all gone.

'Okay Mr Prentice you heard the comment at the end of the tape what did that mean?'

'Yes I knew they were going to be killed yes I knew okay, I'm done for.'

Jim wrapped up the interview then charged him with rape and conspiracy to murder Janet Crosby and prepared the remand in custody report; then called Langton.

Langton was over the moon as he said 'you need to get this wrapped up Jim as Yvonne has been on the blower, she needs to brief you next week.'

91

Jim thought fuck me to the states again what a result, he then thought of Jackie, but knew he could buy her something nice on the expenses.

Jim got Vicky to finish up with the procedures of fingerprinting and photographing Prentice. He then said 'how would you like to help put this job together if Langton agrees?' 'Oh Jim that would be great, what a fantastic job thanks.' 'No problem, but it's a lot of work; Langton will want things done right. I have another job with the Home Office looming up which means I will be away.' 'Oh what's that Jim?' 'Sorry, I don't know yet, just bag carrying for some enquiry I think.'

Jim refrained from letting Jackie know about the spooks till the week-end was over; he just wanted to be pleased and to please her.

Jim informed Langton that Vicky would help put together the file she was a competent detective. Langton agreed and called for a meeting with them both the following day.

Jim then started to write up the log with regard to the interview then gave a copy to Langton for his policy log. Langton reached for the bottom drawer and before Jim could object he had poured two fingers of Islay. Jim was sipping the glass when there was a knock at the door. Jim handed the glass to Langton to hide as he called 'come in' with that the door pushed open and in walked the Chief. 'Sit down please gents' said the Chief as Jim and Langton began to stand up.

The Chief was beaming, 'another good job well done, come on Langton where's the scotch let's have a toast?' Langton opened the drawer and poured another glass and handed them out, they all toasted the job; the Chief then asked Langton to bring his policy log to his office in an hour, then he left.

Jim then discussed the interviews as Langton scribed the log. Langton then said 'I know what this is about; I bet the Chief has got a number 10 interview again; he will be asked to try and keep the MP's name out of the limelight.' 'Yeah another cover up, any other villain would be poleaxed.' Langton nodded as he scribed his log.

Langton spoke with the Chief's secretary as he waited for him to clear the last issue. The green light then came on; she stood and opened the door inviting Langton in. The Chief invited Langton to sit down and as if by a reciprocal arrangement, he poured two glasses of scotch. The Chief toasted Langton on a good job, but he passed it down to Jim. The Chief acknowledged the referral as he raised his glass. They then went over the policy log as the Chief took copious notes. The Chief then said 'who knows about the back bencher, as I anticipate questions that will be asked from the top, can we hide his name?' 'Well sir, there's the interview team. Then of course the others involved especially Prentice, the Small's and last but not least, Sumner, and of course the other women present, they will all know each other.' 'God what a mess so, in effect there is no way of hiding this.' 'I don't think so; there are too many eyes and ears involved.' 'Okay just testing the water, so I can batt off the anticipated questions. Thanks I will keep you updated. Oh and by the way as you are aware 'Box needs' Jim again.' 'Yes I spoke with the intelligence head earlier last week.' 'They think a lot of Jim; you need to be careful they don't poach him.' 'They've already tried, but he has stayed loyal to us.' The Chief raised his glass as they drank the dregs, then Langton left.

The following morning Jim picked up Vicky and the drove to HQ's. On route Jim said 'get on the right side of Langton and you could have a friend for life, he likes a job done well, he can also be a pain in the arse over getting it right. Do you drink scotch?' 'I love it, especially single malt.' 'That's a great start; if I were you I would get him a bottle of his favourite, any one of the Islay brands; that will soften him and show you're on the same wave length.' 'Thanks Jim, I'll do that.'

They arrived at HQ's where they met in Langton's office Jim introduced Vicky, they shook hands; then sat down as Jim outlined the case and where they had got so far. Vicky was making copious notes of the meeting.

Jim had identified all the men in the video sequence and one of the women Lynda Small, but there were two other unknown women to find, Vicky responded confirming she had their first names and would speak with Lynda at the next remand hearing to see if she would name them fully.

The meeting was just about to wrap up when Jim said to Langton 'Oh yes guv, Vicky enjoys a scotch as well, so you can have a dram without fear.' With that Langton opened his drawer and poured a drop into three tumblers, then passed them over, toasting the job and the follow up which Vicky would do. Jim and Vicky finished then left the office; he sat Vicky down and went over the issues that still needed to be completed.

Jim was half way through the briefing when his phone went and saw it was Yvonne. He walked away as he answered it. 'Be at the same hotel Birmingham next Tuesday 4 pm bring an overnight bag, but also have a case at home packed ready to go, things have heated up and your services are required.' 'That sounds good my service is required.' 'Bugger off Broadbent. Tuesday 4 pm' the conversation over; the phone went dead.

Jim finished off with Vicky then headed home for a long week-end. Jim arrived to an empty flat which was expected, so he checked the fridge for the ingredients that Jackie had left out ready to be cooked, he saw mince and a bolognaise sauce so presumed it was going to be spag bog.

He went and changed then put on an apron wearing just jockey shorts and tee shirt. He fried off the mince and added the sauce then let it simmer away as he measured out the spaghetti and heated up the water. He watched the water come to a rolling boil as he thought of Yvonne and the way she boiled over and took every bit of him to the max.

The water was ready as he entered the stems of the spaghetti thinking he was like the stalks being slowly entered into the heat of the boiling water. He kept thinking what was going on in the states that the spooks couldn't handle internally?

Just as he was drifting off into another fantasy world, when he heard the door go and pretended not to have heard it, just like Jackie did when he came home; he felt her hands on his bum as she rested her head against his back then wrapped her arms around him giving him a big squeeze. Jim turned and kissed her and gave her a squeeze, 'get changed nearly ready babes.' 'Okay, I'll open the wine.' 'Make it a nice one.' 'I only get nice wine' as she laughed. Jim dished up and bought in the piping hot plates and a kitchen roll to use as napkins, as it would probably get messy. 'You look sexy in an apron Jim.' They laughed as they ate their fill then relaxed on the sofa as they watched TV; one of Jackie's favourite soaps was on. Jim sat watching and thinking, this is really exciting.

He just couldn't get his head around how people got so engrossed in such drivel; well that was his opinion anyway.

They were both tired and just crashed to bed. Jim woke up half way through the night to find he was nearly pushed out of the bed. Jackie had taken up all of the space leaving him on the edge; he managed to turn half over as he said 'shove over Jack.' Jackie never woke she just rolled away and turned over.

Jim woke to his alarm to find he was on the edge of the bed again with Jackie snuggled up to him. Jim got out and showered then heard Jackie in the kitchen as the aroma of cooked eggs, bacon and black pudding reached his nose. Jackie just smiled as she plated his full English and handed him the plate. He made coffee for them both then he wolfed his breakfast down mopping the plate with bread and butter.

Jackie was slowly coming to life as she sat opposite Jim cupping her hands around her coffee mug, they chatted about the week-end plans.

Jim left it until Sunday to tell Jackie about the looming US trip and the spooks briefing in Birmingham with the probability of an overnight stay. But when Jim finally told Jackie she was none too pleased, but she accepted it, as she knew Jim relished the excitement of working with the spooks. But inwardly she was afraid not knowing what he was involved in.

CHAPTER TWENTY

Vicky sat looking at the still facial photos taken from the video sequences of the two unknown women Julie and Maria; she had a number of flyers made of the facial features, and gave them to the intelligence section who pinned them on their notice board seeking information as to the identities. It didn't take long before the identifications were made.

Vicky obtained the addresses where they lived then did a drive-by checking the cars parked in the drives of the well to-do houses, she took the car numbers and checked against the PNC; then checked the voters register, confirming the occupants of the houses concerned which, also included the first names of the two women in question.

Vicky got back to HQ's; on route she had purchased Langton a bottle of Islay, to start off on the right foot; she placed it in her shoulder bag to prevent prying eyes. She knocked on Langton's door and was invited in, then she began to highlight her findings; then lent over and took out the brown paper wrapped bottle and handed it over; she didn't speak just nodded as Langton smiled. 'Shut the door please Vick' as he opened his bottom drawer taking out his already opened Islay which was nearing the end of its life and poured two tumblers a quarter full handing one to Vicky. 'Good health Vicky and welcome to my team.' Vicky raised her glass 'Cheers guv and thank you.'

'Okay what have you got Vick?' Vicky smiled at him coyly 'well guv this is the identity of the other women on the tapes, I have checked their addresses against voters and car registrations; it all matches up.' 'Okay what do you need?' 'I think an early call tomorrow morning would be good, I will need two teams me on one with a couple to assist, then another team for the other address if Jim's not available?' 'No I'm afraid Jim will be out of the game for some time, so I will get you some manpower. In the meantime get a briefing report completed; by then I will have a team nominated by this afternoon.' Vicky finished her drink then stood up smoothing down her skirt smiled at Langton picked up her bag then left his office. She found a type writer and rattled out a briefing, it didn't take long as she was a competent touch typist. Vicky was looking forward to the arrest as she knew that once arrested the fun would begin.

Langton called Jim expressing his approval at his choice in Vicky; he commented on the following morning's arrests. Jim bid him good luck and wished he could be there, but he had received a briefing from Yvonne which he had to work on. Langton again gave a questioning remark 'are you sure you're not giving her one?' 'No I'm not I told you, you just won't let go will you?' He laughed as he put the phone down.

Vicky's team was assembled for a briefing for the next morning's early door knock. Langton stood in background as Vicky gave out the briefing highlighting the evidence that could possibly be found at the addresses. The addresses look top end so they could expect top end lawyers as well. Vicky then explained that she required video players in each interview room she also nominated different police stations for each prisoner to be taken too.

Langton gave a thank you to Vicky then gave a serious warning to those assembled that it could hit the press big time, so do everything by the book.

That was it, Vicky nominated the interview team for Maria; she would take Julie. She then handed the file out with the photos of both suspects inside.

The morning came as Vicky and her team stood outside of the house, it was all in darkness, they started to walk along the short gravel drive when the bedroom light came on upstairs. Vicky rang the doorbell she waited a couple of minutes, the landing and hall lights came on then footsteps could be heard, the door opened. Vicky instantly recognised Julie Sangster from the video sequence; she wasn't the good looking figure in the video, her hair was all over the place and was in a dressing gown looking half asleep. 'Julie Sangster?' 'Yes who are you?' 'I am a police officer and I'm arresting you for conspiracy to rape.' Vicky cautioned her as per the book then stepped inside as the other two members of team entered and closed the door. 'What rape what are you talking about.' 'All will become clear when I interview you.'

A call came from upstairs 'who's at the door darling?' 'It's the police I'm being arrested.' 'What?' Then Vicky saw a male figure hurrying downstairs 'what is all this about?' Vicky said 'Your wife I presume?' 'Yes it is; what's this all about?' 'Your wife has been arrested and will be taken to the Central police station, but before we do we will need to make a search of the house.' 'Where's your warrant?' 'I don't need one as your wife has been arrested in the house that gives me the power to search for evidence in connection with the alleged offence.' The husband backed down after the confident statement from Vicky. What struck Vicky as strange was he never asked why she was being arrested. Nor was Julie kicking up a fuss the way she had anticipated she would.

Vicky went upstairs with Julie where she searched the bedroom as Julie dressed, she noticed a big television and video recorder on chest of drawers; she opened a drawer underneath the TV and found rows of sex tapes and ordinary movie films. Vicky looked at Julie who just looked down not saying anything. Then she opened the next drawer down and found a number of homemade video cassettes.

'What's on these Julie?' 'Just some holiday pictures that's all.' Vicky removed them and piled them up saying 'I'll take these and have a look to make sure.' Julie blushed as she knew what was on them; scenes of her and numerous men and other women in sexual positions.

The search concluded Vicky went downstairs with Julie. The other officers had kept the husband busy whilst they had searched the downstairs and had seized some photographs of Julie in the arms of other men and women and with some of the women tied up.

The husband said as they were leaving 'I'll call Peregrine he will be there when they interview you this is outrageous.'

Vicky kept quiet in the car on the way to the station other than 'it looks like being a long day.' Julie never responded just kept her head down low.

They arrived at the station where after being booked-in she was placed into a cell to await the interview.

Vicky got all the tapes and placed them on her desk then had breakfast; a full English as the early start had given her a big appetite.

She had just finished when she received a call from the front counter confirming Sangster's brief had just arrived. Vicky met the brief at the front counter and invited him in. He was a tall well-dressed man, not the archetypal brief, more in keeping with a barrister. As soon as he introduced himself with the plumb in his mouth accent she knew this had to be done by the book.

He produced his business card and stated his name was Peregrine Farquharson. Vicky looked at his business card and saw the address as the Temple Chambers in London which confirmed her suspicions as being correct.

He was polite and not the pushy arrogant person she expected. He just said quietly can I see my client please. Vicky decided to keep him that way as she nodded then showed him the way to the custody suite where he signed-in and was shown to an interview room. Vicky then prepared the room where the interview proper would take place then confirmed the video recorder was working.

Vicky knew that the consultation with the barrister would take a while so went upstairs to the CID office where she began to look through some of the tapes seized from the bedroom. They were indeed sex videos. They were in the main of Sangster and other men and women, who all looked consensual, nothing forced. Some included her husband; then she saw something, that made her smile, as she said 'Yes' to herself. Then the call came in that confirmed the consultation was finished. She went into the main office where she nodded to a DC who she had asked to assist her in the interview. They went downstairs as Vicky set up the video player with the first tape.

Then the door opened as in walked the dejected Sangster along with the barrister followed by the DC.

They were invited to sit down; Vicky then made the introductions and commenced the interview.

'Julie Sangster just so you are clear why you are here, you have been arrested for conspiracy to rape; you were cautioned at the time, but I will caution you again.'

Vicky rattled off a word perfect rendition of the caution which she had used so many times before.

'Do you understand?'

Julie looked at the barrister who nodded.

'Yes, I understand.'

'Okay, how do you know Charles Sumner?'

'No comment.'

'You do know him; also how do you know Stuart and Lynda Small?'

'No comment.'

'How many times have you been to the house at 76, Tall Pines Road?'

'No comment.'

'I will show you later how I know you have been there. Okay Julie, what I'm about to show you on video are a sequence of events, watch the video and then I will ask you some questions.'

Vicky nodded to the DC who pressed play on the video player; the whirring sound died away as did the white noise on the screen; the scene opened to the bedroom where naked men and women stood waiting. Then the door opened as in walked Sumner leading Janet Crosby. She was blindfolded. Then two women Julie and another stripped the clothes off of the fighting and struggling Janet, who was taken to a bed and held down by Julie and the other woman who tied her to the bed whilst she was raped by the men present.

Vicky looked at Julie whose face was as red as beetroot from blushing as she looked down. Vicky nodded to the DC who stopped the tape.

'Okay Julie you do know Charles Sumner he is the one leading the woman in, oh by the way her name was Janet the one with Sumner; that name is important; you will see why in a minute how important it is. You also know Lynda and Stuart Small, because that is their house at 76, Tall Pines Road.'

'No comment.'

'Now as you can see Janet was a non-willing participant in the proceedings as she was held down by you and another whilst she was raped by the men one after the other. That Julie is why you have been arrested for conspiracy to rape.'

'No comment.'

'As you can see, there are four other tapes to be played. I can tell you now that they all contain the same scenes but with different women. Yes Julie conspiracy to rape.'

Julie looked at the barrister, who requested an adjournment.

Vicky gathered up the tapes ejecting the one in the machine as well. They waited for some twenty minutes then the barrister confirmed they were ready to carry on. Once back in the interview room the barrister said that his client would like to make a statement on the videos.

Vicky nodded as she thought she is going to say the women consented to the sex because they liked to be involved in rough sex. She was right as Sangster gave a nearly scripted account of how the women liked to be roughed up and enjoyed rough sex.

'How did you know the women liked being roughed up?'

'They told me they did.'

'Oh so you spoke with them did you?'

'Yes I did.'

'Was that before or after the sexual encounters?'

'Oh afterwards they all said they loved it.'

'Okay let me show you this video sequence after the rape of Janet Crosby, yes I say rape, just listen to one of the men in the room, you will know him, his name Reginald Prentice; just listen as he is heard to say something, you are standing next to him, just listen?'

Vicky fast forwarded the tape to the section then pressed play; the voice of Prentice is heard 'who is going to do this one; it must be exciting hearing someone die.' Julie is seen to squirm at the comment made by Prentice.

'Now Julie, you are also being arrested for conspiracy to murder.'

She was again cautioned by Vicky and this time she was ready to go for the throat.

'So Julie as you see this knocks consensual sex out of the window, you knew she didn't consent, nor did the other women you held down whilst being systematically raped by the men present. They didn't consent because after being raped they were murdered, that is why none of them complained; they couldn't, they were all dead!'

The barrister then interjected and became very insistent that his client was innocent and wanted it recorded that Vicky was becoming aggressive in the interview.

'Oh I wouldn't go too far with that if I were you!'

'What do you mean by that, is that a threat, are you threatening me detective?'

'No just making a comment that's all.'

'What does that mean?'

'Okay, if you want me to tell you I will,'

Vicky opened her brief case and took out another video cassette and after ejecting the one inside placed it in then pressed play; a sex scene was shown with Peregrine Farquharson, the barrister representing Julie taking her from behind looking pleased with himself as he was smiling for the camera.

'I want that tape?'

'Sorry that is evidence for the prosecution; I now believe you have a conflict of interest in this case?'

'I will make that decision. I want to speak with your senior officer?'

'I haven't finished my interview yet.'

Vicky then carried on.

'The women on the five tapes are all dead, their bodies have been recovered from woods nearby; five deaths to satisfy some underlying sexual desire. You knew they were being brought to the room to be raped, you knew afterwards they would be killed, you knew that didn't you? You knew damn well they were going to be murdered didn't you?'

'No comment.'

'Okay this interview is now concluded, I will prepare charges and you will be in court in the morning.'

The barrister was now looking sheepish he knew if that tape was entered into evidence and produced at court his days would be numbered as a barrister.

Vicky then smiled as she withdrew the video cassette from the player as she said 'if you would like to see the senior officer now I will take you?' She knew she had him by the bollocks and was calling his bluff. He replied 'no not at the moment.'

Vicky prepared the charges then after reading them out placed her back in the cells, then she went upstairs and punched the air shouting 'yes, yes, yes.' The other detectives knew she must have had a result.

Once she had calmed down she got on the phone to Langton explaining the tape and the barristers comments after he was shown the video sequence of him shagging his client. Langton replied nice one Vicky; get here ASAP please, and to bring the tape.

Vicky was hoping to have a meeting with Steve the DC, who had gone to arrest Maria, but knew that was out of the window for the moment; so she grabbed the file papers and the tapes and went to HQ's where she met with Langton. He shook her hand and said the Chief will be here in a moment, can you set up the tape so he can see it, he's going to inform the Temple Chambers Head of this.

Vicky set it up, just as she had finished the Chief arrived and requested a look at the sequence. Vicky pressed play and pointed out whom Peregrine Farquharson the barrister was and who Julie Sangster was in the compromising position they were in. The Chief thanked Vicky then invited her into Langton's office where she outlined the interview and the way the barrister had reacted.

The Chief thanked Langton and Vicky as he left the office. Langton said 'well done Vicky.' He opened the bottom drawer and poured a large scotch each as he toasted her for the good job she had done and how Jim had been right choose her for the role.

Langton enquired about Steve, Vicky confirmed that Maria had been arrested, but she had not heard from him, so that was a good sign.

Vicky finished her scotch and left the office. She finished off her papers; she tried to ring Steve again, but was informed he was still wrapped up in the interview.

CHAPTER TWENTY/ONE

Steve stood with Georgina a uniformed officer at the door of Maria's house, it was all in darkness; he rang the bell and saw the upstairs lights come on, then the landing lights as he heard footsteps coming down the stairs. The door opened half way as a sheepish looking woman looked around 'Yes what do you want?' Steve put his foot in the door as he said 'police Maria, I need to come in and talk to you for a moment.' 'Come back later when I'm dressed.' She went to close the door but, his foot prevented it, as he pushed his way inside then said 'Maria I am arresting you for conspiracy to rape.' 'What? Oh do behave.' Georgina then took Maria upstairs to get dressed; once dressed Steve joined them upstairs in the bedroom.

'You live alone Maria?' She sat at the dressing table brushing her hair. 'Yes, but what's that to do with you?' 'Just asking that's all.' He then started to look through the drawers and the wardrobe. Then in the corner he found a box of video cassettes with handwritten notes on.

'What are these Maria?' 'Video's; are you blind?' 'Okay the hard way then, what's on them?' 'Just some holiday video's' 'been on lots of holidays then?' 'I'm taking these as part of the investigation.' That hit a note with Maria as she began to colour up. Steve took the box out then found some photographs in a folder, he opened the folder and took out the photographs as he did he saw Maria in all kinds of sexual poses performing sexual acts on both men and women. Steve thought she has got a nice body, as he looked over at her as she sat blushing.

The search completed she was taken to one of the other stations where she was booked-in, then placed into a cell. Steve took one of the videos and checked the content. He sat and watched as he saw Maria rough handling a woman who was being held by a man, she cut her clothes off her and performed sexual acts on her as the woman struggled. Maria slapped her then she became compliant, then the man had sex with her.

Steve thought good stuff then had a full breakfast; after a fat boy's; he and another detective interviewed Maria.

'Okay Maria you have been arrested for Conspiracy to rape you are under caution you understand?'

Maria nodded

'Is that a yes?'

'Yes I understand.'

'Your full name is?'

Maria Glennister.'

'Do you want a brief?'

'No don't need one.'

Steve having spent time reading the briefing notes of Vicky, so was prepared for the interview.

'How do you know Stuart and Lynda?'

'They're friends of mine.'

'How long have you known them?'

'A couple of year's maybe a bit longer.'

'How long have known Charles Sumner?'

'Not long about a year or so.'

'How many times have you been to Stuart and Lynda's house?'

'Quite a few times.'

'For what reason?'

'Mainly parties.'

'What kind of parties?'

Maria knew he was playing the game with her but, she had no way of stopping it.

'You know damn well what kind of parties.'

'Sex parties?'

'Yes sex parties; I like sex okay.'

'Yes I understand. I am now going to show you a sequence of a video so you know what and where this is leading okay?'

'As you like.'

Steve operated the video player as the scene opened to show the group of naked men and women including Maria standing waiting looking at the door, when in came Sumner with Janet blindfolded as Maria and the other women stripped Janet then held and tied her down whilst the men raped her.

'Okay that scene; tell me what that was about?'

'You saw it was a game the woman liked being subjected to humiliation and raped, it was a sex game.'

'Okay I have four other tapes here all with different women depicting the same scene and the people present going through the same procedure. Are they all into sex games the women that are led in, were they all into being humiliated and pretend rape?'

'Yes, it is quite common.'

'So what you're saying is that all the women consented to the acts depicted on the video?'

'Yes it was just a sex game, have a look in any sex magazine; there are adverts for this kind of party.'

'Okay, tell me why all the women are different in the videos? Why aren't they part of the other videos either as victims or taking part when other women are engaged as victims?'

'I don't know, I didn't organise the parties, I just took part.'

'Tell me then if these women were so willing to be subjected to this kind of treatment why have they never stayed behind to laugh and joke about what had happened?'

'I don't know I never asked.'

'The tape we just saw; the woman's name was Janet and she left in tears and it didn't look like tears of joy either, it looked like she was petrified not full of the joys of spring like your suggesting; she had just been raped and you knew she had been raped; you held her down whilst she was being raped by the men, then you engaged the men as well, not a game Maria, it was rape wasn't it?'

'No it was a game.'

'No Maria look at this section of tape when one of the women is released, she attacks Sumner who punches her face causing her a nose bleed then punches her again; just watch as she is dazed and falls sliding down the wall leaving a blood smear as she falls, that is not consent that is force.'

Maria just looked down and made no comment

'Okay we will watch the other tapes then let us see if any of the other women are jumping for joy at the thought of the party and having fun shall we?'

Steve played the tapes and then he went for her throat.

'Now all those women were raped and you knew they were being raped; you knew they were suffering, you knew by the screams and the tears running down there faces during the rape and then being led from the room crying their eyes out that they had been forced. No Maria not a game it was rape which you participated in by holding the women down.'

'No you don't understand it was a game they enjoyed it they all did, so did I.'

'During the rape of Janet, yes the rape not the game, the rape, when it was over one of the men in the room is heard to discuss who was going to kill Janet, and how it must be good to hear someone dying. Not a party Maria; victims were led there, raped then murdered, you are also being arrested for conspiracy to murder.'

That was it Maria finally broke down and cried and said.

'I'm so sorry I got wrapped up in the sex games to start with, but then Stuart and Charles wanted it to be more exciting and real, so started to bring in women and forced them and raped them. I didn't know they were going to be murdered.'

'Oh Maria I think you did; why did the women not complain about being gang raped. They couldn't could they? They were all dead and you knew they were going to be killed didn't you?'

Maria sat and cried, her whole world now collapsed she was now looking at life in prison.

'Yes I knew Charles had gone too far, but everyone just kept quiet and went for it, yes we all knew; there I've said it, you happy now?'

'Thank you Maria, just a couple more questions, can you name all those present in the videos, we know some, just need you to confirm the others?'

Maria then rattled off the names of those present including the backbencher.

Steve then finished off the interview then stepped outside of the interview room, where he punched the air and shouted 'yes, what a fucking result.'

He then went and prepared the charges, conspiracy to murder and rape, once charged he rang Vicky who also said 'yes well done, thanks for the update.'

Langton appeared from his office as Vicky put the phone down; the beam across her face didn't need a question. 'Good news Vicky?' 'Yes guv, Steve has cracked Maria she has coughed she knew of the murders and rapes.' 'Good girl, well done, Jim will be pleased, he'll be over then moon.'

Vicky went home to her flat which she shared with her boyfriend Tom. Vicky opened the door although she was knackered from the early start; she almost floated in with the result of the day. Tom was not in the police so had no idea of the elation a good result caused in the psyche, but knew from her beaming smile she was over the moon. As he

110

took her coat he gave her a hug which she accepted and kissed him passionately. They eagerly started to undress each other as they hurried to the bedroom where they had an intense lovemaking session. Vicky just lay there afterwards looking at Tom as he slept; she felt a sense of achievement after her days work and smiled as she wrapped herself around him, then nodded off to sleep.

CHAPTER TWENTY/TWO

Jim arrived at the Marriot hotel in Birmingham, where he booked in and was met with a big smile from the receptionist he looked at her name badge which read Kirsty. 'Thank you Mr Broadbent for staying with us again I hope you have good stay.' 'Well thank you Kirsty for your greeting' as he smiled at her.

He went to his room and hung up his shirt and trousers then had a shower and shaved, he splashed on his aftershave which caused a stinging sensation. He dressed casually then he texted Jackie to say he had arrived okay and would let her know the situation as soon as he knew. He got a message back almost immediately thanking him for the text.

His phone then pinged as another text came through, this time from Yvonne stating she would be there within the hour and would meet him for a drink in the bar at 1700 or thereabouts.

Jim checked his watch and seeing he had an hour to spare, went for a short walk; he smiled at Kirsty as he passed reception, he thought fuck me I could give her one as well; then thought of the demands that Yvonne would be putting on him very soon. He walked for a while, not far, just enough to get some fresh air; then he turned around and walked back to the hotel. He arrived just to glimpse Yvonne entering the lift she didn't have time to turn before the doors closed, he watched the floor counter and saw she was on the same floor, as he thought; not too far to walk after he got kicked out; as he smiled to himself.

He then went to the bar where he ordered a coffee and sat at a table, he picked up a paper scanning the headlines of the world news as he tried to see if there was anything happening that would cause rumblings in the corridors of MI5, which could have been the reason for the meeting with Yvonne, but nothing was evident just the normal conflicts throughout the world hotspots; not that he had expected anything to jump out at him really.

He sat drinking his coffee, as he cast his eye around the foyer and caught Kirsty giving him a second glance. He then saw Yvonne arrive as he raised his hand; she acknowledged him and walked over to his table, he watched her walk and thought she still has got a good body, not young and firm, but built for comfort. Jim stood up and shook hands as he tickled her palm. She coloured up as she said 'behave Jim.' He smiled 'coffee or something stronger?' 'Oh a double vodka and tonic, with a slice of lemon, it's been a hard day.' 'Could get harder?' 'I'm hoping so I need something to relieve my stress.' Jim thought oh I could relieve you right now.

He came back having ordered the drinks at the bar, he sat down and looked at her and said 'you look worried, anything wrong?' 'Lots Jim, but nothing you can help with.' With that the barman came over with the drinks as Jim signed the bar tab and room number. Jim raised his glass of double measured scotch as he chinked against her glass of vodka.

Yvonne opened her small document case and said 'read this Jim; the first page will give you an insight into the issues involved.' Jim took the page and read it and was half way down when he looked at Yvonne who just nodded, he didn't speak as he returned to reading. When finished he looked at Yvonne and said 'is this for real?' 'I'm afraid so. Now you see why I need someone on the outside, someone without allegiance to any staff on the inside of the secret services.' 'Wow this is heavy duty stuff.' 'Yes Jim and dangerous, so be careful, there is big money involved in this, also top players as well, so be careful.' 'Where does Barney feature in this?' 'An American undercover agent has infiltrated the main players, so he cannot afford to be seen with anyone outside of the people he is mixing with; Barney is his handler, but can only be debriefed very infrequently; what Barney has been told so far, squarely implicates one of our agents who has a relative in Parliament; not sure where he stands in this at the moment, but we cannot take any chances.' 'What's my role?' 'Work alongside Barney and report back to me by scrambled phone; I have a sim card here, it retains your same number; talk to me only once you have inserted the sim card. Trust no one Jim other than me and Barney and be careful.'

'I thought you said this was to do with the assassination of a UN official, there's no mention of that in this document?' 'No Jim that was a ruse put out by the CIA to cover increased activity of the secret service, which would give our suspects the ability to work on their operation knowing they were not in the limelight so to speak, but in reality they were being watched.' 'A double bluff then?' 'Sort of, it appears to be working; there is a lot of traffic between the suspects, now they think they are not being looked at, it's looking good.'

Jim saw the seriousness in her eyes, but he lightened it by saying; 'does the condemned man have a last request?' As he laughed; 'that could be arranged after another double vodka.' Jim raised his hand to the barman who bought over another round of drinks, Jim signed the tab again.

They both chinked their glasses as they chatted away; when they finished their drinks they took the lift to third floor; they kissed passionately in the lift then went to Yvonne's room where they engaged in love making till the early morning; Yvonne was making up for all the years she had gone without sex. Jim was good, he took her to places

114

she had never been before. Most of her love making previously had been wham bam thank you mam leaving her wondering what this sex thing all about. Then she met Jim, wow the earth did move; she never knew she had so many sensitive areas which heightened her vaginal expectations. She had never experienced someone so thoughtful to her needs either; Jim made sure she was satisfied first.

Jim slept heavily, when he awoke he was alone Yvonne had gone, having left a note saying 'thank you Jim, I will call you soon to let you know when your flight is; your credit card will be updated again. Barney will call you in a couple of days to bring you up to speed.'

Jim returned to his own room a couple of doors away and showered then went down to the restaurant where he had breakfast. He called Jackie to update her on his arrival time; and would talk when he got home.

Whilst at the table he changed sim cards; after about twenty minutes he called Yvonne, she answered 'just testing the sim card, it works fine and thanks for another good night.'

'Can't talk now Jim, but yes another good night in your experienced hands, you must tell me sometime where on the list I am in the women you have slept with?' 'Oh not many I read a lot.' 'Oh do bugger off Jim; look must go, bye for now.'

Jim went to reception and checked-out as he admired the good looks of Kirsty who smiled nicely at him 'I hope you enjoyed your stay Mr Broadbent?' 'Thank you, very nice,' as he shook her hand and kissed the back of it. 'Oh thank you kind sir' as she smiled even deeper, with a sparkle in her eye. 'Till the next time Kirsty thank you.' 'I look forward to it.' Jim waved as he left thinking, fucking hell what a looker she is.

Jim then drove back to HQ's where after the long drive he met with Langton who updated him on the interviews of the two women and how Vicky had done a cracking job; she had been an excellent choice of his.

Jim then updated him on the information he had read in the one page document. Langton 'this is heavy duty stuff Jim just be careful.' Jim acknowledged the warning highlighting the same sentiments from Yvonne.

Jim then rang Vicky requesting a meeting with her to talk over the interviews; he then made his way to Central policed station, where he met Vicky in the canteen where they discussed the interviews; they were then joined by Steve. They both outlined the interviews and Vicky mentioned how she had viewed the tapes from the chest of drawers; on one of the tapes she saw the figure of man giving Sangster one; he ended up being the barrister representing her at the interview; she was able to get the tape in during the interview. She played the tape highlighting it as a conflict of interest; she also stating the Chief was contacting The Temple Chambers regarding the find. Vicky said 'you should have seen his face when I played the tape.' 'Good girl well done; great job.'

'How was yours Steve?' 'Not as exciting as Vick's, but Maria tried to say that it was all play acting and the alleged victims were all willing partners to the act, but that got chucked out when the blooded nose of one of the women was shown, also when the conversation was heard about who was going to do the woman in; plus the five bodies in the woods, after that she cracked admitting she knew. So I charged her with conspiracy to murder and rape.' 'Another great job well done; right tomorrow night Nags Head please and have a beer.' They both nodded and smiled, Jim then went to find Jackie, he was just walking out when she came into the canteen, they greeted each other as Jim out of sight patted her bum and said 'just coming to find you, you want a coffee?' Jackie smiled and nodded.

They sat as Jackie looked worried sensing something was worrying Jim, 'what's wrong Jim?' 'Oh nothing just a long debrief last night and tired. Oh before I forget I'm meeting Vicky and Steve for a beer tomorrow night, you want to come?' 'No thanks, you go, but don't drive if you've had a few.' 'Okay, no problem.' Jim then went home early and had a couple of hours sleep catching up from the night before.

He decided to get a takeaway so called the local Indian for their normal order. Not long after Jackie came in and sniffed the air, 'Oh Jim I'm whacked out, I thought you would have started dinner by now?' 'Just ordered an Indian it'll be here soon so get changed.' She smiled and gave him a big hug and kiss. Shortly after the meal arrived, they sat eating and drinking wine. Jackie kept quizzing him about the spooks meeting, but he kept batting it off. He didn't want her worrying whilst he was away. The time had flown by; Jackie was whacked out and as soon as she hit the pillow she was gone. This was good as far as Jim was concerned as he was still getting over the effects of being ravished by Yvonne; so he crashed as well.

The next morning they both ate a small breakfast as they were still full from the previous evening's meal. Jim then reminded Jackie of the Nags Head.

Jim was half way through the day when his phone went, he saw the callers ID, it was Barney, 'hey Barney how you doing?' 'Fine Jim, look I need you here soon, like next week, I have spoken to Yvonne she said you had been briefed?' 'Yeah, what's the hurry?' 'Not on the phone, but my man has got something red hot and it's going live here and in the UK, so you need to get here to check out the faces as they will be in the UK soon.' 'Okay I'll await Yvonne's call; see you next week. Oh yeah, just so you know my phone now has a scrambled sim card inserted.' 'Okay Jim thanks but, still rather brief you on this side of the pond.'

Jim then went to see Langton where he filled him in on the phone call from Barney. Langton looked at Jim 'are you sure you're not giving Yvonne one?' 'You ask me every time; no I'm not.' 'I'm still not so sure; anyway, we will have to wait for her call.' 'I'm going to the Nags Head later to buy Vick and Steve a well done drink, you coming?' 'Sorry not tonight I'll see them when you're away enjoying yourself.' 'Jealous are we?' 'Bugger off Jim; have a good night.'

Jim arrived at the Nags Head it was like Déjà vu; reminding him of the old days. He saw loads of colleagues he knew and had a good session toasting Vicky and Steve on the good job, but his capacity was nowhere near as good as it used to be and it wasn't long before he was pissed. Although he did remember Jackie's warning about driving so, called a cab and arrived home staggering; he all but crashed through the door and ended up sleeping on the couch where he landed.

He awoke in the morning with his neck cricked and back aching, he was busting for a piss as well, he just made it to the toilet, nearly pissing himself; he looked in the mirror as he was relieving his bladder and thought what a state; then had pangs of conscience about how he had treated June all those times.

Jackie awoke and entered the bathroom and said 'You smell like brewery I hope you never drove home?' 'No I cabbed it, so can you drop me off at the Nags Head to get my car?' 'Yep will do you want a fry up?' 'Please I'm starving.'

Jim ate the full English that Jackie had prepared and patted his tummy as he burped; he excused himself 'that was lovely Jack thank you.'

Jackie dropped Jim off at the Nags Head; after collecting his car he drove to HQ's where Langton was on the phone as he said 'He's just walked in looking the worse for wear, yeah he was on the piss last night.' Langton mouthed Yvonne. 'Yes; I'll pass you over.' Jim took the phone. 'Okay Jim next week you got a pen and paper.' She confirmed Heathrow; the flight number and time; 'the tickets will be collectable at the AA desk just be careful Jim.' It was a short and sweet conversation then she was gone.

Jim said to Langton, 'well that's it next week and I'm off again.' 'Jim, Yvonne said to tell you to be careful; there is big money involved and big players, so tread carefully.' Jim nodded 'yeah Yvonne has already eluded to that, thanks for the warning.' 'Right clear up your backlog of enquiries and bugger off, and spend a couple of days with Jackie, I'll sort that out with her D/I.' Jim nodded 'I'll keep my phone on anyway, just in case you need anything.'

Jim cleared his desk then saw Langton's secretary, she was looking nice not that she never looked nice. 'Hi how are you, I'm away again soon so will give you some dict when I'm back!' She laughed as she walked by shaking her head as she smiled to herself. Jim watched her as she walked into Langton's office admiring her bum.

Jim cleared his desk as his phone rang, it was Jackie, 'how did you manage that Jim; I've been given a couple of days off?' 'Just call it charm, see you later; let's go for a nice meal, your choice, see you later.'

Jim got home as he did so he received another call from Barney, 'Hi Jim, I need you to get back in with Carole-Anne, that shouldn't be difficult, I've laid the ground for you, she is expecting you to call her, she's on a different number I will text it you, call her as soon as you land, I'm not going to meet you; get a cab to the same hotel, then call Carole-Anne. I think I'm being tailed so need to distance myself from you. Just be mindful of your surroundings Jim, this is getting heavy now with the suspects getting paranoid. Okay have a good trip, once I am sure the tail has been eliminated I will meet you; this number and yours are scrambled so they are secure. Cheers Jim.' Barney hardly drew a breath and before Jim could answer he was gone.

What the fuck was he getting into; he couldn't tell Jackie she would worry herself sick at the thought of all the warnings he had been given on both sides of the pond.

Jim waited for Jackie to come home, he confirmed her preference; then booked a steakhouse restaurant for later. Jackie pushed him back into the bedroom where they went for an epic session pleasing each other with their favourite preferences. Jackie grabbed his head forcing it between her

119

thighs relishing the pleasure he gave her; she had a massive orgasm covering his face. She in return took his shaft in her mouth working her head rhythmically then she felt his hips go solid as she felt him grab her hair holding her there; then he exploded in her mouth as she swallowed greedily. As she felt her hair being released she took her head away and made sure she had feasted all of him. This felt good to Jackie her heart was beating fast as she lay on Jim's chest watching it rise and fall with his breath.

Her breath settled she closed her eyes drifting away slowly on Jim's settling heartbeat. This was nice she was drifting on a cloud being wafted on a gentle breeze, she could feel the warmth of the sun on her face; this was oh so good. Jackie didn't want to move this was the best she had felt for a long time.

Then she felt Jim stirring, she turned over wishing the dream not to end; but had to get up; they finished by having a shower then dressing and headed for their meal.

They sat and toasted each other with a nice glass of wine as they consumed their steaks. Jim likened it to the last supper as he cut through his blood red steak absorbing the juices as it melted in his mouth.

Jackie was asking all sorts of questions in relation to how he wangled her getting time off. Jim just informed her that Langton had arranged it.

Jackie didn't want to, but she began to pump him about the American trip; he let her know he had no idea until he got over there, but probably another mole hunt and dry run stuff as before. He couldn't tell her, he couldn't.

The few days passed so quickly and before long Jim was dropped off at Heathrow, terminal 3; he picked up his tickets from the American Airline office, then went through check-in at the business class desk. He went through the security check-in; once airside he found the business class lounge. He casually watched the information display board. The flight was on time so hopefully that would ease the tension of hanging around. He called Jackie letting her know all was okay. They chatted for a couple of minutes then Jim saw the boarding gate number highlighted for his flight; so said his goodbye and promised to text her on his arrival.

The business class was the way to travel as he stretched out his six foot frame leaning back the recliner knowing there was no one behind him. He just relaxed and went to sleep; the stewardess had seen him sleeping so covered him with a blanket. When he awoke he was surprised to find the blanket on him. He was then tended too; being offered a meal and a glass of wine which he duly accepted. Finally the journey ended as he saw the distant sky line of Washington DC out of one of windows. The seat belt sign went on as he buckled up; then he adjusted his recliner to the upright position.

He went through the normal immigration procedure which took longer than before as he never had Barney to fast track him through. He was finally processed then went to baggage collection; the carousal was well underway as he waited for the repeat circulation; he collected his case then caught a taxi to the Washington Hilton, where he was efficiently booked-in. Once finished he went to his room where he unpacked. The air conditioning was on full, making the room chilly so, he turned it down as he rubbed his hands together to get warm. His clothes unpacked and hung up he decided to go for a stroll to absorb the sunshine.

He sat on a street bench and called Carole-Anne 'Hi babe's its Jim here; I've not long arrived, your colleague said I should call you.' 'Oh high Jim; you must be tired after the journey, we can meet this evening if you like or make it tomorrow?' 'How about a beer and bite to eat later?' 'Meet in Maddy's bar as before, say 6.30?' 'That would be good babes, looking forward to seeing you again.' Jim thought of later; as he imagined how things were the last time he was here.

Jim went back to the room and tried to have a crash for a couple of hours, but he wasn't tired so had a shower then went to the lounge and had a beer at the bar. He scanned the area for any likely signs of being followed, but saw nothing obvious.

He decided to walk to Maddy's bar which blew away the cobwebs, he arrived just after 6.15 and ordered beer he sat at the bar keeping one eye on the door and the other on the attractive barmaid, who was wearing a tight low cut blouse highlighting her ample cleavage, she also wore tight trousers which hugged her pert bum. Jim nearly jumped out of his skin when he was tapped on the shoulder, he momentarily thought, oh no jealous boyfriend, but thankfully it was Carole-Anne. 'Admiring the view Jim?' Then she kissed him on and the cheek. He laughed as he put his hand on her bum and squeezed one of her cheeks; then ordered her a beer as well; they sat at the bar for a moment then she dragged him to a table so she could get his full attention. 'You look gorgeous Carole-Anne' 'the same gorgeous as the barmaid?' 'Oh now come on, that was just a bit of window shopping; I bet you do it as well when you see a nice hunk of a guy; admiring his physique I bet you do?' 'Just winding you up Jim' 'well you got me.'

'Okay Jim let me just say, I was briefed by Barney this afternoon and will divulge all later, but I need to know how much you have been told?' 'Virtually nothing; so I need grass roots the lot.' 'Okay you need to be put in the loop, lets grab a takeaway on route to my place, what about an all American Pizza?' 'That suits me just fine.' 'Yep there's one on the way.'

Carole-Anne looped her arm through Jim's as she walked along the sidewalk then stopped off at a Pizza bar, he let Carole-Anne order for him, as she knew the favourite toppings. Jim carried the box as they walked a couple of blocks to her apartment. Once inside they exchanged a generous kiss and petted each other then, Carole-Anne pulled away as she hung up her coat up then dished up the triangles of pizza. Once finished they washed their hands and drank wine. Then before Carole-Anne could talk they were undressing each other in the bedroom and engaging in their favourite sexual positions.

Jim was knackered as he lay panting from the exertion as the jet lag began to creep up on him. Carole-Anne needed to brief him before morning due to the dangers involved.

Carole-Anne grabbed a couple of cold beers then got back into bed; Jim twisted off the tops as he tipped the neck in appreciation.

'Right Jim the bottom line is that one of the UK agents has been linked to one of ours, who is in league with one of the South American cartels which is supplying massive amounts of cocaine to the US and looking to open up a route to the UK. The difficulty is that a relative of the UK agent is an MP. At the moment there is no suggestion he is involved, but he could be; whether he would be privy to overseas operations we don't know, but other senior MP's may have sight of the potential operations and could put the two names together, and mention something.' 'Wow big stuff where do I fit in this?' 'Barney wants you to cover some of the meetings, sometime in a week or so, when all the main players will be there; then go back to the UK. He will then let you know where the players will be so you can point them out to Yvonne.' 'I don't understand, one of yours could do that?' 'Sorry Jim I don't know the in's and out's, I'm just the messenger,' 'sorry I just question things too much, so come here.' He then grappled her tickling her as she giggled kicking her legs up and down. He then kissed her then travelled south kissing her breast then to her navel finally to the place of desire. He could hear her moaning softly as his tongue probed her depths. Carole-Anne instinctively grabbed his head as she arched her back pushing his tongue further into her as she orgasmed, she cried 'oh yes Jim don't stop, oh fucking hell yes.' The session lasted into the night as they continued to satisfy each other.

'Oh Jim please don't go back stay here and make love to me forever.' Jim smiled as he said 'who will cover the meeting then?' 'Touché Jim,' he laughed as she lay on his chest, her head rising and falling with his laughter. She played with his chest hairs twining them around her fingers then kissing his nipples.

Carole-Anne began to move and sighed as she went to the bathroom, Jim watched her slim figure disappear, then heard the shower; he went after her and soaped her body washing her lovely breasts, then dropped his hand between her legs as she parted them feeling his finger probing inside, she took a deep breath then let out a deep satisfying sigh, then pushed him off, 'fuck off Jim I got to work all day.' Jim got out and checked the bathroom cabinet, his disposable razor pack was still there and a bottle of his aftershave; he then went through his ritual pouring some of the lotion in his hand and waited for the stinging sensation as he slapped his face 'brrr' he said as he rubbed both his hands onto his cheeks drawing them down as he looked at the reflection in the mirror; as he did so he saw Carole-Anne coming out of shower, she said 'that smells nice mmmm, very sexy.' He turned to look at her with the come on eyes. 'Don't you dare Jim, no bugger off; no leave me alone.' She laughed as his hands roved over her body then patted her bum, he knew she loved her bum patted and spanked, so gave her a playful slap, then squeezed her cheeks, she threw her arms around his neck; she already felt herself moistening as she said 'well alright, but just a quick one or I'll be late.' They engaged in another passionate session as she cried with pleasure then had no time for niceties as she dressed and brushed her hair, she had no time for make-up she would apply that on route and at the office.

Jim lay there watching her dress; hopping as she put her shoes on, then she threw an envelope at him, 'read this Jim,

124

I forgot to tell you, this is your legend for being here if anyone asks. You're a friend we met and became lovers you're here rekindling it, which is true, and this is your job history not that anyone should ask. Right also in here is a sweeper use it in your room, I sweep mine every day just in case, you never know, look gotta run call you later bye.' With that she was gone slamming the door as she went.

Jim walked back to his hotel and swept the room as soon as he entered, it was clear. He then sat at the desk and opened the A4 manila envelope as he read the legend; he had allegedly met Carole-Anne on vacation in South Carolina, close to Myrtle Beach; they hit it off during the two weeks. They met again in Washington and he was now back to carry on the relationship. His legend was a freelance security advisor working with a UK security company; he sometimes visited foreign countries to undertake research.

Jim then called Jackie, 'hi babes, yeah a rough night with jet lag, but should be over it soon. No not sure how long babes; just be sure I will keep you up to date. Okay keep well and speak soon, sleep tight.'

Jim then called Yvonne he confirmed he was keeping up Anglo Yank relations. He smirked to himself as he thought of Carole-Anne. He also confirmed the first meeting had been made and he had been given the brief. Yvonne also confirmed his credit card had been updated with a healthy sum. Jim thanked her, confirming he was looking forward to her debriefing him as he smiled to himself. Yvonne in her normal calm voice said 'Jim, I have sent by courier a pack of business cards, with a security company details on including a UK address and telephone number. If anyone calls that number it will be answered as the company; we use them all the time; you are a freelance employee in the field. Only give the cards out sparingly and only if asked.' 'Okay is there anything else?' 'Not for the moment, just be careful Jim; speak soon let me know of any updates? Just be careful.' That was it she was gone.

Jim lay on the bed with jet lag beginning to kick in as he fell asleep. He woke a couple of hours later by his phone ringing, it was Carole-Anne 'you okay Jim.' 'Yes just had an hour, oops sorry, no two hours' as he checked his watch. 'Okay Jim meet me tonight at Maddy's then we can have a meal as I need to update on some issues that have just come to light, see you at 6.30 bye for now, oh by the way what a great night that was, thank you; I needed you to bring the best out in me, see you soon.' Jim smiled to himself relishing the night's activities and his ego being inflated.

Jim rested back and had another hour, then showered, shaved and got dressed ready for a meal, he put on a shirt and slacks and a light jacket. He then thought, wow all this, and being paid for it as well. He decided to walk to Maddy's again, as he did so he felt the effects of jet lag beginning to wear off. He arrived and ordered a beer as he sat at the bar admiring the same barmaid who was wearing a low cut top and a mini skirt, she had great legs, she was absorbing the admiring looks she was getting from the punters.

Jim this time kept an eye on the door and clocked Carole-Anne as she walked in and ordered two more beers one for him and one for Carole-Anne. Jim stood up and greeted her and kissed her on the cheek. They sat at a table and chatted, Jim said 'were you late this morning?' 'She slapped his arm as she laughed 'nearly, just made it on time, but it was good.' They held hands and discussed her day and her meeting with Barney. It was then she said 'it looks like Barney is being followed, so until he can identify by whom, he cannot meet you and apologises, but knows you will understand.' Jim nodded 'any idea at who they might be?' 'Maybe; I'm not at liberty to say at the moment, but will let you know as soon as I can.' Then she said 'right Jim food, I'm starving how about you?' 'Yep I'm as hungry as a horse.' 'That's good there's a great steak house not far from here, we can get a cab and get you re-charged with energy.' She laughed as they left Maddy's and hailed a passing cab, within a couple of blocks they were at the restaurant.' The smell as they went in was heavenly. Jim loved steak, he loved it cooked rare, the rarer the better, he would always order blue, if the restaurant cooked it that way, but some wouldn't due to fear of being sued for food poisoning. He was enjoying the grilled steak aroma and the noise of meat sizzling. They stood in line to be escorted to a table. The American service sprang into action; a young waitress went through her routine 'Table for two?' Jim said 'Please.' 'Follow me, here you go, my name is Angela I'm your server for this evening, please let me know if there is anything you require; can I get you drinks while you study the menu?' Jim looked at Carole-Anne, and said 'beer?' Carole-Anne nodded. 'Two beers please; thank you.' 'Yes sir' as she handed over the menu's, she highlighted a couple of specials; then left, allowing them to study the choices.

Jim looked at the menu, he liked the look of the Aberdeen Angus Sirloin, he chose that and Carole-Anne chose a fillet. Angela returned as Jim ordered his blue and Carole-Anne's medium rare.

Then they chatted, Carole-Anne looked around and said 'Jim you may need to fly down to Miami to cover a meeting with all the suspects, including the MI5 agent. Then it is understood, they will then fly to Columbia then back to the UK; there is no need to fly to Columbia we have someone there to cover that; your job is to photograph the players, did you bring with you the sunglasses camera?' Jim nodded, 'yes they have come in very handy a few times.' 'Good, you won't look out of place wearing them in the sunshine state.' 'Are you coming as well?' 'Not sure if I can, but will try.' 'It would be more natural a man and woman rather than a man on his own.' 'I agree.' 'Come with me; get your bikini on and get some sun?' 'I'm sure Barney can swing it for me, I'll ask him.' 'Just as long he doesn't get any of your clothes off?' 'No Jim, that's your prerogative you're the only one to get into my knickers.' 'Good girl.' Then the steak platters arrived with the trimmings, baked potato, butter and a pot of cream cheese. Jim said 'wow look at the size of that.' Carole-Anne laughed as she said 'American portions.' They tucked in as Jim commented how good his was, Carole-Anne chewing on a mouthful just smiled and nodded. Angela did the rounds asking if all was okay. They ordered more beer then ate their fill. Jim looked at Carole-Anne 'you want a sweet?' 'No Jim I'm full' 'me too babes.' Angela collected the plates as Jim said 'coffee please.' They drank the coffee as Jim raised his hand for the bill; he paid by credit card and left a good tip. The waitress looked at Jim and said 'thank you sir.' 'My pleasure it was a lovely meal; thank you.' As they left the restaurant Carole-Anne said 'she likes you Jim; smooth you are too.' 'Just being polite' 'I bet you could get into her knickers as well' as she laughed, 'no, only yours mam.'

They started to stroll back to her flat, which walked off the meal it left them feeling less full than when they first walked out.

They got inside as Carole-Anne opened her purse and took out a mini sweeper as she put her finger to her lips, then she scanned the room. 'Okay all clear.' He then grabbed her and pulled her to him as he kissed her passionately she responded then they ended up back in the bedroom pleasing each other for the rest of the night until they lay exhausted. 'Oh Jim you are so good, where have you been all my life, what have I been missing? But it's been worth the wait.' 'I like pleasing you; it pleases me to pleasure you.' 'Oh and then some; come here.' She hugged him and snuggled her head on his chest listening to his heart beat. She closed her eyes and was in heaven. Then she thought; I'm going to Miami with him, I can't let this opportunity go. Then she fell asleep still listening to his heart beating.

Jim felt comfortable with his arms wrapped around Carole-Anne cuddling her, he felt in some way at home. He did occasionally get a pang of conscience about Jackie, but this was good, dare he say it even better than Jackie. Then he fell asleep.

He awoke in the morning having hardly moved, Carole-Anne was still laid on his chest; he was now busting to go to the toilet, so eased his way free from her grip then just about made it. He looked at his watch and saw 6 am he went back to bed and snuggled up to Carole-Anne feeling her warm soft skin, he ran his hand over her back feeling her smoothness then reaching the pliant flesh of her bum as he gently squeezed the cheeks. Carole-Anne was awake, but was so comfortable with his gentleness; she just relaxed under his expert hands. She had to get up and get ready, but couldn't, not yet, this felt oh so good. She just lay there with her eyes closed drifting off into some dream like state, half in this world and half in some other peaceful place. She thought oh Jim please don't stop, as his hands ran up and down her spine causing a tingling sensation each time he reached her bum.

She couldn't stay any longer 'oh Jim that was so nice thank you so much I really enjoyed it' 'my pleasure my darling.' 'Oh Jim I love your accent and your manner, it's so refreshing you are a true gentleman.' 'Now you're taking the piss.' 'No Jim you truly are.' 'Well thank you mam.' 'Yes you could be my Sir, yes Sir Jim Broadbent, I like that.' 'Go on bugger off' as he laughed at her suggestion.

Carole-Anne showered then dried her hair and wrapped a towel around her head. Jim showered and shaved. They had some fruit and toast for breakfast; they left the apartment together, he kissed her as she hailed a cab 'call you later Jim; I'm not going into work tomorrow, so we can do something if you like?' 'Love to, let's do another sightseeing tour like before shall we?' 'Okay till later.'

Jim felt a little uneasy, he didn't know why; he felt he was being watched, so he decided to take a cab in the opposite direction to his hotel. He travelled a few blocks he still wasn't sure, so asked the cabby to stop as he paid the fare he nipped into a department store and then out the other side, he slipped into another store, where he stood in the entrance as he watched for anyone suspicious exiting the store he had just left. He watched, he then saw a man come out, he looked up and down the street; and then he met up with a woman who was also looking around. Were they clandestine lovers? He didn't think so; they didn't have the normal lustful look about them.

He decided to test it, he made no attempt to hide or show he suspected them, as he casually walked out of the store, then set off down the street. His suspicions were correct, he was being followed; the man and woman separated and began following, the woman on his side of the street the male on the other. He stopped, they stopped; he went into a store so did they. Once he was completely sure he took out his phone and turned on the camera and took a couple of shots of the followers then turned on his sunglasses camera when he got near to them taking a couple of close up shots.

He sat on a street bench and texted Carole-Anne 'I'm being followed; I was picked-up outside your apartment.' He quickly received a reply 'I expected it, no problem just make sure you don't show you're aware of them; will call soon, don't go back to the hotel, go to Maddy's have a coffee. I will call you, when I do, be prepared to leave when I say.' He confirmed the request. This was like Déjà vu when Barney did the same thing on his previous visit.

He caught a cab to Maddy's then sat inside drinking a coffee at a table facing the door; he wanted to be aware of who was coming in and out for self-preservation. He drank his coffee it was nice and creamy; he was eating the complimentary biscuit when he received a text from Barney 'leave Maddy's in twenty minutes, when outside stand still and call me; I will tell you what to do.' Jim confirmed he had received and understood the message. He checked his watch, confirming the countdown time.

Twenty minutes up, he went outside where he stood to the right of the entrance and called Barney, 'okay Jim, my teams on you; so walk back towards the hotel, just casually not to slow or to quick just like a tourist, we need to identify your tail.' 'Do you think it is the same team as the ones following you?' 'More than likely, we are about to make a big bust so identifying the ones on you will be a great advantage; talk later.' Jim then set off looking in various shop and office windows looking at the reflections, he was able to pick out the classic 3 man team who were working the A,B,C method of foot surveillance; he tried to spot the watchers watching the watchers, but they were good, he never saw them at all. He arrived back at the hotel, checking at reception for messages; he didn't expect any yet, so wasn't disappointed.

He went to his room and swept it, it was clear. He just flopped on the bed and dozed off for a couple of hours. He was awoken by his phone ringing, he answered; 'Hi Jim it's Barney, good job we've made the swoop and identified the suspects. I will meet you in reception in an hour as things have moved on.'

Jim met Barney with big handshakes and man hugs 'hey Jim great to see you.' 'Likewise Barney it's good to see you too.' 'They sat and talked; Jim enquired who the surveillance team were? 'They were a private agency; they wouldn't disclose who they had been contracted by, but they were totally embarrassed that they had been spotted, they were also shitting themselves as they believed they would now be targeted by them; whoever them are, but it had to be the persons involved in the drugs deal.' 'Are you sure it's not from within your lot?' 'Could be, so will keep a watch on the suspected member, here is his photo.' Barney handed over a photo of their agency guy meeting with the MI5 agent; then he showed him another picture of a meeting between them and one of the suspects involved in the smuggling cartel.

'Okay Jim our suspect agent is called Martin Kowalski; yeah I know, with a name like that, he should be Russian, his parents came from a long line of immigrants, from an eastern bloc country, Poland I think. Your guy is called Trevor Jones-Smyth; he is over here now on some alleged intelligence mission. As said they have met that guy pointing to the photograph who looked South-American and probably Columbian, we haven't fully identified him yet, he's probably an intermediary anyway, but it's getting closer to a big deal as all the indications are pointing that way.'

'Okay Jim I want you to go to Miami next week with Carole-Anne and get close to the suspects; get as many photo's as you can of them together, we will equip Carole-Anne with some covert photographic gear as well; whilst you use your sunglasses. Don't push getting to know them, although if the situation presents itself then take the opportunity.' 'Won't your guy know Carole-Anne; the surveillance team may have sent pictures of me and her together?' 'No she is not well known in the section that he works in, and certainly we don't think in the time that the team were on you, they had sent back any photo's also when we swooped they never had any cameras and their phones were clear,' 'wow that is a bit risky isn't it?' 'That's the name of the game Jim; make the best of what you have got.' 'Have we got any form of back up?' 'Only my telephone number, if you suspect things have gone wrong; let me know and I will get a local agency to get you out.' 'Now this is real James Bond stuff,' as they both laughed. 'Just be careful Jim, enjoy yourself as well, but be careful. I know you will enjoy Carole-Anne, I know you will.' Jim smiled as he nodded 'she's a nice girl.' Barney nodded as he said 'she speaks highly of you Jim.' They wrapped up the meeting when Barney stated that Carole-Anne would book the same hotel as Kowalski once she knew it. They shook hands as Jim returned to his room to study the photos.

132

Jim then called Yvonne he explained his meeting with Barney including the taking out of the surveillance team. Yvonne was not surprised as she reiterated his need to be careful. She then went on to talk about Jones-Smyth, he was in the states on a mission which was confidential; the part about him going to Miami was not in his brief, so if he turns up there, it will confirm he was involved in the drugs importation; endorsing my suspicions.

Jim then called Jackie saying he was going to be at least another week before heading home. He then asked her if she had anything in mind for a gift; anything special she had always wanted. 'I just want you back safe and well, but if you really want to buy me something, a nice watch would be nice, something for special occasions.'

Jim then went window shopping checking out the jewellery sections in the department stores. He returned to the same store he had been to on his previous trip; where he bought Jackie the bracelet and necklace. The assistant recognised him instantly as she said 'you back again sir?' 'Yes mam; I'm after a nice dress watch for a special lady; she was most impressed with items I bought for her last time.' 'Well thank you sir; you're in luck we have a good selection of watches and I am able to offer you a good discount as a returning customer, follow me.' Jim went to the other side of the large square counter where he looked through the big glass display, the assistant slid back the door on her side and took out a couple of watches, two gold and two silver, saying 'I can offer you 25% discount on these, but unfortunately only these as they are now coming to end of line, so we have discounted them for returning customers.' Jim looked at them and knew Jackie preferred gold. One of the ones shown he was sure she would like, so he bought it. The gold face was encrusted with gems that sparkled in the light. The assistant took the watch to the counter as she adjusted the time and set the date. She made a phone call with her back turned to Jim. He couldn't hear what was being said; she must have trusted him as she had left the other watches on the counter. She returned, handing him the watch as she explained the operation of the hands and the date adjustment, then said 'good news sir, due to your previous purchases the manager has agreed a 33% discount.' Jim looked at the heavily made up, 50 year old assistant who smiled at him. 'Thank you so much for your kindness.' 'Oh it has been my pleasure sir,' as she smiled at him.

Jim handed over his credit card then signed the receipt after she had slid the machine across the face of the card impregnating the details. She very carefully and slowly wrapped the watch in gift wrap paper and then very neatly tied a bow of pink ribbon and placed into a small carrier bag. She handed it to Jim as he smiled; he took her hand as he kissed the back then thanked her again. The assistant was all aflutter smiling at him. Jim smiled back then he left the store. The assistant stood with her hands clasped together as she watched Jim leave, her mind was way up in the clouds. Then she was brought back down by another customer.

On the way back to the hotel Carole-Anne called Jim making an excuse about later; he knew from her voice that she had received her monthly visitor, she reminded him of the way Jackie sounded when all she wanted to do was sit hugging a hot water bottle.

Jim then went back to the hotel and called Barney asking if he wanted a drink, but he declined the invitation. Jim was alone so went to the hotel restaurant where he sat and ordered a meal and a bottle of wine. The restaurant was busy with both residents and non-residents. The waiting staff and wine waiters were rushing around with what seemed like ordered chaos.

Jim was sat people watching, when he saw an attractive woman sat on her own reading a book as she ate her meal, she was dressed as if she was meeting someone or going onto a show after the meal. Jim finished in the restaurant. He went to the bar and ordered a scotch, a single malt to compliment the meal and the wine; he sat in a lounge chair and relaxed. He then saw the woman from the restaurant sat at the bar. He couldn't help himself, so he went to the bar. He stood next to her looking at her very expensive dress and jewellery. 'Good evening; may I compliment you on your dress, it is very nice, you off to a show?' She looked at Jim with a sort of down the nose look and didn't answer. 'Oh sorry, I was just paying you a compliment.' He then turned and sat back down at his seat. The woman turned and walked over to him 'Sorry, compliment accepted; it looks like I have been stood-up' 'Oh please join me; sorry I'm not dressed for the occasion, just having a casual day.' 'Thank you; if I may join you that'd be nice.' 'I'm Jim and you are?' 'Christina.' 'Nice name; where in the states are you from?' 'Ohio, Cleveland.' 'Okay, as you guessed from the UK not far from London.' They chatted about different things as Christina began letting her defences down as she became more comfortable in Jim's company.

Christina explained that she was always being hit on so, had developed an outer shell which she used to bat off those who tried it on with her; at least that's what she told Jim.

Jim should have guessed it, but he didn't, he was too wrapped up in her classy nature and well healed appearance also her looks, she was ravishing, he was being sucked in and he was enjoying the ego inflation.

He never knew it, but he was being groomed and professionally so; her sultry looks with deep blue sparkling eyes were burning into his, giving him a stirring his loins which had made him nearly drop his guard. All he could imagine was him in bed with her; she was openly flirting with him and getting him worked up. She made an excuse as she went to the toilet. He watched her as she swayed her hips for him provocatively; her long shapely legs and high heels accentuated their shape. He thought fuck me what a body; I think I'm in there.

Then he thought with a loud bang in his head, this had been too easy, what the fuck, then he thought honey trap, why hadn't he seen it coming? Why had he let his guard drop? He quickly called Barney of his suspicions. 'Okay Jim no problem let's just see if she is on the other side. See how far she will go push her a little, get her phone number. If she wants to bed you on the first date then you will know; no one does that these days, not if they are as classy as you say she is.' 'Okay she's on the way back; speak soon.' Jim took a picture of her using his sun glasses; the light was just good enough. She commented on the phone call. Jim just stated a work commitment for tomorrow; she began pumping him for information about his work. He just went with the legend he had been given. But she kept on at him through a series of questions in a roundabout way. Jim then knew he so nearly fell for a honey trap; he looked at his watch and gave a false yawn and said 'you will have to excuse me I have a busy day tomorrow, nice meeting you; look give me your number perhaps we can have a bite to eat somewhere later in the week if you'd like that?' 'I'd love to Jim' as she wrote down her number handing it over; she placed it into his hand as she gave a meaningful, but gentle squeeze. 'Till later Christina, this has been a pleasure, if I wasn't so jet lagged I would invite you for a night cap.' He smiled at her as she leant over and kissed him on the cheek. 'Maybe next time we can have a night cap in my hotel?' 'I would like that.' She smiled coyly as she stood up, seductively smoothing her dress. 'Till later Jim, I look forward to it?' Then she left the hotel knowing he was watching her swaying her hips. Jim watched her thinking she looked like Marilyn Monroe with her sexy walk and nice hips.

Jim got to his room and thought fuck me what a body, as he down loaded the picture from his sunglasses camera.

Fuck me I could have given her one. He then emailed Barney the picture and her contact number.

Jim knew his weakness was a good looking woman, but he had now entered a different world, one he was not used too. He never had to watch out before; now he was in the world of double dealing spies and secret agents; this was so surreal. He could have unwittingly blown something, as he smiled thinking she could have blown me. He was just glad he had woken up to the threat in time.

Jim then lay on the bed contemplating how close he had come to being caught in a compromising position, with a threat being made to disclose the photos to Jackie; his life would have been in tatters and his cover blown. No more Yvonne, no more trips abroad and above all no more expenses. The thoughts were racing around his head.

He then called Carole-Anne enquiring how she was, she was none too pleased at his late call having been woken up, but confirmed she was okay.

He lay on the bed as the alcohol and latter ends of the jet lag began to take its toll as he fell asleep not waking till the morning.

He called Jackie enquiring if she was okay, she confirmed she was, but was still worried about him. Jim talked for some twenty minutes; then she had to go to a meeting.

Jim showered and went for breakfast, albeit he couldn't get over the sweet cakes and muffins on display, albeit he had taken a liking for waffles and maple syrup.

He looked around the restaurant looking at the guests; they were all sizes and cultures. He was trying to spot any likely suspects; everyone appeared to be busy chattering and eating so he gave up and just relaxed.

Barney called him, 'hey Jim lets meet; I'll pick you up outside the hotel in twenty minutes okay?' Jim acknowledged him then went back upstairs and changed into something more in keeping with a tourist, a pair of slacks and bomber jacket.

Barney arrived in a black SUV, he wound down the electric windows, 'hey Jim, jump in' Jim opened the door and climbed in as he shook hands. 'What's up?' Jim enquired, 'Just need to brief you on some movements that have occurred.' 'Did you check out that woman's details I sent you?' 'Yes, she is one of ours; she was used to see if you would fall for a honey trap.' 'You bastard, she was gorgeous I could have given her one.' 'Ha ha Jim, you were nearly served up on a plate, but it was to show how easy it is to be lured into a trap, not everything is as it seems.' 'Fucking hell she really played the part, she looked really up for it as well.' 'No Jim; you wouldn't have got her into bed, but she is a cracker isn't she?' 'My god Barney, I can see how easy it could happen, especially after a few drinks.' 'Anyhow that's now past; I want you and Carole-Anne to sit down and work through your history, the hotels you stayed in whilst on holiday, what you did and who you met, the works, because if you get separated and you're asked questions I want you to confidently know that each other will give the same answers; not that I think it will happen, but just in case. You're purely down to monitor although it's best to have all bases covered just in case.' 'Okay we can work on that.' 'I may get someone to test you as well, before you go, so get your heads together, not just kissing either.' 'I'm just keeping up Anglo-American relations.' As they both laughed.

'Okay Jim the serious stuff, when you're in Miami they will have watchers out on the ground, this is a multi-million dollar deal so, they will take no chances, just remember, life has become cheap, so don't put your head above the wall to be shot at.' 'Okay, thanks Barney, good stuff!' 'Right, Jones-Smyth has made contact with another Columbian; then he spoke with Kowalski. The wiretap is working well, they have discussed meeting in Grand Beach Hotel which is where Jones-Smyth said he had booked a room, so I suggest you book one as well, you can be just another tourist couple.' 'It doesn't sound cheap?' 'No it isn't but, it's on Uncle Sam.' 'I'll get Carole-Anne to book it; she can use her covert business credit card.' 'Okay anything else?' 'Yes, yesterday was to show you how you have to be aware at all times, don't let your guard down, because the moment you relax, you can be sure someone will be there to reel you in.' 'Okay I have that firmly in my head, but fuck me Barney she was tasty.' Barney laughed 'yes she is very tasty and happily married, so your luck is out.' 'What a shame.' 'Anyway your plate is full I suspect, with Carole-Anne?' 'You ain't kidding she is a handful and no mistake.' 'Okay Jim, just remember sort out the legend with Carole-Anne and once you're in Miami the game is fully on. Forget James Bond, this is for real; people to the cartels are very dispensable, just remember, they pay off who they want, and they get what they want; so make sure you sweep the room every day and make sure you leave nothing out that can identify who you really are.' 'Okay I think I'm up to speed, I will call Carole-Anne later and start to go through our timings.' 'Okay Jim I'll drop you back now, we will have that beer before you go to Miami.'

Barney dropped him off at the hotel then sped off in the archetypal SUV of the secret service. Jim went to reception checking for messages; the package sent by Yvonne had arrived; he signed for it then went to his room; he went through the sweeping procedure, which was almost second nature now; but this time, there was a slight reading as the needle hovered between green and amber; he walked around the room, he couldn't get any real fix, then he realised it was emanating from the adjoining room, he held the device against the wall, the meter went into amber nearly touching red.

He couldn't think straight, was he the target or was it next door, or was the device next door installed so it picked the conversation in his room. He called Barney, and just said 'all the indications are going into to the red; so better just watch and see, before making any sudden investments.' Barney acknowledged him and said 'keep quiet about it, as to go public could cause a blip on the horizon.'

Jim went outside the room and into the corridor walking towards the lift, and called Carole-Anne asking if she was okay she confirmed all back to normal. Jim made a time for a get together at Maddy's.

Jim went back to his room and opened up the package and looked at the professional business cards, he peeled off a couple and placed them in his wallet.

Jim met Carole-Anne at Maddy's where he discussed the meter reading indication and the implications of his finding. Had the device been placed in the next door room to listen in on his conversations?

Carole-Anne needed to meet with Barney to discuss the finding, as it could have far reaching consequences; there could be another leak or another freelance agency involved. 'Okay let's get back to my apartment and do a full sweep, I have an extra sensitive metre which will pick up any device there or close by.' They finished their drinks then walked back to her apartment, Jim grabbed her unexpectedly and stood her up against the wall of a building and kissed her. She tried to stop him, but he had the advantage of surprise. This wasn't passion this was his chance to view the street and check on any suspects following them. He held Carole-Anne tight as he said 'just keep still, I think we are being followed.' Jim confirmed they were; he had picked out a two man team, one on their side-walk the other on the opposite side. 'Okay let's cab it somewhere; until we can contact Barney.' Carole-Anne nodded as they waved down a passing cab. Carole-Anne directed the driver to the Italian restaurant where they had eaten previously. Before entering Carole-Anne contacted Barney, giving them their location. She received his instructions; which was to do nothing make it look normal, just carrying on as usual don't take any notice of the followers. Barney indicated he would get them identified.

Carole-Anne passed on the instructions from Barney to Jim as they went inside and were shown to a table. Jim didn't like the situation he would have preferred the followers to have been taken out, but not his call.

They sat and ate their meal, Carole-Anne said 'I'm off tomorrow remember, so where shall we go?' 'Okay, how about somewhere on the coast, what about Chesapeake beach? Get up early and go, we can use your car what do you say?' 'How do you know I have a car?' 'Haven't you?' 'Yes, but hardly ever use it, it's easier to cab it; I keep it in the underground car park. Okay Chesapeake it is, but we will have to make an early start because the traffic in the morning is horrendous anywhere around Washington.' 'What's early?' 'Be away from here by 6am at the latest.' 'What?' 'It's your idea not mine.'

They arrived back at Carole-Anne's apartment; to make it look good they kissed outside before entering. Once inside Carole-Anne swept the apartment as normal, it was all clear. They toasted their night and the meal, then went to bed grappling each other out of their clothes and engaging in their favourite sexual exploits.

Jim set his phone alarm for 5am then cuddled Carole-Anne to sleep. Within a couple of hours the alarm sounded as they rose bleary eyed and looked at each other and laughed, shook their heads and went back to sleep as they cuddled each other, feeling the warmth of each other's skin. They hugged as they drifted off again, satisfied with the comfort of togetherness.

Carole-Anne was falling head over heels for Jim; he was all she had looked for in a man, good looks, charming with a sense of humour; something she had never found all in one package before. She felt secure wrapped in his long powerful arms, snuggled into his chest. She lay drifting off on a cloud as she calmly thought; I wonder how many women he has been with to get experience like this? He had found sensitive areas on her she never knew she had. No other man had given her the number of orgasms she had had with him. She slowly drifted off in a mist of comfort.

They finally awoke and stretched as Jim reached under the covers tickling her as she giggled at his touch, she turned to him and looked with the look of come take me, I'm ready. Carole-Anne felt her passion growing as she began roving her hands over his chest then began following her hands with her mouth kissing and licking his chest following the hair line to his navel, she looked towards his eyes with a smile that said devilment; her eyes twinkled with desire. Then she took hold of his semi firm member, she took it into her mouth, she worked him with her hands and tongue, then he went rock hard, she loved the taste of him. She could feel his urgency building as he was squirming and tensing, then his hips locked as his breathing shortened, she loved the control she had over him. Then he let go as she took his load feeling the warm salty liquid fill her mouth as she swallowed relishing the taste, she likened it to salty peaches.

She then worked her way up then began breathing into his ear then took his hand placing it between her legs feeling him penetrating her manipulating her G spot as she threw her head back and sighed deeply as she had orgasm after orgasm soaking his hand. She lay back with a satisfied grin as she snuggled into his chest.

They stayed in bed for another hour then got up, showered then went to Maddy's and had a good cooked breakfast. They decided to take another tour bus; one of the Old town trolley buses. They caught a cab to the bus station and spent the day locked in each other's arms. Jim had almost forgotten about the surveillance tail; he casually looked around, he caught sight of only one guy; he had spotted him the previous day, but only the one this time. He tried to detect the other guy without looking like he was searching, but he only spotted the one. This gave him a satisfied feeling; perhaps their sightseeing and lateness out of bed was an indicator that their cover of being rekindled lovers was working.

Jim sent a text to Barney saying 'only one today.' The reply came 'okay just go with it.'

The day went quickly as they spent time looking at the tourist areas; these old buses were good as they allowed you with the same ticket to hop on and off as you liked.

The situation seemed so right, he was beginning to get strong feelings for Carole-Anne, his life at home was good, but this American dream was exciting; then he thought of Jackie, with a pang of conscience as he remembered how she had dragged him from the life of unhappiness to one of bliss.

Carole-Anne said 'what you thinking about Jim?' 'Oh nothing just wondering how the case I was dealing with back home is going.' 'Hey forget about that; you're here with me now.' They both laughed then continued with their day.

Jim then received a call from Barney, 'Jim you and Carole-Anne fly down to Miami and book into the Grand Beach Hotel get Carole-Anne to book it; you will be there a good week before the subjects arrive so will give you good cover.

CHAPTER TWENTY/THREE

The flight to Miami was straight forward, a direct flight lasting just over 2 1/2 hours, then a short taxi ride to the Grand Beach Hotel. Jim thought this was like a honeymoon and that's what they would say they were doing, a pre-honeymoon trial. 'Oh Jim how romantic, and all paid for by Uncle Sam, shhhh!' as she laughed hugging his arm. Jim smiled as they arrived. The cab driver smiled at them as Jim paid the fare; the driver said 'hey you guys have a great time.' Jim smiled as he said 'thanks, we sure will.' They booked-in at the reception desk Jim mentioned they were testing out the hotel for their honeymoon. The receptionist looked at them and said, 'look shhh; don't tell anyone, I'll upgrade you for the same price, the room has a sea view.' Jim and Carole-Anne smiled as they were handed the electronic keys; then made their way to their room. On opening the door Carole-Anne said 'wow, this is some upgrade, look at it!' Jim smiled thinking, this is some pad. They pulled back the curtains looking at the clear blue sea of the Atlantic through the full length windows then stepped out onto the balcony. 'Oh Jim this is wonderful.'

Once they had unpacked they decided to go for a swim in one of the hotel pools. They were right about the sunshine state, it certainly was, it was hot, especially walking outside from the air conditioned hotel. The pool was refreshing, more like a bath than a pool. They swam a few lengths then played games splashing and diving underwater trying to trip each other up, just having fun.

Jim rested by the side as Carole-Anne undertook another length of the pool, when she returned she said 'oh Jim I can't believe this is all paid for, this is fantastic.' Jim smiled as she rested on his shoulder.

The week went by with them sightseeing including a trip to the Keys where they spent a day and night. With lots of sunbathing

They kept on testing each other on how they met and what they had done in Myrtle Beach, so it became second nature and not having to think about it, or worry what the other would say if questioned.

Then Barney called 'The subjects should be with you tomorrow, so get snapping.' That was it nothing else. Jim then sat down with Carole-Anne where they went over their legend again and how they met.

The honeymoon so to speak was over this was now going to be full on; now they had to be guarded, although at the same time looking relaxed. Jim checked the room safe and ensured it was secure, he took a fine piece of thread which he placed in the door which would fall out if the door was opened, then he locked it; he made sure Carole-Anne was aware of it as well; showing her where to place the thread if she opened the door for any reason. 'Look babes we don't know who we are dealing with, so just in case, we need to ensure we are not in the firing line so to speak, we must make a habit of sweeping the room and checking the safe every day.' Carole-Anne nodded saying 'you're right, darling we must make sure everything fits into the right place.' She smiled and grabbed hold of him sealing her lips over his as she pushed him back on the bed and took him inside her. He smiled 'you just raped me.' Carole-Anne smiled as she threw her arms around him 'and you loved it, all of it.' 'That's beside the point mam; you just took me, and used me for your own pleasure.' They both laughed and fell asleep not waking until the early evening.

They went for an evening meal at a nearby steakhouse as they replenished the energy expended with prime steaks. Jim had been keeping a constant lookout for their previous tail; but he was absent; he didn't know if this was by accident or by Barney's design, having him whisked away at the airport? Perhaps another option was, they were now being watched by a new more professional team; either way they had to keep up the appearance of being on honeymoon; which wasn't difficult for him with Carole-Anne. Although he had to sneak away from her to ring Jackie, as she was continually pulling her hair out with worry about his safety. He tried to placate her ensuring her that he was okay. But nothing he said could prevent her from worrying about him; she was also in need of his attention as she was getting frustrated. Jim blessed himself, the father son and holy-ghost as he felt a momentary pang of conscience as he looked heavenwards; then returned to Carole-Anne and her charms.

CHAPTER TWENTY-FOVR

Jim was sat in the lounge reading one of the many American newspapers and magazines when his attention was drawn to the reception desk where he saw three distinctive Columbians all very well dressed in top of the range clothing carrying leather cases which must have cost a fortune. They clicked their fingers as the bell hops ran around them all expecting a good tip for carrying the luggage to their rooms. They went to the lift which whisked them up to the 4th floor. Jim thought this has to be them, it must be; they oozed money.

Jim contacted Carole-Anne 'hi babes I think the package has arrived from down south.' 'Okay, I will meet you soon; I'm going to have my hair done, be back later.' Jim ordered a coffee and sat reading the paper.

He was not going to show any interest in the party, he knew his assignment which was photos. He also knew with the money these guys had, they could buy information about who was staying at the hotel; they could easily plant bugs having bought access to his room from the cleaners. Most of the cleaning staff looked either Mexican or South American and were probably on the minimum wage or below, so anything extra would be taken without question.

The hotel lounge was busy with new arrivals checking-in; all bringing numerous cases. He couldn't get over the loudness of some of the Americans; they sounded like they were on some film set, shouting into a megaphone.

Jim decided to go for a swim in one of the many pools; he changed and scribbled a note for Carole-Anne, but knew having been to the hairdressers, there was no way she would join him.

He went into one of the pools and swam enjoying the warm sun and the warmth of the water, although he looked out of place with his gleaming white skin reflecting the sun's rays. Most of the people on the loungers soaking up the warmth were bronzed, maybe out of a bottle but still bronzed. He then thought he should have done the same, slapped on a fake tan from a bottle.

He went for a swim as he cruised up and down the pool; he took in some of the beauties that were sun worshipping, some really lovely women; he thought he had gone to heaven.

He found a lounger and put more oil on as he lay back and soaked up the rays. He rested back and closed his eyes for ten minutes, when he heard the silence broken by the Columbians speaking Spanish as they grabbed vacant loungers and chatted ten to the dozen. Jim could pick up the odd sentence, but as soon as two of them were talking at the same time he was lost. He gleaned that the meeting was for manana so they could relaja esta tarde y fiesta esta noche. Some ten minutes later Carole-Anne appeared in a wrap-around sarong and pulled up a lounger next to Jim. 'Hi babe's hair looks nice when you going back' he laughed as she slapped his arm. 'No looks nice they have done a great job.' 'Well thank you kind sir.' She removed her sarong revealing her bikini which emphasized her figure. 'Wow babes you look gorgeous.' She sat down as he handed her the oil and watched as she rubbed it in 'you need a hand with that.' 'Only on my back and hands off my butt as well.'

They lay soaking up then rays with Jim trying to half listen to the conversation of the Columbians, then in the end he gave up.

Once half-baked Jim and Carole-Anne retired to their room and showered although Carole-Anne wore a shower cap to protect her hairdo. Jim smiled at her hat as they got ready for dinner. Jim had taken a few snaps with his sun glasses camera of the Columbians so downloaded them and emailed them to Yvonne.

The meal was good as they walked along the beach absorbing the warm evening air blowing off the sea. They hugged as they strolled back to the hotel; the breeze picked up, blowing Carole-Anne's hair all over the place; she eventually gave up trying to hold it place.

They arrived back at the hotel where Carole-Anne went to the restroom to try and salvage her hair. They had a nightcap at the bar. The lounge seats were comfortable; sitting close to each other they chatted whilst casually checking out the other guests. After a while they both yawned and laughed which was the signal to call it a night.

The staff in the hotel had heard they were a honeymoon couple and they were given knowing nods and smiles.

They entered the room where Carole-Anne gave it a scan, confirming it was okay as they completed their bathroom ritual then went to bed, they were both whacked from the day's activity so went straight to sleep. Later Jim felt a nudge in his back, 'Jim you awake? Jim you awake? Bleary eyed he grunted 'what!?' 'Oh Jim I need you now.' 'What!' He turned over to face Carole-Anne, who pulled down the duvet and kissed his chest absorbing his manly scent she slowly kissed her way down allowing him time to respond then went down on him taking his half sleeping member in her mouth and began working her tongue till he went hard. Jim was moaning at the sensation of her lips caressing him as she ran her tongue over the head, she was so good, so, so good, he knew she liked her hair pulled when down on him. He kept her there by gripping her hair, he could feel he was nearly at the point of no return, when all of a sudden she stopped and waited as she smiled at him waiting for him to settle, then sat astride him, she was ready for him as she guided his member into her, then she went for it and shouted 'yes yes yes' as she fulfilled her desire, then she kept going till he came inside her. Carole-Anne collapsed on his chest her heavy breathing matching the rise and fall of his. 'That was nice Jim.' Jim smiled a contented look as he went back to his disturbed sleep. Carole-Anne just closed her eyes satisfied with the warm feeling of Jim's chest against her face. This to her was the closest she had ever been to heaven. She floated off on a cloud feeling warm and contented; closing her eyes smiling to herself as she drifted back to sleep.

The morning came as Carole-Anne woke first; she turned the room kettle on and poured the sachets of coffee into each cup and the cartons of long life milk. Then she woke Jim up with a smile and the warm smell of hot coffee. Coffee was slowly sipped. Carole-Anne looked at Jim as she rested on her arm; not saying anything just looking. Jim smiled and said 'what?' 'Nothing, just admiring you and thinking how lucky I am.' 'Oh do bugger off' as he laughed. He then said 'you raped me again last night.' Carole-Anne laughed as she slapped his arm 'and you loved it didn't you?' 'That's beside the point you raped me, took advantage of me.' They continued to have fun bantering with each other. When finished their coffee they showered and dressed being mindful of the days ahead and the reason they were there.

CHAPTER TWENTY/FIVE

The restaurant was busy with customers so they had to share a table with a couple from Maine who were retired and travelling with the sun. They made small talk with them, they immediately picked up on Jim's accent, as they talked. Jim noticed the Columbians walk-in they managed to find a vacant table and sat together. It was then that he caught sight of Jones-Smyth entering the restaurant; he nodded to the Columbians and sat an adjacent table. They started talking as he shook hands with the nearest Columbian. Jim pretended to clean his sunglasses and took some pictures for Barney and Yvonne. Carole-Anne had her handbag camera with her, she was also snapping away.

Jim couldn't believe that this was all that was required of him; surely any agent from the CIA or DEA could have accomplished this, he couldn't help but think that there was something he was missing, some part of a bigger jig-saw puzzle, but what? No matter how he tried to piece things together nothing made any sense at all. Carole-Anne and Jim went back to the room where they emailed the pictures to Barney and Yvonne. When finished they just looked at each other, as Carole-Anne looked back at Jim with tears in her eyes 'surely this can't be it Jim can it?' 'I thought the same there must be more to this than meets the eye.'

Jim received a phone call from Yvonne at the same time as Carole-Anne did from Barney. 'Jim, now we go to phase two, Carole-Anne is being spoken too as we speak.' 'Yeah, she has just received a call from Barney.' 'Okay Jim, the

CIA agent Kowalski is making his way down as we speak, he suspects there has been a leak and he is being set up, so he will be doing loads of checks on people and watching for anything out of place. All we want, is you to snap a couple of pictures of him with the others and then you're gone, we want him and all the other parties together then we will have enough to start a good conspiracy trial against him and Jones-Smyth. But, be careful Jim there is big money involved which buys people like chocolate.' 'What then?' 'You fly home. What do you expect a holiday?' 'Just asking that's all.' Then the phone went dead.

He saw Carole-Anne was still in deep conversation with Barney. Then she came off the phone, and hugged Jim, 'Oh Jim darling I'm going to miss you, I have fallen so in love with you.' Jim hugged her as she began to sob heavily into his shoulder soaking his tee shirt.

She then looked at him and kissed him passionately then pushed him back to the bed saying 'this maybe the last time we can really be together,' she placed the do not disturb sign outside the door, then all but tore the clothes of Jim, then she made the most of him.

They were just about whacked out from the early morning session which had been so intense. They lay on the bed in each other's arms with Carole-Anne's head on his chest as she played with the hairs, listening to his heart beating. Nothing was said, it was a sad time for them both. Jim laid there and then thought of Jackie as he had another pang of conscience, but that soon passed, although he knew he had to call her soon as she would be worried. He knew she would be rampant by the time he got home.

Carole-Anne stirred and suggested going for a swim, Jim nodded then turned over for a sleep. Carole-Anne changed and went to the pool leaving Jim to sleep.

Carole-Anne oiled her skin and lay on a lounger adjusting her sun glasses to get a tan on her face; then soaked up the rays.

Jim woke up shortly after and took the opportunity to call Jackie, he got a load of abuse for not calling, she just let rip at him. 'Look babes I have been up to my eyes in it and have just had yet another meeting and broken away, I should be back very shortly.' 'You better be Jim, I've just about had enough of this, you being away abroad all this time, with me being here all on my own; you better watch out, I might find someone else.' That was it she switched off the phone. He said to himself 'fuck me, I wish I hadn't bothered.' He changed and went and joined Carole-Anne. He rubbed oil on himself then laid back and chatted; then the Columbians came to the pool and started swimming they started jumping in and generally splashing about to the annoyance of some of the guests who objected to being splashed as they sizzled in the heat if the day.

It was then that he saw Jones-Smyth in company with Kowalski as they selected a lounger, they sat watching the antics of the Columbian's Jim snapped away at them managing to get a handshake in as well. All he needed now was the Columbians together in conversation and the job was done. That would probably be later in the evening. Then his mind went back to venom spat at him by Jackie, not saying he didn't deserve it, but he hoped if tonight panned out, he could be gone in a couple of days. Although he loved the American lifestyle and the easy living he was enjoying at the moment; he thought if he could swapped sides and work for the spooks he could try for an American posting, living with Carole-Anne. Fuck me what a triangle he thought. He really didn't want to hurt Jackie though, she had been so good to him; the pangs hit him again. Someone was going to get hurt. He was then interrupted by Carole-Anne, 'Jim this is nearly over my darling, oh how I have enjoyed this so much, I have fallen deeply and madly in love with you, but you're going to leave me, tell me honestly, have you a woman at home in the UK?' 'I won't lie, yes I see someone now and again, but nothing serious.' 'Okay, I thought so, as long as it's not serious; cause I might ask for a transfer to our London office then we could be together for ever Jim.' Jim thought fuck me! Then the Columbians got out of the pool and stood around talking and shaking hands with Kowalski and Jones-Smyth. He managed to get a couple of snaps which then officially completed the job.

Carole-Anne looked so sad, he felt so sure she would burst into tears there and then. Jim made his way back to the room. Carole-Anne stayed a few more minutes to allow Jim time to call Yvonne.

'Hi Yvonne yes got the shots all together around the pool, probably get them together tonight as well but. There is enough here to show association.' 'Well done Jim don't book a flight yet just hang tight for a couple of more days.' Carole-Anne came into the room looking like she had been crying. 'I've spoken to Yvonne and she has asked me to stay on for a couple more days I presume Barney will do the same?' 'Oh Jim I do hope so.' Jim then downloaded the photos and emailed to Yvonne and Barney.

They showered and changed and went for a drink before going for dinner. They decided to eat in at a surf and turf restaurant; there was a good selection of food including shellfish on the menu. Jim laughed as he made a joke about stocking up for the next session. Carole-Anne slapped his arm as she laughed, 'there's no oysters you better double up on the prawns and lobster.'

They sat and ate their fill; cracking open lobster and crab claws and enjoying the sweet meat. The wine went down well as they contemplated a dessert, but holding their stomachs they looked at each other and shook their heads. They sat holding hands over the table, when in came the Columbians with Kowalski and Jones-Smyth in tow. They sat at a nearby table they nodded in recognition; Jim broke the ice as he said 'the lobster is really good,' as he picked up the sun glasses off his head and flicked them on. Jones-Smyth said 'hey you're English where you from?' Jim thought 'oh no' 'Just outside Birmingham, this is my wife to be we are on a pre-marital visit. Jim fiddled with his glasses as he took a couple of good close up snaps. Then laughed saying I won't need these now as he slipped them into his pocket. Jones-Smyth said 'you here for long?' 'We've been here a week and at the end unfortunately; in a day or so we'll be gone; anyway nice chatting' as he called for the bill, it arrived as Jim paid by credit card then said his farewell.

Carole-Anne could feel their eyes on her bum as she walked out, for some reason it made her feel uncomfortable; albeit she was used to being ogled at; this time for some reason it made her feel uneasy. As they got outside she said 'what a load of creeps; just because they've got money.' 'We could be in there.' 'No you don't Jim; that's not our brief.' 'I know, just saying, a chance meeting no introduction I bet I could.' 'Jim, these Columbians are arseholes they kill people for looking at them the wrong way.' 'Relax it was only a comment.' She grabbed hold of his arm as she said 'I don't want to lose you Jim, you mean so much to me.' Jim thought fuck me this wasn't supposed to happen.

They got back to the hotel and had a nightcap in the bar which went down well. Then they made their way to their room. Jim downloaded the pictures and sent them to Yvonne and Barney. Then he joined Carole-Anne in bed and cuddled her to sleep. As if on cue in the early hours of the morning he was shoved in the back again, 'Jim you awake? Jim you awake?' Jim turned over not opening his eyes as she threw back the covers and went down on him again, he felt her warm lips taking his length in her mouth, his passion was now fully awakened as he felt the blood rising he grabbed her hair as she moved her head up and down, she could feel he was getting ready as his breath was shortening. Carole-Anne didn't want him to cum in her mouth; not this time, she wanted him inside her. She could feel him rising so pulled away. She looked at him with seductive eyes then she crept up his body kissing his chest until she reached his mouth where she took his tongue working it like his penis. She was allowing his rising load to settle back down before straddling him.

Once she was satisfied he was sufficiently settled, she sat astride him entering him inside her, she was so ready for him; the anticipation of him inside her after working him with her mouth was so exciting, she was really ready. Carole-Anne straddled him then rode him, working her pelvis watching his facial expressions; she had numerous orgasms then saw him close his eyes tightly then felt his hips go rigid as came inside her. She rested her had on his chest feeling it rise and fall with his breath, she felt so satisfied. Jim then went back to sleep not waking too early, but just as he was about to turn over his phone went, it was Yvonne. 'Well done Jim, book a flight from Miami to Heathrow I will get you picked up, then I will need a debrief, not overnight sorry to say, I will meet you in the car then my driver will drop you off wherever you need to go; you will be jet lagged; things are moving on quickly now.' 'Okay I will text the flight details when I know them.'

Jim hugged Carole-Anne 'that's it babes it's over I've been ordered back for an urgent debrief.' Carole-Anne burst into tears as she hugged him; she sobbed for a good ten minutes on his shoulder. Then she said 'thank you Jim for the best time of my life; I doubt if we will meet again, not like this anyhow.' 'You never know babes?' Jim then rang reception asking if they could book the next available flight from Miami direct to Heathrow. The desk rang back some 40 minutes later, 'earliest flight tomorrow afternoon leaving at 4pm is that okay Sir.' 'Yes that's fine, please confirm it, you have my passport details? Okay thanks.' Another call came in some ten minutes later with the flight details and arrival time at Heathrow. He texted Yvonne, she texted back; 'on second thoughts I'll get Langton's driver to pick you up and I'll meet you at Langton's office at 2pm.'

He then saw Carole-Anne on the phone he presumed to Barney. She turned and said 'tomorrow Jim the last day, well half a day then goodbye, oh I'm so sad; Barney has booked a flight for me it's at midday, so even less time together.' 'Come on then let's get going, do some sightseeing and do some silly things.' Carole-Anne was tearful as she got ready then they toured the city on one of the open top hop-on and hop-off buses; they travelled through the Art Deco area and then along the beach coast road. The day was fun as Carole-Anne made the most of it, knowing this could be the last time she ever saw Jim again. They hopped-off the bus at the end of the day and had their final evening meal before retiring to bed and fulfilling their desires.

They awoke in the morning then packed as they made their way downstairs, they checked out as Jim asked if his suitcase could be held in a secure place till later.

He then requested a taxi for Carole-Anne; he went with her to the airport then asked the driver to wait then hugged her as she broke down in tears then hurried off to departures. Jim returned to the hotel. He had breakfast in one of the beach restaurants. He called Jackie; 'Hi babes I'll be home tomorrow morning.' Jackie apologised for the day before and made sure he understood the reason for the outburst. Jim accepted her apology promising he would make it up to her.

Time had gone by and so he collected his case and caught a taxi as he watched the scenery of Miami city centre go by, he took stock of the warm weather and the tall buildings on the way to the airport knowing it would be a long time before he felt heat like this again. On arrival he thanked the driver palming him a good tip. 'Hey man, have a great trip.' Jim smiled as he acknowledged the driver's comments.

He went through the booking-in procedures then boarded his flight and flew back to Heathrow on the redeye flight. He had booked business class again, so was able to stretch and sleep as he covered himself in a blanket and dropped off. He kept wondering what he had been asked to do. It made no sense; any agent, even a private agency could have done what he had done and for a minimal price. He eventually slept relishing his time with Carole-Anne. He awoke as the cabin crew were preparing for landing.

He went through passport control then exited through the arrivals doors; where he saw the driver holding a card 'Jim B' in big letters; he acknowledged the driver. He was driven home as he made small talk. He entered Jackie's apartment where he started to unpack. He texted Jackie to let her know he was home; informing her he had a meeting at two with Langton. The texted reply was 'okay, later.' He thought mmm she's still not happy, so he took out the watch he had bought her and left it on the table just in case he got home late.

He had a couple of hours but didn't really sleep just nodded, then showered and went to Langton's office. He was keen to know the result of the search for Sumner.

CHAPTER TWENTY/SIX

Jim arrived at Langton's office as he yawned from the redeye flight; the jet lag was quickly catching up on him even though he had slept. Come on in Jim you must have had a great time you can't be tired having had an all paid holiday on the company. Jim smiled 'it was difficult keeping up Anglo-American relations.' Langton smiled 'As I understand; anyway Yvonne is on the way she called earlier, she said things are not as they seem.' Jim frowned as he looked at Langton who put his hands up in the air, 'don't ask, cause I don't know either; that's all she said.'

'How about Sumner Guv has he been nicked yet?' 'No he appears to have done a complete runner. I even asked Vicky to get her man on it, but he came up short as well. Although I must say she was a good choice of yours to carry on where you left off, she's done a cracking job; all the indications are that it will be a guilty plea; those sex tapes have made everyone put their hands up, they don't want a jury to see those.' With that Langton's phone went, he answered, then nodded to Jim 'she's here.' Jim nodded and went to collect her.

Jim was greeted by a big smile from Yvonne, they shook hands then went to the lift, as they got in they were joined by others. Yvonne said 'good trip Jim, you have a nice tan?' 'Very nice thanks.' The others got out at the next floor the doors closed as he squeezed her bum, 'bugger off Jim.' He smiled 'You want me to debrief you again in Birmingham?' 'Not at this time Jim, but soon I can't say anything yet, but soon I will be able too.' The floor indicator pinged as they reached the top floor.

They entered Langton's office where the normal greetings were made then coffee arrived. Yvonne opened the meeting by saying; 'Jim did a really good job, it enabled us to identify a double agent.' 'What double agent.' 'Sorry Jim I can't say, but the backbencher relative information I gave you was not correct, it was mentioned to only you and one other, to see if it came back, and it did; we knew it wasn't you, because of the way it was received; we were able to backtrack to the suspected source.' 'Was there a drugs deal?' Yvonne smiled 'of course.' Jim looked at her and frowned watching her sip from her cup, she was lying; he had been used again to smoke out another mole, but where, and who? Was it this side of the pond or the other side? He wasn't sure of anything anymore. 'Was that the reason I was followed in Washington by the poorly trained surveillance team?' Yvonne tugged at her skirt, to cover her knees. Jim had identified this over the course of time, as one of the signals she gave out when she was lying or about to lie, or as they say, being economical with the truth. 'Things happen for many reasons Jim, some, if not most, I cannot divulge to you; suffice to say, there are good and sensitive reasons why it happened the way it did.'

'So will I get to know what was going on in Miami?' 'Not yet; perhaps later on, when Barney has finished his operation.' 'I thought this was a joint operation?' 'Oh it is, or should I say was; anyway I can say no more.' This frustrated the hell out of Jim; he always wanted to know insides of a ducks arse; all the why's and wherefores'? This way of working was so alien to him.

'I would like to thank you Jim and Mr Langton for allowing you to work with us at short notice.' Langton piped in 'that's our pleasure Yvonne, Jim is at your disposal, obviously work commitments permitting.' Jim had the impression he was a ping pong ball, being tossed from one side of the room to the other.

'Yvonne then said 'okay we have another issue which will require you to go to Portugal this time. That's all I can say at the moment, it will take a little while to get organised, so just a preparatory warning; it might also be handy to get a bit of Portuguese behind you, just the odd phrase, buy some tapes or DVD's.' Yvonne stood up and shook Langton's hand saying 'thanks again a great job.' She picked up her document case then opened the door as Jim showed her out. He walked close to her, as he said 'I could give you one right now.' 'You will have to wait, I will call you soon. Once in the lift he squeezed her bum as she murmured 'I would like you, how you say; to give me one too Jim.' The lift arrived at the ground floor as he took her visitors badge then he bid her goodbye shaking her hand as he tickled her palm watching her smile invitingly as she let her hand savour his touch; then she left as her driver picked her up at the front door.

Jim went back to see Langton, who beamed a smile at him 'you are, aren't you?' 'Oh do bugger off Guv, you ask me that every time, no I'm not.' 'What was the trip like?' 'Yeah it was magic, just magic,' as his thoughts momentarily drifted back to Carole-Anne. 'But now, I haven't got a clue what the fuck I was doing there, have you?' 'No more than what was spoken about just now; the only conversation I had with Yvonne whilst you were away, was to make sure you were okay and longevity of your stay; other than that, I am as much in the dark as you are.' 'I couldn't work like that guv, not knowing the whole picture, it would do my head in.' 'Well get used to it as it looks like another job looms on the horizon. Oh by the way how is Jackie?' 'Oh bugger; I better get home, thanks Guv will be in tomorrow, can you arrange a meeting with Vicky for say 11ish so we can run through any issues that may throw up the whereabouts of Sumner?' 'No problem, see you tomorrow, don't rush in.' Jim gave a thumbs up as he left. He passed

Langton's secretary who looked at Jim, she was expecting his banter and he didn't disappoint her, 'hello miss, you want some of my dict tomorrow?' 'I'm ready for it now,' she retorted throwing the ball back in his court, as she laughed. 'Sorry need some sleep, you okay for a long one tomorrow.' She laughed as she went into Langton's office. She knew he was watching her bum so gave a little wiggle.

Jim thought if she wasn't Langton's secretary I'd give her one; then he thought no way, it's way to close home.

Jim got home just as Jackie did; the only difference was he felt like he was walking on air from the jet lag. Jackie threw her arms around him and dragged inside planting a huge kiss on him as her tongue went deep into his mouth where she searched for his and started to undress him pushing him to the bedroom, he couldn't back down, she was so rampant and needed him inside her; she wanted her favourite first she undressed sat on the edge of the bed and dragged his head between her thighs forcing his head as far as it would go. 'Don't you dare stop Broadbent, this is for going away and leaving me, this is your penance. Oh fuck me Jim yes please, oh my god, yes Jim don't you dare fucking stop, fuck me Jim yes yes, yes.' She then exploded soaking him, then she took him, savouring his length as she worked him expertly with her tongue she listened to his moans and his breathing. She wanted more, so manoeuvred into a 69 position; she had further orgasms soaking his face, then she heard him moan and felt his hips lock as he came in her mouth, she swallowed him ensuring she had tasted every drop. Afterwards she rested her head on his chest as she played with his hair. Jim was exhausted from jet lag and quickly fell asleep with Jackie still resting on his chest.

The morning came to the smell of eggs and bacon, being cooked, Jim had missed this; he heard her scream 'Oh Jim, thank you so much, how much did this cost?' She paraded her new watch on her wrist into the bedroom. 'Jim this must have cost a fortune, how will you explain this away?' 'Leave it to me.' 'Thank you so much darling.' She kissed him and said 'I am going to pay you for this tonight.' She laughed, bringing the watch to her eyes peering over the top seductively. Jim thought, oh no not again, as he tried to smile.

After breakfast Jackie rushed around then went to work as Jim slowly started to get ready. He sat at the table and opened his A4 book and began reading his notes trying to bring himself back up to speed with the case before meeting Vicky at 11am. There was nothing startling; it was just good to refresh his memory for later.

Vicky was already in Langton's office as Jim entered; she said 'looks like you've had a good time by your tan?' 'It was hard work, but enjoyable thanks, and before you ask, no I can't discuss it.' Vicky smiled saying 'Oh okay enough said.' The discussion then continued on with regard to the documents and the committal case having been submitted to CPS also a top QC had been chosen for the trial. Langton confirmed that the Chief had been in contact with the head of chambers regarding Farquharson; there had been no shortage of QC's queuing up for the case, especially after he had been suspended and word spread as to the reason why.

Jim smiled at Vicky she acknowledged his and Langton's gratitude for a job well done, but they all knew that a file of this size once a QC got hold of it, would mean mountains of further enquiries and statements to take.

Vicky and Jim went out into the office where they sat and went through all the notes with regard to the whereabouts of Sumner, but nothing came to light, not even Vicky's informant Tim, could get a handle on where he had buggered off to.

It was now just a waiting game; although there was no doubt, he was on the Costa del Sol, shacked up with some bird or being hidden by friends.

Jim arrived home to see Jackie bopping in the kitchen he slapped her bum, then she turned and shoved him backwards to the bedroom where she gave him one of the best blow jobs he had ever had, after she had finished she hugged him and said 'that's for my lovely watch darling.' He smiled as he hugged her and said 'anymore jewellery you need.' She laughed and slapped his arm, 'come on dinner will be done; you can service me later.'

CHAPTER TWENTY/SEVEN

Jim went to see one of his long term informants, he hadn't seen him for a while, he was one of those that needed a gee up to get him going; as he only rang when he needed some cash; although he was always spot on with the information he gave.

'Hi Joey, you okay?' 'Yes Jim fine thanks; what's going on, not seen you for a while?' 'You should be you telling me what's going on?' 'Okay, look there's an armed robbery planned for next week, it's a cash delivery job, one of the big banks, Barclay's I think, they are having a big replenishment; you know, the main one in the High Street.' 'Who's up for that?' There's some tasty names Jim, some real hard nuts, shooters, sawn-offs the lot.' 'Come on then the names and when?' 'They are doing a recon tomorrow and planning it for next week.' 'You involved?' 'No just offered up the job.' 'How close are you?' 'Pretty close, know what I mean.' 'Come on mate you involved?' 'No, straight up Jim; scouts honour.' 'Fuck me that count's for a lot Joey, so when were you going tell me about this one then?' 'Honest Jim, was going to call you tomorrow after they had sussed it out proper, no what I mean.' 'Yeah right; and what is your cut going to be?' '10K for the job and the getaway route.' 'Right I want names, shooters and motors okay; like yesterday.' 'Okay Jim but, one of the main players is Braxton,' 'Who Colin Braxton?' 'Yeah, one and the same.' 'But he's only just got out from a ten stretch, you sure?' 'Absolutely; look, they may have someone inside the bank so don't go sniffing around asking questions, as they will get to know about it. Apparently there's a big delivery next week, close on five mill; that's why they are going for it; one man and a trolley full of dosh.' 'Five mill now that is a serious touch.' 'To right and have a guess what, one of them is dressing up as a woman and will be outside the bank wheeling a pram with a sawn-off in it; he will be the confrontation with a back-up coming up from behind.'

'Fuck me Joey you know a lot for not being involved?' 'Yeah I know; they asked me, but I said no; I was happy with 10k for the info.' 'Just be careful Jim, Braxton is a tasty villain; he's looking to hop over to Spain after, so he won't be fucking about.' 'Okay Joey what time is the delivery tomorrow?' '10.30 that's the normal time; there will be loads of people on the street, a couple of shots in the air and everyone will be scattering in confusion; then into a tranny with loot and gone.' 'Where's the change-over vehicle and the slaughter.' 'Not sure about the slaughter, the change-over is in the lorry park next to the transport café near the motorway junction.' 'Yeah I know it, good man; okay you know what I need; how many handed, shooters, and motors okay?' 'See what I can do.' Jim then gave him a wedge of his own money then went back to HQ's.

He went into see Langton and explained the potential job, 'Fuck me Jim nothing like short notice is there.' 'He wouldn't have told me the little shit if I hadn't have met him.'

'Okay I'll ring the crime squad see if they can cover this, we can't cover it.' Jim nodded, 'it will be good to see some of them again.' Okay can you script this up ASAP; I will need to brief ACC Ops and get his sanction to go with it, at least tomorrow is a dry run so we have some breathing space,' 'what if it isn't? What if that's what they have told certain people, so if there is someone who is loose mouthed they'll have the job done and be in the Costa's sunning it up, whilst the old bill are planning the interception for the following week.' 'Good thinking Jim, okay script it up now and I'll start making calls.'

Jim saw Langton's secretary and smiled at her as he said 'you want some now? Some of my dict?' He sidled up to her. She laughed and said 'Oh come on then if you must give it to me,' as she laughed. Jim then dictated the information as he knew it. As he was getting to the amount of money and firearms, she looked at him, 'this is a big job Jim; I know of Braxton from other reports; he is ruthless.' 'I know, he commands a lot of respect.' The report was finished, although he left out the change-over location as that involved Joey and would complicate matter;, he read it and took Sandy's hand and kissed the back of it. 'Thank you once again for taking my dict so quickly and efficiently.' She coloured up as she 'Oh bugger off Jim, but you know I always like your dict.' Sandy liked the light hearted banter; all she got normally was serious stuff from Langton. He laughed at Sandy as he went to Langton's office; he had anticipated the need for a couple of copies so photo copied couple more off.

He knocked Langton's door and was called in. He saw Ops there in all his braid. 'Come in Jim and sit down.' Ops said 'we meet again Jim as he shook his hand. Jim had a lot of time for Ops, he had worked his way up through the ranks not one of those university fliers. Jim handed them both a copy of his report.

The room went quiet as they read the report making notes as they did so. Ops said 'I notice you made mention that your source is not involved in the robbery, although he has played some role, in it?' 'Yes I only put that in to show you how close he is although I could leave him out if you want?' 'Can you run off another report leaving any mention of him out, just say he's not involved; and destroy these,' Jim nodded and took reports then shredded them. He just caught Langton's secretary before lunch, she quickly rattled off another report leaving out the sources involvement. He then returned handing out the newly typed reports. Langton suggested calling the crime squad and the firearms commander to get the job at least on the radar. Ops nodded and made his way back to his office saying 'page me when they are all assembled I need to inform the Chief, just so he is aware.'

Chris from the Regional Crime Squad attended and discussed the job; if he was sure it was the right job for the squad, he would script it up; then look at the plot for the team the following day.

Ops had a meeting with the Chief where he discussed the pros and cons of the job. The Chief asked the same question are we sure there is no agent provocateur, or participating informant in this?' 'No sir, DS Broadbent has assured me that as far as he is aware it is straightforward information, the Chief looked side wards at Ops and said 'as long as there is nothing to come back and bite us?' 'Take it as red I will ensure all the t's are crossed.' 'What if it is tomorrow?' 'The crime squad have been called, so has firearms Ops, we will cover it tomorrow as if it is a go, and hopefully that will give us a week to set it up properly, I am due to meet them in Langton's office as soon as they page me.' With that his pager went off and he excused himself, 'Can I have your green light sir?' The Chief just nodded then said 'Yes.'

The meeting went well; then Chris and the firearms ops headed out to plot the bank and get positions to strike, if the job came off tomorrow.

Jim obtained an up to date picture of Braxton and photocopied a couple for the briefing the next morning. Just as he was putting more paperwork together when he received a call from Joey, 'must be quick, look it's a five handed team, Braxton will be the guy with a sawn-off coming from behind; the guy dressed up is Graham Sexton, he will have a sawn off as well, the van driver, and the other two in the rear of the transit will load the loot.' 'What colour is the transit?' 'An old white one, just like a builders van.

168

That's it must go.' 'Hold up Joey, is tomorrow a dry run still?' 'As far as I know, but they are acting funny getting things prepared for the off. So I would cover it tomorrow just in case.' 'Fuck me Joey; hold up a minute, is the change over the same location as discussed?' 'Look can't stop, it's as I told you.' That was it he was gone.

Jim then waited for Chris to return so he could write up an operation order. He called Jackie informing her he would be late.

CHAPTER TWENTY/EIGHT

Colin Braxton was an across the pavement armed robber, he was hard and commanded a lot of respect inside prison, and out; he had seen more bird than an aviary. His favourite weapon was a sawn off, it looked the part and made a lot of noise; also when looking at the wrong end, it was a frightening sight. 'Point a sawn off at someone and you get instant respect,' was one of his favourite sayings.

His last job was a disaster; too many people involved which got to the ears of the old bill and the job ended up in an ambush. He had set the job up, a Security van heist; a transit blocked-in front, with another behind, preventing the van reversing; he had jumped out of the front transit and blasted the front windscreen of the Securicor van with his shotgun shattering the screen, but the bullet proofing prevented the shot from penetrating the screen. It was then that the old bill sprung their trap; they arrived in their own transit with more fire power than Braxton's team had; so they put their hands up. Someone had grassed them up big time. Braxton was seething, although he never did find out who it was. He served a ten stretch for his part; the judge had given him the biggest slice for his life of crime.

This was his big one; he had already bought a place near Marbella in the hills, so this job would see him comfortable for a while. He had also got a tickle going with a prostitution racket, using a couple of local massage parlours with a pimp running them on his behalf; which kept a wedge coming in as well.

The team met in a back room of the Blind Beggar pub, it was a haunt for villains. They huddled around the table. 'Right I want this job to go down nice and sweet, the shooters are for conformity, don't go blasting anyone unless they have a serious go. Okay Graham, you looking pretty outside the bank with the pram and sawn off you understand?' Graham nodded.

'Pat you drive the tranny, go slowly until the jobs gone down; don't go drawing attention; we don't won't the old bill sniffing around for speeding right?' Pat nodded 'understood Col.' 'Right we follow the van in and pull up short on the other side of the road and wait for it to unload the cash onto the trolley, then just as it is pulled towards the entrance of the bank, I will jump out of the tranny as Graham pokes the sawn-off under the guards nose, I will come up from behind to ensure no one else interferes. Then Pat, you drive across the road and the two in the back load the trolley into the rear then we pile in the tranny and we're off, job done; it should take twenty-thirty seconds max, any questions?' Pat said 'is the change-over place the same?' 'No I'll tell you where, when we've done the job.'

Braxton raised his hand to the barman who poured another round of drinks and placed them on the bar; he sent Pat to bring them over. They raised their glasses and chinked them to a successful job and some well-deserved sun for those going to Spain.

Braxton had arranged for Joey to nick another transit any colour other than white, false plate it; he would let him know when to drop it off at the lorry park; this was an ideal location for the transfer, leaving the keys in a magnetic box under the driver's side wheel arch would prevent someone having to carry the keys on them and the risk of losing them.

Braxton wanted Pat and the others to believe he had made an alternative location, it would keep them guessing.

The last thing he wanted was the old bill there waiting as they changed vehicles.

Braxton got home and kissed his old lady and had a quickie before getting some sleep; not that he could, as he was on edge. His old lady had already packed her essentials, most of her clothes and Colin's were in the villa in Spain; she would be gone in the morning travelling by cab to the coach station then to Birmingham airport. She would be in the air; on a flight to the sun before his job went off. Colin's ticket was on kitchen table, he would be joining her after it was all over. She needed his money to keep up the appearance of a villain's wife. Although towards the end of his ten-stretch she had to draw her horns in a bit, and spend less, as the safety deposit box was nearly empty. No bank accounts for the old bill to snoop around, the money she spent was money from good friends if they asked.

Colin woke up early having caught a couple of hours sleep, he was tired, but his adrenalin was beginning to seep into his system, he could feel the thumping of his heart in his ears as he picked up his happy bag, which contained a pump actioned sawn off, overalls and a mask. Braxton called Joey 'right mate pick me up now.' He kissed his old lady goodbye as she got into a cab saying 'see you in the sun,' shortly after Joey arrived. 'Right mate take me to a lock-up and pick up the change-over tranny, I moved it so no one other than me knows where it is; then I will drop you off at the Blind Beggar at 9.30 so the gaffer can see you. Not that I don't trust you, I just want you where eyes are on you, you understand?' Joey nodded then said 'no problems Col or do you want me to take your Missus somewhere?' 'Fuck off Joey did you hear what I just said?' Braxton had an aggressive tone to his voice. 'Yes mate no probs; Blind Beggar 9.30 I'm there.' Joey picked up Braxton then drove to the lock-up under his directions. Once there Braxton said 'right Joey hands up.' 'What?' 'Put you're fucking hands up now, do as you're fucking told.' Joey put his hands up as

Braxton patted him down. 'Fuck me Colin you are paranoid, you think I'm wired up, what the fuck is going on?' 'Sorry mate just suspicious of everyone, since the last job.

'I was talking to others inside, who said trust no one.' 'Do us a favour Colin, me a grass; leave it out son.' 'Right you drive the tranny, wear these gloves no traces okay?' 'Yeah no probs. Where we going?' 'The lorry park.' 'Okay see you there, you picking me up? 'Yep I'll be behind you.' 'Not mercenary Colin, but when do I see my slice?' 'Here's 5k now and 5k on completion, I'll make sure you get it okay.' 'Joey nodded, knowing if it went down he wasn't going to see the other five.

The drive to the lorry park was uneventful it took about 40 minutes; Joey parked up at the edge of the lorry park so as not to be in the way of the lorries and cause attention, which could have the old bill sniffing around. Once parked up Braxton put the key in a magnetic box and placed under the driver's side front wheel arch, it clunked as the magnets grabbed hold of the metal.

They dove back to the Blind Beggar which took about the same time. Joey knocked on the pub door just after nine; the landlord came down and said 'you're early?' Braxton watched as the gaffer let him in then gave a thumbs up sign as the gaffer waved acknowledging him. 'You want a coffee Joey?' 'Love one please I'm gasping; just milk no sugar.' 'What's this all about anyway Joey, Colin just said make sure you stay here?' 'No idea, I think he might be shagging some bird and doesn't want anyone knowing where she lives; I don't know could be anything, I think that last stretch did his head in,' as they both laughed.

What Braxton didn't know was the crime squad were watching the lock-up where the white transit was hidden and had plotted it up. The adrenalin was now running as all the villains turned up. Chris put a call into Jim 'fuck me Jim they're all here, it could be going down today.' 'Cheers Chris, keep me updated.'

173

'Fuck me guv the full team are at the lock up, it looks like it's on for today.' Jim called the firearms team to get them on standby.

Braxton was giving the last of the briefing 'right I'm telling you all one last time, no one makes any phone calls till we are at the slaughter and then only when the split has been made, you all understand, fucking tell me you all understand?' There was a mutual agreement rumbling through the team. 'Right just so as your all clear; Joey is at the Blind Beggar, he is under the eye of the gaffer; so just in case anyone thinks about making a call, I will personally take their fucking knees out, you understand?' At the same time he racked the action of the pump action sawn off. The look of fear as they all looked at the mad eyes of Braxton said it all. Then all of a sudden Graham came out of the lock-up office in a blonde wig and a dress on, there was raucous laughter from everyone which broke the tension. Pat said 'me first darling give us a kiss.'

Braxton shouted 'right last run through, time is getting close,' he then reiterated the plan and emphasised 'any sniff of the old bill then we abort, everyone understand?' There was an agreement; he then said 'the signal for old bill is right hand straight up in the air full stretch you all understand.' The consensus was 'yes.' Then they all put their hands in the middle one on top of the other as Braxton said 'okay let's do it.' They all put overalls on got into the white transit and made their way to the bank, waiting at the bottom of the main street.

Chris had given his briefing at 6 am; 'Okay listen up, this is a hurry up job, so here goes. We have with us a firearms team who will be deployed in our cars, there job is to take out the bad guys so don't you be getting in their way especially if they try and take out the security vehicle elsewhere.' He then gave out the briefing and the locations, he also warned about the guy dressed in drag pushing a pram, emphasising there was no better cover than a woman pushing a pram, so be mindful he/she will be searching the streets looking for the old bill, so keep your eyes open for her, I mean him; which caused a ripple of laughter. 'Okay guys get ready for the off, happy hunting, and remember to act on my command to strike and get the firearms team in close. Right lets go.'

The firearms team then loaded and holstered there weapons and then joined the squad guys.

That was it the clock was ticking; so a quick round of bacon sandwiches and on the road. The eyeball of the bank was from an office block overlooking the bank. The venetian blinds gave good cover. Firearms op manned the location with one of the crime squad guys as they waited. They were supplied coffee by the office staff who had been given some cock and bull story about a team of fraudsters who were in town hitting banks with fraudulent cheque books and cards.

The clock ticked towards 10.15 when the pram pushing villain turned up and walked up and down, with no one taking a blind bit of notice. As it neared to 10.30 he stood outside of the bank. Just then the Security van began making its way towards the bank with the transit a couple of cars behind. Chris had been giving a commentary to Jim on the surveillance and the location of the transit. This was heart thumping time as the security van got closer the adrenalin pumped more sending the senses into hyper mode.

The security van pulled up outside of the bank as the passenger got out and took the trolley out from the rear, then through the side serving hatch as the cases of money were removed and piled onto the trolley where they were secured with chains interlocking each one to the body of the trolley, then the guard began to pull the trolley towards the bank entrance.

Braxton was watching this and as soon as the guard had finished chaining the cases he was out of the tranny with the sawn off under his coat, he was making ground on the

175

guard from behind when Graham pulled out his sawn off from the pram and rammed it under the guards chin, at the same time Braxton let rip with a couple of rounds from his pump action. This caused mayhem amongst shoppers who scattered everywhere; this caused problems with the tranny as it was hampered by shoppers as were the crime squad vehicles trying to get in close. Then all of a sudden an off duty copper came out of the bank; seeing the mayhem he waded in and was shot by Braxton at near on point blank range. The officer saw the flash and heard the bang which deafened him, fortunately the officer had pushed the weapon away as the trigger was pulled; the shot glanced off his clothing hitting the wall of the bank. The firearms team had a sniper on the roof who took out Braxton and Sexton with two quick shots, both dead within two clicks of each other.

The transit was boxed in by the squad cars as the firearms team surrounded it; the remainder of those in the tranny came out with hands in the air having seen Braxton and Sexton shot and the overwhelming firepower. The firearms team took over making the arrests and making safe the weapons found in the transit.

The off duty officer was seriously hurt, but fortunate for him it had been a cold sharp frosty morning; he was wearing a thick Barbour coat with a quilt lined fleece underneath. The cartridges that Braxton had used were number 8 shot, the type used in clay pigeon shooting, although still deadly, they didn't pack the same punch as number 4 or 5 shot would have done; having said that he was still badly injured and was rushed to hospital.

The news reached Jim and Langton at HQ's where they were waiting with baited breath, Langton having received the news contacted ACC Ops. Who came down to Langton's office where he obtained a full debrief or as much as he could. They both concurred that no one could not have foreseen an off duty officer being in the wrong place at the wrong time. The press were going to have a field day, with headlines; 'bungled police operation places members of the public at risk.' Therefore he called the force press officer in to try to reduce the impact by releasing a statement saying 'that in the highest traditions of the British Police, an off duty officer being confronted with the scene of an armed robbery as he exited the bank had tried to intervene and had been shot, fortunately not fatally. His family have been informed and we will be supporting them during this tragic time. Due to the lethal force used by the criminals the police had no option, but to shoot two of them which is sad, as they both died at the scene; three other criminals were arrested at the scene without injury or any more shots being fired.' Ops asked the press officer to release the statement.

Braxton's wife Carol arrived at Malaga airport and was met by her friend Julie who was crying as they hugged at the arrivals gate. 'What's wrong with you Julie, I haven't been away that long.' Then Carol saw the tears were not tears of joy as she put her hand to her mouth, as she said 'oh no!' Julie nodded 'The old bill have shot two armed robbers and just named Colin as one of the dead.' Carol just sank to her knees and cried. Julie helped her to her car then drove the journey to Carols home. The journey was difficult due to Carol crying and becoming at times hysterical. They arrived at the villa. Julie unlocked the gates, then entered and opened the doors and windows to air the villa.

Carol said 'you know Colin mentioned that this was his last job and he wouldn't go back inside again; oh my god, I think I'll sell the house in the UK and move out here in the sun.' 'Come on out, it's lovely here Carol, we can have good times again.' Carol said 'call me later or perhaps tomorrow, ta, ta for now' Julie then left, as Carol busied herself, starting the BMW and dropping the roof. Then went out for groceries and came back and went to bed crying herself to sleep.

Langton got Jim to organise a car around to the off duty officer's home to take his wife to hospital and arranged with a policewoman to get the kids from school.

Joey was sat in the bar of the Blind Beggar drinking coffee, listening to the radio. The landlord Mickey was doing normal bar work replenishing shelves, and washing glasses. Then all of a sudden there was an announcement on the local radio 'we bring you a news flash, there has been an armed robbery in the High Street outside of Barclay's bank, an off duty police officer has been severely injured and two of the armed robbers have been shot dead by the police. The police appear to have been waiting for the robbery to take place. We will bring you more when we know it.' Joey said 'Fucking hell Mickey that has got to be Colin.' 'Fuck me you better get a move on, what are you supposed to do?' 'Nothing I've done it all although I better move the change-over motor, or just leave it, no fuck it I'll leave it, it's clean anyway.' They chatted for a while then Joey left getting a cab to the lock up to get his car. Once collected he called Jim. 'Hi Jim I heard on the news, fuck me that wasn't supposed to happen was it?' 'No mate; can't talk at the moment just keep your head down there will be people looking for the snout.' 'Okay the change-over tranny is at the lorry park.' 'I will be in touch in a couple of weeks; cheers Joey, remember keep your head down.'

The three villains from the tranny were taken to Central Police station and interviewed, although as anticipated, it was a no comment interview.

Jim knowing the change-over vehicle was at the lorry park. He went to a news agents without any CCTV and bought a local map he put on a pair of plastic gloves opened it up whilst sat in his car. He marked the High Street outside of Barclays bank with a red X, then a blue X with Graham on it. He said to him-self 'fucking got you, you bastards.' He then nipped up to the lorry park and made sure no one was about, he found the key, using his gloves he opened the door and slid the map onto the passenger seat; he left the transit unlocked with the key under the sun visor. He then went to the café and had a cup of coffee. He used the payphone and called the police station saying he was a lorry driver; reporting a transit was parked in the lorry park, it was in the way, it had been there all day, he declined his name, but he knew the switch board would record the phone number confirming its location.

He sat down and finished his coffee, then drove back to HQ's. He spoke with Langton and discussed the interview and how the Central Station CID had done a good job albeit as anticipated they had to contend with no comment interviews, which had only hampered them a little; it was quite a clear-cut an open and shut case; as they had found tickets to Malaga in Braxton's house. Langton nodded as he opened his bottom drawer. He poured a couple of fingers in each glass, then chinked them together, Jim then said 'what were the chances of an off duty copper being there at the time the robbery went down. Have you heard how he is?' 'Fucking bad luck, it was good job it was cold and he pushed the sawn off away as it went off, his clothes deflected the worst. The last I heard was he was out of any serious danger but had serious wounds.' Jim raised his glass in recognition. The phone in Langton's office rang he answered and said 'okay thanks.' He then said to Jim 'they have discovered a suspected change-over vehicle in the lorry park near the motorway intersection and discovered a map in it which had the high street bank marked on it, that's a bit careless,' he looked at Jim as he smiled. 'The map has been taken to Central CID and van for fingerprinting.' Jim smiled as he said 'that's the icing on the cake then.'

The case was presented at crown court some months later where guilty pleas were entered as the evidence was overwhelming. The sentences reflected the guilty pleas with the judge handing down 10 years a piece stating if the pleas had been not guilty he would have handed down far heavier terms of imprisonment.

The injured officer recovered although he bore the scars; he was eventually fit for duty. He was thankful for his luck and although not religious, thanked god for looking after him.

CHAPTER TWENTY-NINE

The murder and rape cases were opened with the dock full of the accused. Vicky sat next to the CPS representative behind the prosecuting QC, once the pleas of guilt had been received. The prosecuting QC gave a very eloquent opening speech, then he gave in detail the circumstances of each person's involvement in the offences outlined. Each defendant had their own QC who attempted to give a mitigating speech for each of their clients. The judge in his red robes and wig which showed the signs of many years of wear sat looking over the top his half-moon glasses as he made notes nodding to the QC's to continue once he had finished recording each note.

The speeches over, the judge looked at the defendants as the clerk said to those in the dock 'stand.' The stern face of the judge as he looked at each white faced defendant who were all shaking anticipating what was coming, they all knew it was imprisonment, and also knew it was going to be for a long time as well.

Stuart Small you are an evil depraved man and the sentence I give you will reflect the seriousness; conspiracy to murder all the victims you are sentenced to life imprisonment on each count, conspiracy to rape 15 years on each count, false imprisonment 5 years imprisonment all to run concurrently. Smalls face dropped as he shook his head.

Lynda Small, for your involvement in this sordid affair, you are sentenced; conspiracy to murder, life imprisonment on each count, for rape and conspiracy to rape 10 years on each count, sexual assault 2 years on each count, all to run concurrently. He then gave similar sentences to the others, leaving Prentice till last; he then lashed into him for bringing the profession into disrepute and sentenced him for conspiracy to murder to life imprisonment on each count with a minimum time to be served 18 years, rape 15 years and conspiracy to rape on each count 15 years to run concurrently. He then boomed take them down out of my sight. Lynda Small had to be helped down as she was almost feinting, as were the other two women.

Vicky thanked the QC and the CPS representative who were complimentary of the way the case had been handled and put together.

Vicky called Jim and gave him the result as she could hardly contain herself. 'Okay Nags Head tonight Vic?' 'Too right Jim; what a great result.'

Jim informed Langton of the result, who was equally as pleased as he said 'Vicky is a good girl she did a good job.' 'She has a lot of potential; we are in Nags Head later, you coming.' Langton checked his diary and said 'Can't stop long have an important meeting tomorrow, but yes be there for just after 6.' Jim nodded as he punched the air. Then said to himself 'I Just want Sumner now.'

Jim called Jackie, 'hey babe's great result today, you coming for a beer at Nags Head later?' 'Yes could do with a couple beers, I'll go home first and get a cab, then we can cab it home then I can drop you off in the morning to pick your car up.' 'Great see you there later.'

Jim walked into the Nags Head, just before 6, Langton and Vicky were already there deep in conversation. Vicky could hardly contain herself as she punched the air. Langton said 'I have just been talking with Vicky, I need someone else to work alongside you especially when you get called away; I think I can pursued the Chief to get Vicky on the team, what do you think?' 'Magic that would be great; what about Central do you think they will let her go?' 'Just leave that to me.' The old team from Central began to drift in, this was going to be a heavy night; the beer was flowing well. Then Jackie arrived to raucous shouts as she kissed Jim.

Jackie and Vicky chatted together with girl talk as Jim was downing his beer the whole pub was alive with banter, jibes and laughter. Langton had slipped away not before slipping Jim fifty quid to buy a round for the lads.

Jim woke up in the morning with a banging head; his mouth was like the bottom of a budgie cage. He looked at Jackie who was equally as spaced out. He got up and went to bathroom and looked in the mirror trying to focus on the image looking back at him. God you look rough Broadbent he said to himself as he dragged himself into the shower. The water cascaded onto his head as he looked up letting the warmth pound his face. Once finished he began to wake up. He then cleaned the condensation from the mirror and shaved, he saw the reflection behind him of Jackie rubbing her hair as she walked into the bathroom 'fuck you Broadbent don't you ever invite me to one of those nights again, you arsehole.' She sat on the toilet with her head in her hands moaning. Jim finished shaving and splashed on his after shave, then turned the shower on and guided Jackie in sliding the glass door closed. He dressed and put some bread in the toaster and made coffee. Jackie came into the kitchen with her turban and dressing gown on. She was getting there, although Jim knew from old, to say nothing till she had a coffee. She had such a vipers tongue in morning until awake, even more so, when suffering from the night before.

Slowly like a blotting paper absorbing liquid the colour was rising in her face, then as if the lights had been switched on she spoke 'oh Jim I feel rough, I've never drunk that much for a long time I can't take those nights anymore.' 'I know babes I feel the same, we have been away from those nights for so long.' 'What's this I her from Vicky you want her on your team?' 'Not my idea Jack, Langton's, she did such a good job, he wants her to work for him so when I'm not there she can carry on the work.' 'Makes sense but, don't you go trying to get in her knickers?' 'Not my type Jack, anyway I haven enough on my plate with you.' 'Yes you do, and don't you forget it.' They ate more toast then looked at their watches and double timed in getting ready. Jackie dropped Jim off at the Nags Head to collect his car then he went to HQ's.

Langton was not at his desk so he cracked on with his paperwork he still had a jackhammer in his head pounding so hard it hurt. He went to see Langton's secretary. 'Oh Jim; rough night was it? No dict. from you today then?' As she smiled; 'have you got an Aspirin or similar for a thumping head?' She opened her drawer and handed him a couple of tablets saying 'they are extra strength; it looks like you need a lie down somewhere?' She jibed at him knowing for the moment she had the upper hand. Jim smiled as he thanked her then took the tablets. It took about twenty minutes to work but, slowly they started to kick in.

Langton arrived at midday and said 'you look rough.' 'You should have seen me earlier.' 'Okay I think I have got the go-ahead for Vicky, I should know by tomorrow.' Jim nodded as he drank more coffee.

The day dragged on he was just about to go home when his phone went he saw the display it was Yvonne. He was going to ignore it, but had to answer. 'Hi Jim I need to debrief you on your last job I can now tell you the truth, and get you to carry on where you left off.' 'What when?' 'Next week in Birmingham again, I will let you know for sure, probably Wednesday.' Jim thought fuck me not again. But she is such a good fuck and really very grateful too.

Jim got home to the sight of Jackie bopping as usual in the kitchen wearing one of his shirts as he crept up behind her lifting the shirt tail, patting her bum, she had heard him, but played along pretending she hadn't. He then slid his hands under the shirt cupping her free flowing breasts in each hand. She pushed her head back as he kissed her throat then breathed warm air into her ear, pursing his lips as he blew gently so his breath tumbled deeply, as his warmth excited her inner ear stimulating the sensitive nerve endings, sending signals rushing to her brain, which caused sensations to race down her spine to her vagina. She sighed deeply feeling herself moisten as she moaned softly as his hands roamed over her body. He knew all the right places to excite her inner feelings. This was heaven for Jackie she was a sexual animal; Jim brought out the beast in her and she loved it. Jackie turned the dinner down then circled around and looked into his eyes, then kissed him deeply, as she licked his ear and said 'take me now, anywhere just take me.' She unzipped his trousers releasing him as she walked him backwards to the bedroom where they indulged in their favourite sexual preferences. Jim lay back panting and said 'wow babes that was good you were ready willing and able,' he laughed as she smiled and looked at him 'no complaints this side either.'

They spent a few minutes hugging each other, Jackie played with hairs on his chest as he stroked her shoulders and spine. Jackie didn't want to get up as this was heaven, but eventually had to. She dished up dinner, as Jim cracked open the wine, they consumed the meal and discussed each-others day. Jim daren't mention the spooks as it would have spoiled a precious moment, so he left it for another day.

The week-end came and went, then Jim threw into the conversation that he may have to meet the spooks again in Birmingham and probably be away overnight again, although he wasn't sure of the day, the indications were probably Wednesday. Jackie looked at Jim 'you going away again babes?' 'I don't think so, it's just a debrief on the last job.' Jackie looked at him 'why can't you tell me about the results of these jobs Jim?' 'Look Jack I'm sworn to secrecy and have signed so many documents regarding the information I'm given. I trust you implicitly, but I cannot risk you accidently mentioning something that could have implications further down the line, cause you know what old bill are like, the gossip factory would be in top gear.' 'I suppose, just I never know what you're doing?' 'If it helps Jack, I never know what the full picture is either, and it frustrates the life out of me as well. I want to know the in's and out of a ducks arse, but that's the way they work.'

Jackie dropped the conversation just relishing the last of the week-end with Jim and his attention, she was also looking forward to the following week-end when they had Jim's kids, they loved her and being with Jim. She doted on them and hoped one day to have one of her own.

No sooner had they gone to bed when the alarm went off for the beginning of another week. Jim showered as Jackie made breakfast. Jim feasted on his full English mopping up the remnants with bread and butter patting his tummy. 'That was good babe's thanks as always.' Jackie smiled not speaking, just nodding at the compliment.

CHAPTER THIRTY

Jim was fast asleep when the phone went by his bedside, he picked it up as he tried to focus on the display, he didn't recognise the number and wasn't going to answer it, but his inquisitive nature wouldn't allow it. 'Hello who's that?' 'Hi Jim its Ricky Briggs, remember?' 'What the fuck. How did you get this number?' 'Never mind that, I've heard you're after Charlie Sumner, well the word is he's in Marbella, meet me later today; I'll call you, to let you know where, don't nick me Okay? I know I'm still wanted, just trust me, as I will trust you.' 'Okay call me later.'

Jim laid back wide awake, thinking about Briggs and Spain; the child abuse case and him doing a runner out of the court dock, then ending up in Spain. He would need to speak to Langton and Yvonne later. He snuggled down under the covers spooning Jackie as he eventually drifted back to sleep.

'Hi Guv, can I have a word?' 'Come in Jim sit down, what's up?' 'I had a phone call last night from Briggs, you remember the spooks' undercover guy. He wants a meet later today to let me know where Sumner is; apparently he's in Marbella, what do you think?' 'Have you spoken with Yvonne?' 'No not yet just wanted your opinion.' 'Speak with her first, she may want him nicked or at least have one of theirs present as well.' 'Okay will do.' 'Here use my office phone.' Jim dialled the number and spoke with Yvonne, as he explained the phone call from Briggs. 'Okay Jim; meet him and get him to call our hot line, he will know the number.' 'Okay will do, is he still wanted?' 'Don't ask questions just meet him and tell him of my request;' that was it nothing more was said then the phone went dead.

'Fuck me Guv she has a strop on this morning; but yes, she said to meet him and get him to call their hot line; she just said he would know it. I knew he was one of their undercover guys.' Langton looked at him and just smirked saying nothing. Jim said 'I bet his record has been wiped clean as well, this is just like Tinker, Taylor, Soldier, Spy.' Jim went out into the office and called the CRO office for a previous conviction check on Briggs. He received the reply; fuck me, as I thought, nothing, not even a speeding fine, absolutely wiped clean.

His phone went, 'Jim, it's Briggs; right meet me at Fox and Hounds on the London Road at 2.30, see you there,' then he was gone.

Jim arrived at the pub and scoured the car park for signs of anyone watching, he picked out an old rusty Transit in the corner, he casually walked over to it, he looked inside the cab; it was covered in out of date copies of the sun most of them open at page 3. It looked like a builders van, although he knew covert vans were made to look that way. He looked around it and in the back, it looked genuine. He then went into the pub, the bar was spit and sawdust, with all types of punters around the bar; the lounge was more for those eating a meal. There was a group in overalls at a table eating pie and chips and swigging beer, cracking jokes and laughing. He presumed they belonged in the rusty builders van. He walked into the lounge as he was more suitably dressed for that side as he sat at a vacant table.

He checked his watch it was a little after 2.30, he presumed Briggs would be checking out the carpark as well, before venturing in. Then Briggs walked in looking cautiously as he did a quick nonchalant 180 of the lounge acknowledging Jim; he got a lager and sat down. They shook hands exchanging pleasantries.

Jim then said 'Look Ricky before we crack on, Yvonne wants you to call the hot line; she said you would know the number.' 'Will do; right Charlie Sumner; here's his address, it's a villa just outside of Marbella, apparently he's renting it off some guy. Nice pad surrounded by high fences and electric gates the full business.' 'How do you know?' 'Jim trust me mate, he's there. But I knew you would ask, so here's some pics of him and his bird around the pool at the villa, and don't ask how I got them either.' 'How longs he there for?' 'Don't know, but apparently he doesn't seem in any hurry to move on.' 'Are you seeing him again?' 'No, but I understand he's up for more of those sex parties at the villa which, might get some Spanish old bill attention.' Thanks Ricky, don't forget Yvonne.' They spent an hour discussing Spain and Morocco; then they shook hands and went their separate ways.

Jim spoke with Langton re Sumner being in Spain and the address. 'Okay Jim we need to get Interpol involved, and get the Spanish old bill to nick Sumner; then get him extradited. I will get the ball rolling. Oh by the way Vicky will be joining us as of a week Monday.' 'Thanks that's good news on both fronts.'

CHAPTER THIRTY⁄ONE

Jim arrived at the Marriot in Birmingham the same receptionist was on duty, she beamed a smile, 'Mr Broadbent, nice to see you again, thank you for staying with us.' 'Thank you Kirsty it's nice to see you again as well.' She took his details then handed him his electronic key as he thanked her, absorbing her sparkling blue eyes which smiled at him. He walked to the lift thinking, fuck me she's a cracker.

He just got to his room when he received a text for Yvonne, 'be there in about an hour.' Jim showered and shaved splashing on his aftershave.

He went to the lounge where ordered a coffee; he read the paper keeping one eye on Kirsty and the other on the entrance door. He looked at the headlines; he noticed something he hadn't picked up before, which announced unconfirmed reports regarding a British attaché who had been released from a Russian prison, in exchange for his counterpart in the UK. This had to be the double dealing suspect Yvonne had referred to in her last meeting. There was no date for the exchange to take place, but for the press to have got hold of it, it had to be soon.

Jim read the newspaper report mentally absorbing the details ready for his meeting with Yvonne. As he was reading the report his concentration had taking his attention from the door, he had failed to notice Yvonne arrive. He glanced at the reception desk; he couldn't help but notice the grey suited Yvonne with her back to him. She turned and visually searched the lounge, as her eyes met Jim's they lit up like beacons signifying instant attraction and a lustful desire as she anticipated Jim being inside her again. She felt herself warming up already with the need. She smiled at Jim as she walked over to where he was sat. Jim stood up and kissed her in the cheek. 'It's nice to see you again Yvonne.' 'Likewise Jim.' Jim raised his hand; the lounge waiter came over then he ordered two coffees.

Jim laid the paper down with the headlines of the Russian UK exchange. He looked at Yvonne and smiled, she looked at the headlines as she nodded. 'It's in the open now, so yes Jim, he had been suspected of being a double agent for some time, so we fed him a number of false stories, but he had someone on the inside who was also feeding him information which was obstructing us in outing him. So we created the false information regarding the UN official who was going to be assassinated this was to muddy the waters so to speak, which caused a lot of traffic back and forward across the pond and with SHAPE. It didn't take long to involve everyone; getting their sources to try and establish the truth.' 'Hold up what about the Yanks they were told about the UN official weren't they?' 'Yes of course they were, but most of what we told you was for your ears Jim and Carol-Anne's. Only Barney was aware of the real truth.' 'Woe, hold up a minute, you created the assassination as a smoke screen for the drugs deal didn't you?' 'That's what you were told Jim.' 'Was the drug deal real? Was anything real?' 'Yes Smyth-Jones was real so was Kowalski, but nothing else was.' 'No drugs deal?' 'No that was false as well.' 'What was I doing there then?' 'Look Jim some things I can tell you, but a lot I can't, let me just tell you that Carole-Anne and yourself have been tested and have passed all the assignments.' 'What, it was a test?' 'Partly, look Jim, we needed to out this suspect so created a story about a major US and UK drugs deal. We knew our suspect had arranged for Carol-Anne to be followed in the US, which also included you.' 'Why Carol-Anne, she's not into drugs or is she?' 'No Jim, Barney created the illusion that Carol-Anne was going to Miami with her boyfriend, but was suspected of using this as a cover to meet the drug suspects.' 'What! I was with a suspected drug trafficker?' 'No Jim, you weren't, that was the illusion created.' 'She was with me all the time.' 'Was she?' 'Well most of the time except when she had her hair done.' 'Think about it Jim, she was out of your sight and you had no idea what she was doing, we had to do it that way, to allow the illusion to grow. She will be approached soon we are sure by a rogue CIA agent who will try and turn her, then Barney will strike, so I want you to have no communication with her until this is over okay?' Jim nodded, as his head raced from place to place.

Jim was even more confused with the enlightenment he had just been told. 'Look Yvonne I'm still confused over this, were the Columbians real?' 'Yes they were Columbians, but in reality DEA undercover agents recruited by Barney to play the role as an exercise, they were not told why, just that they had to pretend to be part of a cartel for a couple of days.'

'Look Jim, you had a nice time in the states paid for by the service so don't knock it.' 'Yes mam, I did, but this way of working is so alien to me. I am used to knowing the whole nine yards when I go on a job.' 'Well get used to it Jim, as this won't be the last time you're used either. Also Barney has nothing but praise for the way that you and Carole-Anne worked together, so there could be more work in the states for you as well.' 'What if I was to be seconded to the states to work alongside Carole-Anne?' 'In your dreams Broadbent; no, I need you here, for many reasons.'

Jim sat thinking, what the fuck was going on; his deep frown and deep breathing was loud as he blew out a gust of air through pursed lips with swollen cheeks acting like bellows which said it all, he didn't have a clue what was going on.

Then something hit him, as he thought about the question he had asked Barney about Kowalski knowing the identity of Carole-Anne and the dangers of her being recognised by him. It made sense now, that's why Barney wasn't concerned, it was all acting to expose the mole that side of the pond. He was just a pawn on a big chess board with Barney and Yvonne working through the many moves ahead, but being kept in the dark.

'Okay Jim let me summarise for you. We suspected a senior MI5 official; we suspected he had been compromised and was trying to turn some of our other agents. Honey traps and wrong doings were his tools for getting other agents to feed him information or be exposed. We used Smyth-Jones as a Trojan horse so to speak, as we set the trap. One of our inside men let slip to the suspect about his suspicions of Smyth-Jones being involved in the planned drugs deal. The suspect then set the wheels in motion as we began to monitor his phone calls and emails; it soon became clear he was in deed our suspect, as soon as Smyth-Jones returned to the UK from Miami; he was approached by the suspect in an attempt to blackmail him, this confirmed our suspicions. That's when we undertook to spring the trap.' 'Fucking hell Yvonne, you could have told me?' 'No Jim I couldn't, we needed your reactions to be untainted so you reacted naturally without hesitation.'

'Now Jim let me have a shower then we can have something to eat.' 'I have a better idea, let me eat you first; then we can shower and have dinner after?' Yvonne felt the warmth inside her begin to moisten at the anticipation. She smiled and nodded saying 'you're on; I have been waiting for this.' They entered the lift as Jim pushed Yvonne up against the side and kissed her deeply.

The lift floor indicator pinged at the correct level; they exited and went to Yvonne's room, as soon as they entered the passion overflowed as they undressed each other kissing with deep desire, Yvonne was on the point of boiling over, her breath was short as the anticipation was bursting, the steam was rising as she felt the desire about to explode inside her. Jim spun her round as he wrapped his arms around her from behind as he cupped her breasts, he kissed her neck. Yvonne's breath was short and heavy as Jim's breath reached the inner depths of her ear sending waves of deep desire rushing down her spine, which was heightened by his hands roving down over her stomach and between her legs. Her boiling point was already there, as soon as he touched her outer vagina lips she orgasmed as she let go; as he inserted his finger she went berserk. Jim pushed her back on the bed and took her foot as he kissed and licked her toes. Her facial expression and breathing told him she was having another orgasm. He worked his tongue slowly up her leg to her inner thigh; this caused her to arch her back anticipating him entering her. Her eyes were tightly closed as she saw flashing lights in her mind's eye as he probed her depths with his tongue.

The night was full of passion as they satisfied there sexual desires to the maximum. They held each other as they rested panting from the exertion. Dinner was now the last thing on their minds as they fell asleep in each-other's arms not letting go until they awoke in the morning. Yvonne lent on one arm as she looked at Jim as he slept, she felt for the time-being complete; well and truly satisfied. Then Jim began to stir; as he opened his eyes he saw Yvonne staring at him. It took him a moment to focus; then said 'what?' 'Just admiring my lover, never to be openly admitted, but yes my true lover, it feels good to have this relationship, no strings, just unadulterated sex.' Jim looked at her, this was the first time she had really spoken this way. 'The feeling is entirely mutual mam.' Yvonne laughed, as she stretched, she yawned as she said 'oh Jim this feels so good, just to be able to relax and not worry about saying the wrong thing, you don't know what it's like having to watch the p's and q's when I'm with people outside of the know.' 'I do to a certain extent, but nowhere near your secret knowledge. You must have an encyclopaedia in your brain of operations and agents in the field?' Yvonne smiled as she got out of bed and went to the bathroom. They were both starving so showered then went for a full English breakfast in the restaurant. Afterwards they sat in the lounge drinking coffee, as Yvonne made a couple of calls. When finished she said 'you will be getting a call from Barney soon there is another issue that he wants you to help with in Lisbon. I think he'll be meeting you there.' 'What, when?' 'There you go again, wanting to know it all, how you say, the whole nine yards; I can't tell you. Barney will enlighten you when you speak to him and before you ask, I don't know when either.' Jim cocked his head to one side raising his eyebrows in a questioning manner. Yvonne just smiled as she shook her head then said 'look Jim, I have to go my driver is on the way, so thank you once again for your attention to detail. I am as always, very impressed.' They went and packed when finished he returned to Yvonne's room but, she had already checked out.

He sat in the lounge and called Jackie informing her he was okay and would be leaving soon although, he had to brief Langton before coming home. Jackie informed him she would most likely be home later as she was tied up in anther abuse case.

He checked out smiling at Kirsty 'everything okay with the room Mr Broadbent?' 'Fine thanks.' He handed over his credit card as she processed the bill; he punched in his pin number. She handed the bill and his credit card to him as he kissed the back of her hand again, then said goodbye. 'Please stay with us again?' 'Be back soon, and thank you.'

Jim arrived at HQ not really knowing how he got there; his head was in a blur, what does Barney want in Portugal? What was Miami all about? Jim was also feeling exhausted from the night with Yvonne, so before going to see Langton he went to the toilets and swilled cold water over his face. Langton's door was closed so he sat at his desk going through his paper work, Langton's door opened as he saw his secretary Sandy leave; she smiled at Jim as she put her hands through her hair for his benefit as she walked to her office with a slight hip sway.

Jim went in as he retorted 'you giving Sandy one guv?' Langton said 'touché; come in close the door. How was your meeting with Yvonne?' 'Well to say I don't know where to start is an understatement. None of what I did was real, it was all false to identify a double agent, or so she says, I don't know what's what anymore. The truth is so elusive, I have never been kept in the dark so much in all my life, and now there's a Yank job in Lisbon soon, the CIA agent Barney will call me. Fuck me guv I'm confused to say the least.'

Langton laughed 'was that from pillow talk?' 'Oh do fuck off guv, you won't leave it alone will you?' They both laughed as Langton said 'okay Interpol have been contacted and the extradition papers are being drawn up by the legal dept. as we speak. I would like Vicky to interview Sumner when he gets here, with you present; I want her to get the experience, because I can see you being away more and more with the spooks.' Jim showed his disappointment as he wanted to get inside Sumner's head, but at least being in on the interview was a result. Jim looked at Langton and was sure he knew more than he was saying. He was being kept in the dark from all sides now. He felt like the proverbial mushroom being kept in the dark and fed on bullshit. Jim cocked his head to one side as he looked in his normal questioning manner raising his eyebrows? Langton just smiled and said 'that's it Jim, anything else?' Jim smiled and shook his head then walked out just as Langton said 'I will get a couple of uniformed officers to fly over when he gets nicked and bring him back.' Jim nodded as he opened the door then sat at his desk.

He browsed through the new documents on his desk, but not really concentrating, so called Vicky. 'Hi Vicky we need to meet to discuss the Sumner interview, say in an hour, yeah here will be fine.' Jim collected all his papers and found a spare office and set them out, he also obtained some dry wipe pens from Sandy. He wrote on the whiteboard the points that needed to be proved. Not that he needed to, nor was he demeaning Vicky's competence, but it never hurt to go through the evidence again to make sure nothing was missed.

Vicky arrived as he made coffee then went to the office and set to work detailing the evidence as he knew it. He wrote on the whiteboard the points to prove in chronological order. 'Okay Vick, lets presume he will have a brief with him so we need to be positive, also devious as well; he will have had warnings about what we've got and what we haven't got; that's why the evidence of Debbie and Sandra will be vital, especially Debbie who he left for dead.' 'Why are you involving me in this Jim?' 'Oh, hasn't Langton told you? He wants you to run the interview with me present.' 'No he didn't, fuck off Jim, your winding me up; are you serious?' 'Yep doubly serious; so any questions fire away now?' They sat down for a couple of hours going over the finer points of the case making notes and cross referring evidence and witness statements. Vicky was scribbling furiously making sure she had it all down in writing, which she would disseminate at her leisure, so it got implanted in her brain. Once finished, Vicky went into see Langton and thanked him for the opportunity. He smiled and said 'right Vicky close the door this is for your ears only. Jim is going to be working away for a while, I can't tell you where, and nor do I expect you to ask Jim where, and neither do I expect you to repeat this outside of this room because if you do your secondment will cease, no warning no second chances. We deal with highly sensitive matters here, so my trust is being put in you on the strength of Jim's recommendation, so pleases don't abuse that trust.' 'Understand guv you have my absolute trust. I hope it doesn't come on top, Jim going away before Sumner gets nicked and brought back here?' 'I have no control over that.' Vicky looked at Langton not sure what to say. Langton opened his drawer and poured a dram in each glass as he toasted her secondment to his department. Vicky raised her glass and nodded in recognition. The toast having been made Vicky collected her papers and returned to Central; she didn't take up her new post until after the week-end so she still had to be present at Central.

She had to fend off the normal searching questions and banter about who she was giving one to at HQ's to get the job. She didn't rise to the bait, just smiled and said 'the list was endless.'

CHAPTER THIRTY/TWO

Yvonne arrived back at MI5 headquarters in Thames House, London, where she met up with one of her senior officials who reported directly to her. Archer discussed the issues of suspected double agents and how they could overcome the latest scandal. Archer was a tall man with greying temples having an air of being snobbish and aloof. This was more of an act on his part, using his Harrow and Cambridge education to keep up the image, but deep down he was a man's man who in private would call a spade a spade. He had worked his way up through the ranks of MI5. Archer was married with the 2.4 children average, living in suburbia with a country retreat.

'Look Yvonne I've debriefed Murphy and as expected he was compromised after being honey trapped in Brussels whilst on a mission. Rather than owning up and suffering the consequences, he lost his nerve, and once having passed one piece of information he was threatened with exposure, he was hooked and reeled in, then the gravy train went on with him getting deeper and deeper.

'He refuses to name any others who are in the same boat, but we suspect there are many others. The foreign powers involved have many women who they use to trap agents with the lure of honey. Then the pictures are shown with threats of exposure to wives and husbands alike, oh yes, he also says there are female agents as well who have been trapped by good looking women and men.' Yvonne was obviously aware of the traps as she authorised them herself,

199

so was not surprised; this was just the tip of the iceberg. 'Okay thanks, let me know if there are any other suspects mentioned or suspected before the hand-over is made. Also who is debriefing Hunter when he gets here after the exchange?' 'I will get the debrief section head to undertake it.' Yvonne nodded as they separated. She went back to her office where she rubbed her eyes; she was tired after her night's passion. Then she said to herself 'what a fucking mess.' She called the technical head requesting he attended and sweep her office. He arrived with a box of tricks as he opened it and operated various devices, which beeped and flashed. 'All clear mam.' 'I want all heads of depts. Offices swept please.' He acknowledged her as he walked out with his box of tricks. Although regular sweeps were undertaken there was no harm in another out of sequence sweep being made.

Yvonne checked her watch, then called Barney 'hey Yvonne how you doing?' 'Fine Barney, I've informed Jim of you needing him in Portugal, so he's expecting your call. Are you all set?' 'Won't be long most of it is in place now, I just need to check on a couple of issues then we are ready to rock and roll.' 'Thanks Barney I will start this end soon as well.'

Yvonne put the phone down then called her driver to take her home. On arrival she said 'that's it for today; take the opportunity of an early finish.' 'Yes mam, thank you.'

Yvonne checked the post then had a long soak in a soap suds bath relishing the previous night as she sipped her glass of red wine. Life's never been better she thought to herself as she closed her eyes feeling the warmth of the water around her. She soaked for a long while, then as the water cooled she got out and dried herself and put one her white towelling dressing gown, when fully dried she discarded the gown and slipped into bed where she slept till the following morning. Her night had been undisturbed; she felt refreshed, but starving hungry, as her stomach growled at the lack of food.

She opened the curtains allowing the sunrise to send shafts light into the room; then went downstairs and decided to cook a breakfast rather than her normal cereals; so made herself poached eggs on toast washed down with a big cup of coffee. Not long after, she was brought back to her real world as her phone kicked into life with a flurry of calls regarding the operational issues she was responsible for.

Yvonne dressed as her driver arrived and parked outside her house and duly waited for her. Then the day started as she sat in the back of the car reading the headlines of the broadsheets to bring herself up to speed with news before arrival at the office.

CHAPTER THIRTY/THREE

The Spanish police arrived in the early morning outside of the villa where Sumner was. They scaled the walls using ladders then crashed in the front door; they found Sumner in bed with a couple of women. The screams and shouts went out, as Sumner was detained and handcuffed; the house was searched where large quantities of cocaine were found. The women got dressed; they were interviewed at the at the police station then let go.

Sumner was not used to the Spanish police, who were rough in their handling of him, not the softly approach of the UK police. He was asked his name, when he declined he was given a slap around the face. When he again refused he was hit in the stomach with business end of a long batten. 'Okay me llamo es Smith, John Smith. The senior officer looked at the faxed copy of Sumner's picture, then he shouted in broken Spanish 'liar, lo eres Sumner' as he showed the faxed picture. Sumner held his head down, it was over he was well and truly nicked. Then his passport was found which was also waived under his nose as the police laughed in his face.

Sumner was rough handled out of the villa as he saw the damage to the front door, he shook his head knowing he was in the shit big time, the villa had been ransacked; he hadn't got a pot to piss in and had to pay for the cocaine that had been laid on him, plus the damage to the villa.

The extradition papers had been sent to the Spanish police. Once examined the papers were endorsed and stamped. Confirmation was returned regarding Sumner's arrest. Langton authorised two officers to fly to Spain and bring Sumner back with instructions not to mention the case he was being brought back for, only to formally arrest him for the murder of Janet Crosby, nothing more. The officers collected their tickets, when they looked at the return date it was the same day. Langton looked at their disappointment and said 'sorry lads just a quick hand over then back.'

The officers arrived at Malaga, they were met by a senior police officer who fast tracked them through arrivals then took them to a nearby police station, where the documentation was checked then rubber stamped for the flight. Sumner was brought out of a holding cell where one of the UK police officers produced his handcuffs as he closed one to Sumner's wrist and other to his, he then informed him he was under arrest for the murder of Janet Crosby cautioned him. Sumner just shook his head saying nothing.

The flight was short and uneventful. Just after they had landed they were met by airport security and fast tracked through passport control, then they were met by a driver who took them to Central Police Station. Sumner was booked in and placed in a cell to await interview. He declined a brief at that time.

Vicky and Jim made the final preparations ensuring the video player was working; then Vicky went to get Sumner.

Jim had lived and breathed Sumner for so long he knew every inch of him.

He was brought in and sat down. Jim looked at him as Sumner lowered his eyes. Jim looked at Vicky as he nodded.

'Right my name is DC Howser and this is my colleague DS Broadbent can you please confirm your name?'

'Charles Sumner.'

'Thank you; just in case you are unaware of the reason why you are here, you have been arrested for the murder of Janet Crosby, I am further arresting you for rape, conspiracy to rape, sexual assault, kidnapping and conspiracy to kidnap, you are under caution for those offences as well, you understand?'

'No comment.'

'Do you want a brief?'

'No don't need one.'

'Okay Mr Sumner, do you know Debbie Andersen.'

'No comment.'

'I think you do, look at this photograph, with your arm around this girl, that's Debbie Andersen, so you do know her don't you?'

'No comment.'

'Now then young Debbie was severely injured and left for dead, but miraculously she survived, the poor girl was so afraid of her assailant when interviewed she declined to name him. But that assailant was you wasn't it Mr Sumner?'

'No comment.'

'Debbie said you and others had raped her as well?'

'No comment.'

'Do you know Sandra Rose?'

'No comment.'

'She was your girlfriend, but you also assaulted her and raped her and also let others rape her as well didn't you?'

'No comment.'

'Now let me see, oh yes, you know Lynda and Stuart don't you?'

'No comment.'

'They live at 76 Tall Pines Road; you have been there haven't you?'

'No comment.'

'You have been to parties there haven't you?'

'No comment.'

Vicky was building up to the videos, but wanted him to sweat the same as Jim would have; she was enjoying it knowing Sumner knew she had more to come.

'Oh silly me I nearly forgot about Janet, you knew Janet Crosby as well didn't you.'

'No comment.'

'Let me show you her passport and her lovely picture inside, there that's Janet, you remember her now don't you?'

Sumner was now shuffling his feet and his eyes were everywhere apart from looking at Vicky. Jim was impressed; she was doing what he would have done.

'Now just to bring back your memory about Janet; let me show you a video sequence of you and Janet so it jogs the thought process okay?'

'No comment.'

Vicky nodded to Jim who operated the video. It showed the naked people in the room and then the door opens with Janet being led in by Sumner. Vicky nodded as Jim stopped the video.

'See there we go Mr Sumner that was Janet, so you do know her, it must have slipped your mind, did it?'

Sumner put his head in his hands, he hadn't realised the police had the tapes.

'Yes I knew Janet; that was a party she liked sex parties.'

'Go on then, tell me about those parties where were they held?'

'At Stuarts and Lynda's.'

'At 76 Tall Pines Road?'

'Yes.'

'So let me recap, you do know Stuart and Lynda?'

'Yes.'

'So just to recap please confirm that you also had a relationship with Debbie and Sandra?'

Sumner was fucked well and truly, how could get out of this, he was just about to deny it when Vicky brought up four more video tapes and placed them on the table, she never said anything just patted them and smiled at him and nodded, as if to say I got you.

Sumner was now deep in thought and never replied. Vicky looked at Jim who put his finger to his lips. Vicky just sat quiet as the thought processes in Sumner's mind were turning over and over like cogs in a machine.

He then said:

'I'm fucked aren't I?'

'Big time Mr Sumner, so shall we?'

He nodded then said

'Ask away?'

Did you know Debbie?'

'Yes I did.'

'Was she your girlfriend?'

'Yes she was.'

'Did you have sex with her?'

'Yes I did.'

'Sometimes by force?'

'Yes.'

'Did you allow others to take her by force?'

'Yes.'

'Did you attempt to strangle her?'

'Yes.'

Did you know Sandra Rose?'

'Yes.'

'Was she your girlfriend?'

'Yes.'

'Did you have sex with her?'

'Yes.'

'By force?

'Sometimes'

'Yes and others did before you ask.'

'Thank you Mr Sumner.'

'Did you hit Sandra?'

Sumner nodded his head which was bowed in shame; not for what he had done, but the fact he had been caught.

'Was that nod a yes?'

'Yes it was yes.'

'Okay I can play the rest of the tape if you like, do you want me to?'

'No.'

'Okay what happened to Janet Rose?'

Sumner knew Vicky had more, but wasn't sure how much, could he bluff it?

'I don't know she ran off and haven't seen her since.'

'Okay just so you know I ain't bluffing here is a section of interview with Stuart, where he say's you strangled Janet and then he helped you bury the body in the woods.'

'He's lying.'

'Not so fast Mr Sumner, he then took us to the grave site and the remains of Janet were found. You killed her didn't you?'

'No he must have done, not me.'

'Okay I will play you the rest of the tape shall I, then I want you to listen to the conversation that is heard when the person talking, thinks the tape has been switched off.'

Vicky nodded as Jim played the tape. The scene was watched by Sumner then Vicky nodded as Jim stopped the tape.

'Okay Mr Sumner, that scene shows Janet being raped, by others and you and in order for that to happen she was held and tied down, do you agree?'

'No she agreed to it.'

'Okay listen to the last part of the tape.'

Jim pressed play where Prentice is heard to say 'who is going to do this one, it must be exciting hearing someone die?'

'Now then Mr Sumner you were seen to take Janet out of the room in hysterics then Prentice speaks those words, which together with the statement of Stuart Small plainly puts you as the killer of Janet.'

Vicky smiled at him and cocked her head to one side seeking an answer.

'Yes alright I killed her, you happy now, yes and buried her in the woods.'

Vicky clenched her fist under the table, she felt like shouting yes yes yes; but curtailed her enthusiasm.

'Thank you Mr Sumner, just confirm how you killed her and why?'

'Well that's obvious isn't it?'

'No, not at the moment enlighten me?'

'She had been raped so I needed to stop her from going to the police.'

'How did you kill her?'

'I strangled her.'

'How?'

'What?'

'How did you strangle her, with a rope?'

'No with my bare hands.'

'Thank you; when we recovered the body of Janet we were also shown four other graves and found four more bodies, and those coincide with these four tapes, shall we go through these or do you want to tell me about them, their names, and how you killed them.'

Sumner then gave a detailed account without viewing the tapes of the rapes and murders of the four women. He named them which also tallied with the identification made from dental records and jewellery found on the victims.

Sumner was charged and placed before the court to await trial.

Jim gave Vicky a hug and congratulated her for the interview. 'Oh Jim I'm so glad we went through the evidence before, and being with you on other interviews really helped as well.'

'No the credit is all yours well done. You fancy a beer?' 'Love one thanks.' 'Right you ring Langton and tell him the result and tell him about the beer as well in the Nags Head later.' 'You sure Jim, shouldn't you do that?' 'No you do it; you did a great job, well done.'

'Hello guv it's Vicky, I think Jim should be making this call, but he wanted me to call you; the interview went well, he coughed it, the lot.' 'Well done Vicky good girl and thanks for the call; Jim was right to select you for the team.' 'Oh yes, Jim also mentioned a beer in the Nags Head later.' 'Sorry, tell Jim I'm at a late meeting; enjoy the evening.'

Jim met Jackie at Central 'hey Jack great result today, young Vicky did a great job, we're having a beer in the Nags Head later, you fancy a beer?' 'No Jim I'm exhausted, plus my visitor has arrived, so not up to it.' 'Okay babes I won't be too late.' Jackie knew once in the Nags Head and amongst the lads he would go for it. 'Don't drive home either get a cab promise?' 'Yes babe's promise.'

The Nags head was full of the guys from CID and some from the Drug Squad; that was it, the beer flowed as the banter and piss taking hit the air, the pub was full of laughter and raucous jokes. Jim saluted Vicky for a good job as they chinked glasses. The CID was a great club to be in, the comradery was good. Although the work was hard the hours long and gruelling; when a good result was had, it was a great feeling especially when dealing with the likes of Sumner.

Jim shouldn't have driven, but he did, and just made it as police traffic car was on the slow prowl around the side streets. There had been a change in their department and they were now known colloquially as the black rats. Get bagged by them, then your job was gone. On seeing the car he ducked down as it cruised by. Then he vowed never to run the gauntlet again. He got in and decided to sleep on the couch and let Jackie have an undisturbed night.

He awoke in the morning with a thumping headache as he dragged himself to the bathroom and spooned two big spoonful's of Andrews into a glass, as soon as the water hit the powder, the volcanic reaction rushed up the glass, it bubbled with effervescence as he downed it in one go, the reaction took his breath away as he gulped air as soon as he stopped drinking. Then from the depths of his ankles he let out the biggest belch, it was like an earthquake, the sound rattled around the bathroom. He looked in the mirror as he shook his head at the reflection looking back at him. His eyes were sunken and his hair was like he'd just seen Marely's ghost. He forced himself into the shower letting the power of the water hit him in the face. It was like a thermometer rising, he could slowly feel life coming back to him.

He got out and dried himself as he wiped away the condensation from the mirror with the towel and saw a better reflection looking back.

He shaved and splashed on his aftershave as he felt the stinging sensation of the liquid as it hit his face. Jackie was just rising as she looked into the bedroom she looked rough. 'Hey babes you okay?' 'Not really Jim, I feel awful.' Jim went to her, he put both hands on her shoulders and pushed her back into bed and pulled the duvet over her. 'Right you stay in bed, and that's you for the day; I'll call in let them know you're not well, right don't you dare move, I mean it.' Jackie protested, as was pushed back every time she tried to move. In the end she gave up and cuddled the pillow then went back to sleep.

Jim made the call then made toast and marmalade he took Jackie some toast and a cup of coffee. She was just nodding off as Jim brought it in, 'oh thanks Jim, what did work say?' 'They had no option I just said you were ill and wouldn't be in.' Jackie drank her coffee and tried to eat her toast, but she wasn't hungry. 'I won't be late this evening so will grab a take away on the way home, what do you fancy?' 'Chinky would be nice, spare ribs and fried rice.'

Jim arrived at HQ's where he saw Langton who looked at him and shook his head 'must have been a good night.' Jim nodded 'as far as I remember it was.' Langton laughed; then he stopped laughing 'come into my office Jim.' Jim had seen this look before he knew something was in the offing. 'Sit down; right, I had a long conversation with Yvonne on the phone last night, which is why I couldn't have a drink. She said Barney would be calling you today sometime. There's going to be a meeting in London between him, Yvonne and you. This is high powered stuff Jim. The information regarding Portugal was false though, it has triggered a chain reaction, which is what they have been looking for.' Jim cocked his head to one side and raised his eyebrows, asking silently for an explanation. Langton looked at him and smiled, 'that's all I know Jim.' 'Yeah right, and pigs might fly. I feel like the lamb to slaughter again.' 'I'm sure they will explain all when they see you.' 'Any idea when?' 'Yvonne spoke of a couple of days.' 'Okay I better get the decks cleared.' 'All I know Jim is your last job opened a can of worms, that's all I know.' Jim smiled as he got up and went to his desk.

He sat there still wishing the hammer blows in his head would stop; he went to see Sandy again. 'Oh my Jim, another heavy night was it?' Jim smiled, not with the normal lecherous smile followed by banter, just the knowing smile that she was on the right track. 'Aspirin Jim?' He nodded, saying 'please.' Sandy opened her desk drawer and opened a small brown bottle handing him two white tablets. 'I can only give you two as before, as they are extra strength.' Jim thanked her as he popped them into his mouth and crunched them as he walked out.

Jim got the Chinese meal on the way home. He was met by Jackie spread out on the sofa with the duvet over her as she cuddled a hot water bottle. She smiled at Jim and nodded at the white plastic bag containing the silver foil containers. 'Crack open the wine Jack.' Jim dished up; then they sat eating their food on their laps as they sat watching the TV. Jackie commented on her day of being a lazy cow and loving it, although at the same time feeling guilty. Dinner eaten they retired for the evening.

They hadn't been in bed long, about an hour when his phone went, 'Hi Jim control room, we have a suspicious death at 24, Mill Field Avenue you know where it is?' 'Yeah think so, off Carlton Road?' 'That's the one.' 'What's suspicious about it?' 'The victim has a knife in the back Jim.' 'Okay good start; call Vicky Howser and D/Supt Langton please and ask them to meet me there.'

Jim got out of bed quickly showered then he dressed on the hoof and was out the door; Jackie slept through it all.

Jim arrived at the address as he began to make enquiries with the officers first at the scene, trying to ascertain the background. The street was now like a scene from a TV program with blue lights flashing, police radios blaring out loud, and noisy officers and an ambulance crew talking.

This helped, as neighbours were now awake standing at their gates in dressing gowns and slippers. Jim was busy interviewing the officers at the scene trying to get a full picture before Langton turned up. SOCO were there already in their white suits undertaking their investigation; they had taken a couple of Polaroid pictures to satisfy curiosity. They also confirmed the pathologist had been called. Jim instructed the officer on the door of the victim's house that no one other than SOCO was to enter until they had finished their examination.

Jim asked 'who discovered the body?' 'It appears there had been a party which ended at about midnight, most people drifted away, but a few stayed; the victim was one of those who stayed.' 'Was there any identification on him?' 'Mc Cavity, P Mc Cavity, not sure what the P stands for yet, he has an address in Essex.' 'What's he doing up here?' 'No idea sergeant, I have a list of others who were at the party, so they may be able to throw some light on him.' 'Okay get a telex off to Essex police requesting a home visit and the notification of a body with identification on it in the name of P Mc Cavity and ask them to obtain a photo and get that faxed to us asap, we need to know that the identity on the body is one and the same.'

Vicky arrived looking bleary eyed; 'hi Jim what is it?' Just then Langton arrived 'I'll brief you both together, so you get to know what is needed when you get to be first on the scene.'

Jim waited for Langton 'morning guv, right the known factors so far. This is a shared house; there was a party last night which ended at about midnight, most people drifted away, but the deceased with I.D. in the name of P Mc Cavity was one of the one's who stayed. He has an address on him in Essex, I have requested Essex police undertake a house visit to confirm with the occupants he lived there and also obtain an up to date photo if possible, to ensure we are talking of the same person. I haven't seen the body yet as SOCO are still undertaking their search but, they took a couple of polaroid shots, as you can see he has a knife in the back, he was found in the kitchen; from the position of the knife I would say death would have been pretty quick.' Langton nodded as he thanked Jim for his information.

Jim then set Vicky to task, recovering the names and addresses of all the people who had been at the party from the uniformed officers, and ascertain who normally occupied the house, also to try and ascertain the mood of the party during the night; any animosity? Then get some of the uniform guys to ask the neighbours if there had been any trouble between party goers and them.

Slowly a picture began to emerge of the evenings events; it appeared that Mc Cavity had been a gate crasher, well not fully; he had latched onto a few people when he heard there was a party; everyone presumed he was with someone in their group. He had been pissed which upset a couple of people, although nothing to the extent to cause him to be stabbed.

The morning sunrise chased away the darkness; by this time most of the police cars and the ambulance had gone, the road was cordoned off with police tape as a daylight search was to be undertaken to look for anything which may give a clue as to who the assailant was.

Jim, Vicky and Langton had gone to a local greasy spoon and had a full English breakfast; the stomach noises could be heard growling as they waited for the food. The café soon filled up with builders and painters on their way to work, the noise of chatter and banter filled the cafe. It was obvious who Jim and company were by their dress code, no one took any notice of them, just being mindful of their comments about nicked and snide gear, which was normally one of the main topics of conversations, as someone usually wanted something or, had something for sale that was a shade warm, if not red hot.

Breakfast over Jim received a call confirming the pathologist was on the way. Jim then received a call. 'Essex police have attended the address; confirming the full name was Phil Mc Cavity, but he wasn't living at the address anymore, he had moved out some 10 months ago to an address near the City, he was a bit of loner he didn't mix much with them, according to the residents.'

Jim then informed Langton that they had for the moment the real identity although, something wasn't quite right, something smelled; his sixth sense hackles were pricking the back of his neck again. Jim then said 'this doesn't seem right guv, I don't know why, it ain't right.'

The pathologist finished his examination as he confirmed the post mortem would be at 8 am the following morning; from his preliminary investigation the knife wound was undoubtedly the cause of death, but as in all cases confirmation would be withheld until after the full post mortem.

The day was spent interviewing the partygoers and neighbours, trying to build up a picture of the night and who did what and where. Jim was trying to place people in certain positions at midnight; just the normal reconstruction process. It was painstaking, firstly trying to find all the witnesses and secondly trying to get those who were found to recall their actions, especially when they had in the main all been pissed; there appeared to have been a lull at midnight when everyone was crashing to sleep, which was the point when the assailant had struck.

The incident room had been set up with the normal action teams undertaking the tasks in hand.

Vicky got home after a hard slog, it had been a long day; she had been at work for some 18 hours and was now fading fast. Her husband was looking at her as she collapsed into bed not saying much, then she set her alarm for 6 am 'what time you going in tomorrow?' 'Got a job that is important, not nice, it's a post mortem.' 'What? You shouldn't be doing that, it's not your place; I'm going to complain. Who's your boss now?' 'Leave it, I want to do it. This will be part of my new job now so, just leave it. I'm tired and have a heavy day tomorrow; so just leave it will you.'

The morning came with the trepidation setting in. 'Okay Vick you can do this gal, come on' as she talked to herself silently under her breath as she showered and dressed; taking heed of Jim's words, she wore an older suit which had seen out it's fashion sell by date, but it would do for today.

The drive to the mortuary didn't help with the anticipation setting in, as she felt the butterflies whizzing around inside her; they were now growing in size and number.

'Morning Vicky, how are you?' 'Nervous if I'm honest Jim.' 'You'll be fine, look if you want to be sick just go, don't hold it in; there's nothing to be ashamed of; they get easier the more you do. Langton's just parking his car he'll be here in a minute; you got your note pad?' Vicky nodded as she tried to smile

Langton arrived as he shook hands with both saying 'We ready then?' They both nodded as he opened the door as they entered. Vicky took a deep breath as she went in front of Jim. Jim then grabbed her bum as she went in front she turned scowling at him she was about to shout obscenities at him when he said 'that took your mind off it didn't it?' She looked at him and saw him laughing at her. She nodded then said 'get you back sometime for that.' He was right though, at the moment he grabbed her, any thought of the post mortem had gone as she had focussed on Jim in anger. Then she laughed at him.

The pathologist was ready as was SOCO, 'Ah lady and gents shall we start?' He checked his watch then commenced by switching on his Dictaphone, nodding to SOCO who nodded back. 'Okay the time is 8am; we have the body of who we believe is one Phillip Mc Cavity a 25 year old male. From the initial examination at the scene I concluded he had been stabbed in the back with what looked like a kitchen knife, probably a carving knife, pointed with a 9 inch thick blade. From the outside it looked like it had penetrated the heart between the fourth and fifth ribs.' He took a scalpel as he nodded to SOCO who was taking photos of the proceedings. He nodded as the scalpel slid down from the sternum opening up the thorax exposing the stomach and the intestines.

Vicky held her hand to her nose as the internal organ smell hit her nose. Jim looked at her and nodded as she nodded back, but inside her stomach was rolling over and over. But she busied herself making notes.

The pathologist then opened the sternum with a set of cutters then placed a spreading tool to open up the rib cage fully. He examined the heart, confirming the knife had indeed penetrated the heart through the fourth and fifth ribs and had just exited the other side. 'Death would have been instant; no medical help at the scene could have or would have saved him, he would have been dead by the time he hit the floor. The amount of force to have penetrated the outer clothing and then through the rib cage would have been immense I would say probably inflicted by a male rather than a female.'

He then went about removing the internal organs as he placed the blue/grey intestines onto the slab, then he removed the liver, kidneys and spleen. He took samples for toxicology testing. The stomach was opened as the contents were emptied into a container.

Then one of the mortuary assistants cut back the scalp hair by cutting at the base of neck, then around the ears and pulled the whole scalp forward exposing the skull then he used a spinning blade to cut around the skull then removed the skull cap and exposed the brain. SOCO was taking photos by the dozen as each procedure was taking place.

Vicky at this stage was feeling queasy at the sight of the skull cap being removed; although she just about managed to keep it down.

Once finished Jim, Langton and Vicky met outside where Vicky took a great lung full of fresh air. She looked at Jim who smiled and said 'you did well, good girl.' She smiled back and said 'you grabbed my bum?' 'It worked didn't it?' 'Yeah, it did.' Langton said 'right Jim get some breakfast and I'll see you both back at HQ's.' Jim nodded as he went to another greasy spoon and had a slap up breakfast. Vicky just had toast which she just about kept down. She watched Jim as he mopped the left overs on his plate with bread and butter, not believing he could eat like that after what they had just witnessed. He looked at Vicky and smiled and said 'what?' 'You grabbed my bum.' She smiled 'but thanks it did work, it took my mind off it for a while.' 'Like the old saying; if you got a pain in the head, get someone to stamp on your foot, then you'll forget about the pain in the head,' He laughed as he said 'Nice bum though!' 'Don't get any ideas you.' They both laughed.

They travelled independently to HQ's Jim arrived first and went to see Langton 'come in Jim close the door.' Jim could see the seriousness in his face. 'For your ears only,

Barney is coming over in a couple of days; he will be staying at the Savoy I think, if not there, at the Dorchester.' 'Fuck me; how the other half live guv; all on Uncle Sam no doubt?' Langton nodded 'Look Jim, Vicky's okay, what I don't need is you fucking off not yet, she's only just wet behind the ears, she needs a couple more cases behind her.' 'Yes I agree, but she is competent don't put her down, she'll surprise you I'm sure.' 'Anyhow Barney should be calling you probably tomorrow okay?' Jim nodded then said 'I've got a feeling about this case, it ain't right, something doesn't fit somewhere along the line.' 'Like what?' 'Ain't got a clue, but why would some computer geek be at a party miles away from where he lives then get stabbed for no apparent reason? It doesn't add up, I must be missing something somewhere, surely I am?' Langton nodded as the door was knocked he called out 'come in.' It was Vicky, 'Come on in Vick, well done today, you'll get used to it the more you see, I was just telling Jim how you are settling in well.' 'Thanks Guv, yes it's all new to me, I'm normally at the lower end of enquiries on a big job like this.' 'Okay crack on will speak later.'

Jim was not entirely happy that Langton was being entirely upfront with him, he was sure he knew more than he was saying.

The fingerprints of the deceased were taken and run through the Scotland Yard index but turned up nothing.

Jim requested he be allowed to travel to Essex to interview those in the house where Mc Cavity used to live and show the photo him. Langton shook his head, 'no Jim, Essex police have already done that, it would just be duplication.' Jim was now sure he was being treated like the mushroom again. On previous murder cases he would have been sent all over the country for less than this.

The enquiries with the party goers were slowly petering out with all of them saying the same thing. Mc Cavity had latched on to them and gone to the party. It was as if there had been a ghost who stabbed him, then floated away. There was some kind of conspiracy going on, not only amongst the party goers, but also Langton. What the fuck was going on?

The one thing that did come out of the interviews, this was a party of high end people; the house was shared by people from wealthy backgrounds, some post graduates, so not the type to be looking for a fight. The deceased would have fitted into this group, but what was he doing so far away from the City? This was now beginning to get to Jim so he went back to see Langton. 'Look guv this isn't stacking up, there is something not right, I think interviewing the staff where he worked, would be a good idea, to get some background information on him and interview his work colleagues, that may turn up something?'

Langton just point blank refused it. Jim walked out thinking about other cases he had dealt with where Langton would have detectives sent all over the country on enquiries like this.

Langton shouted 'Jim, come back in please.' Jim came back in and closed the door as Langton opened the bottom drawer and poured a couple of scotches. 'Right Jim for your ears only, I knew you would be digging; this job has got really serious connotations attached that will reach far and wide.' Jim looked at Langton as he took a big slug of his scotch as he poured another. Mc Cavity was an MI5 implant in the City. He was being used to infiltrate a company which was handling off-shore finances for the Russians and the Americans.' Jim looked at Langton with a smirk on his face waiting for the punch line, but none was forthcoming. 'He had been discovered, he had done a runner. He was up here visiting a friend then he got caught up in the party revellers; he was trying to hide from someone. He had been targeted and silenced by someone at the party.' 'Get out of here, what some assassination squad in suburbia leave it out guv?' 'That's why Barney is rushing over and why I can't allow you to go sniffing around and digging up things that could stir a hornets nest. Just do the preliminaries not to deep okay? Yvonne will be briefing you later today.' Jim was still expecting the punch line, or a 'gotcha' although none was forthcoming. He finished his scotch and went out into the office.

Vicky was looking at him expecting some words of wisdom; he just nodded and handed her an action, a mundane issue for her position. She looked at him with her eyebrows raised waiting for a comment, but there was none. She just collected her things and went out.

Jim's phone went he saw from the display it was Yvonne. 'Yes Yvonne; Langton has half-filled me in on some of the issues.' 'Right Jim, I want you to meet me at the motorway services Watford-Gap northbound in 2 hours, you know my car?' 'Yes mam, but that's pushing it?' 'In 2 hours please.'

Jim grabbed his keys and was on his way, there was no way he would make it in 2 hours especially with the traffic. The backlog eventually began to clear and he made it some ten minutes late. He found Yvonne's car after a bit of searching; he parked next to it and got in the rear. Yvonne told the driver to go for a coffee and bring a couple of take away cups back in about twenty minutes. The driver obviously used to this type of situation walked off with no complaining or look of surprise.

'Jim your late, I don't like lateness.' This was said for the benefit of the driver, it was also a side of Yvonne he had never seen before.

'Right Jim Barney is coming over because Mc Cavity was one of theirs a CIA agent recruited by agents out of Langley, we thought we had recruited him, but he was spying on the Russians and us for the CIA when we thought he was spying on the Russians for MI5.' 'What?' 'Yes Jim we all do the same. All modern powers do it, but the difference was, he was a double agent.' 'Who with?' 'The CIA and MI5.' 'What? He was your agent and the yanks turned him back on you?' 'Yes Jim exactly that; we recruited him, but we also think he was in the pocket of the Russians as well.' 'Oh leave it out mam; this is really James Bond now.' 'Yes Jim and you lot shouldn't be involved, Mc Cavity was taken out, in the wrong place.' 'What do you mean wrong place?' 'Sorry ignore that, I can't say Jim; I have told Langton the minimum investigation nothing more.' 'What about Barney?' 'Don't worry he will be shown pictures that clearly identify Mc Cavity as a double agent with the Russians, he won't want to reveal that he was spying on us. You know none of this, you understand?' 'Okay I get the drift.' Jim was trying weigh up the pros and cons of what Yvonne was saying. 'That's it Jim, nothing else, so don't go pushing too hard on the investigation side, you can live with Mc Cavity, a gate crasher got involved with an unknown party goer and upset him and got stabbed as a result of an argument. You can make an appeal, for anyone with any information to come forward; you know normal drill?' 'What about the coroner?' 'Leave that to me he will be given the nod so to speak.'

Jim then said 'what about Portugal?' This hit a note in his head; what was Portugal to do with the yanks and more to the point with the spooks. Yvonne smiled. 'Okay Jim the issue of Portugal was circulated within a tight circle, with undertones to make certain people react if they suspected what we had muted was true, and Mc Cavity was the person we suspected as being a double agent; he didn't let us down he reacted as we thought he would, our suspicions were correct.' 'But why was he killed?' 'I can't tell you Jim as it's a national security secret.' 'Look Yvonne I'm not stupid, is this issue with Barney real or just another smoke screen?' Yvonne smiled and just nodded 'all will be revealed in good time Jim.'

With that the driver returned as he handed the styrene cups to Yvonne and Jim. Yvonne shook Jim's hand and said 'be on time the next time we meet please.' Jim took his cup and got into his car and drove home.

What the fuck had just happened. Investigate a murder, but not too much; how often did this occur? The drive back was a blur it was full of questions. He bypassed HQ's and drove home where he saw Jackie arriving at the same time. 'Oh hi Jim, phew what a day, you fancy a takeaway?' 'Yeah I'm easy babes, whatever you fancy.' 'How about a Pizza for a change I really fancy one?' 'Sounds good; plenty of pineapple on mine please.' Jackie called the local Domino's and ordered to their liking. It didn't take long to arrive, but in the short time before it did, Jackie could see the frown on Jim's face; she cocked her head to one side as she raised her eyebrows. Jim looked at her and said 'sorry babe's miles away, how was your day?' 'What's wrong Jim you have that look again; that look of disbelief.' 'Don't ask Jack I can't discuss this one, sorry I can't; I'm sorry, I just can't.' With that the intercom rang as Jim pressed the button and received the two Pizzas and settled the bill.

They ate and drank wine as they chatted about Jackie's day and the continual increase in child abuse cases she was dealing with, 'You know Jim, one of these kids is going to die one day, then the press will have a field day, because no one cares, or seems to care. We are overloaded, but keep getting staff cuts so we are dealing with more with less time; social services are the same. When the balloon goes up everyone will be pointing fingers at the police. I've had enough, I feel like telling the press before it happens, I'm not going to be made a scape goat of; it ain't going to be me or any of the others, I've made a list of times I have asked for more help and been declined. So when the investigation starts I will wave that under the noses of the investigators. I'm so bloody angry and tired Jim, so tired, those poor kids.' 'Let me see if my press colleague is interested in a story, don't go making any noises, or they will be sure to blame you for the leak.' Jackie nodded, 'too late for that they all know my feelings on the matter.' 'Just keep quiet for the moment till I have spoken to my guy.' The evening ended with them crashing and sleeping.

The following day he received a call from Barney, 'hey Jim I'm in London you fancy a beer tonight.' Jim thought, Yanks they have no idea of distances in the UK. But he knew from his time in the USA, they thought nothing of a 50 mile drive for a meal. 'Can I call a bit later; I have a lot on my plate; I will try my best?' 'Hey no worries I have two beds in my room at the Savoy crash there if you like.' 'Okay will be in touch soon.'

Jim went to see Langton, who had just returned from seeing the Chief. 'Come in Jim and close the door.' Jim entered as Langton said 'the Chief is not happy with the way we are being dictated to over the murder of Mc Cavity, in fact he is seething, as this will mean in effect an unsolved murder on the forces books which doesn't look good on his stats, especially when asking for more financial assistance when next year's budget is submitted.' 'But our hands are tied by the spooks.' 'He is fully aware of that and is going to speak to the Home Secretary about it.' 'I had a call from Barney this morning; he is in London and wants a meeting later. Are there any other issues not to mention?' 'No Jim, just go along with Yvonne's brief.'

'This is crazy guv, we have a spooks hit squad taking out a double agent, and we can't properly investigate it in fear of stepping on toes.' 'I know Jim, that's why you were brought into the spooks arena, so things can be said, that otherwise would be hidden from everyone's view.' 'Big responsibility though guv.' 'That's why you were chosen because you can keep your trap shut.'

'On a different matter, I had a call from someone, from the press asking about the staff reductions on the sexual offences team. I made no comment, but when I mentioned it to Jackie she confirmed that there would be a massive investigation soon as her dept. was on the point of overload with only lip service being given to the kids and their suffering. I think someone should look at it just in case the balloon goes up.' 'Who was it?' 'No idea some freelance guy it sounded like, it was definitely someone from the press though. Who else would ask that kind of question, and why ask me, they must have a sniff of something?' 'Okay Jim, leave it with me I will speak with Ops and see if the department can be bolstered, but as you know cuts are being asked of every dept.' 'Ye guv, although it wouldn't surprise me if someone in the Social Services who are under the same pressure has let something leak to the press.'

Jim felt good, he didn't want the press walking all over Jackie's department with all sorts of innuendo's being made; so a threat like this could tip the balance in her dept.'s favour.

Jim drove to outer London then caught a tube to Charing Cross then cabbed it to the Savoy. Jim looked at the opulence of the interior with the hustle and bustle of the reception: he thought, where's the recession? There were up their own ass customers demanding this and that, with concierges running around pandering to the rich in the hope of a great tip.

Jim then caught sight of Barney, they met with man hugs and hand shaking; then got a beer and sat down. 'Hey Jim great to see you, it's really good; oh yeah and before I forget Carole-Anne says hello and wants you to call her.' Jim nodded 'good to see you too Barney, I will call her.'

Barney looked around and said 'this is a mess Jim a real mess?' Jim didn't know whether Barney was aware of what he had been told. 'Not sure what you mean?' 'Have you been briefed by Yvonne yet?' 'Only to say you would be over, although she did intimate that it possibly had something to do with the murder case I'm dealing with?' Jim knew that Barney would be looking for the signals to tell him Jim was lying; so he kept his eye movements and hand gestures to a minimum. 'Look Jim, I need to brief you on this as a matter of urgency.' 'Go on?' 'Look Mc Cavity was a double agent, perhaps even a triple agent.' 'Get out of here, no way, was he?' Jim was trying not to give an Oscar performance. 'Look Jim, he had been recruited by MI5 to infiltrate Russian financial movements, but we had already recruited him, then the Russians had him honey trapped; as I said a real mess.'

Jim looked at him as he shook his head 'where does that leave us Barney, our relationship and our trust?' 'The same place it has always been Jim, nothing has changed at our level, I just need to straighten the fall-out from above; as there has been a lot of sabre rattling over Mc Cavity mainly by MI5 blaming the Russians, but they can't do anything until the full handover of Hunter and Murphy is made, otherwise that would be a shot in the foot if they persisted in asking too many questions which prevented that from happening.' Jim looked at Barney as the light started to brighten in his head. 'Are you saying Mc Cavity was silenced by a Russian hit team who knew that MI5 couldn't accuse them, because of the exchange of prisoners?' Barney nodded, saying 'that's about the sum total of it, their timing was precise, and by the time the prisoners are exchanged the trail of the death squad will have gone.' 'Fuck me.' Jim exasperated.

'You fancy a meal Jim?' 'Love one, what you fancy?' 'What about a Greek restaurant?' Barney responded 'sounds good to me.' Barney grabbed his bomber jacket then took the next cab in line hailed by the doorman. Jim asked the cab driver to take them to a good Greek restaurant. The driver, a cockney with all the gift of the gab, took them to the best one he knew; like most drivers he got a nice drink from the restaurateur for every customer driven there.

The restaurant looked nice, very well decorated and clean. They were met by a staff member who showed them to table. The waiter spoke good broken English. They ordered Kebabs with all the side dishes as well. The food was good and plentiful as was the wine.

The conversation skirted around Mc Cavity and the reason why Barney was here, only occasionally touching on it, then quickly moving on.

Jim then quickly realised that the spooks, CIA and KGB played the same games with each other, as they did with other foreign powers. They were all involved in the same infiltration and spy games seeking out each-others secrets; perhaps not to the same level as with the Russians and Chinese, but still with a degree mistrust. Both countries leaders were staunch allies although the Russian secret service, spooks and CIA always quietly testing each-others systems.

'How long are you here for Barney?' 'Not sure yet, maybe just a few days or even a week.' 'Perhaps we can meet up again sometime and do some sightseeing, although I expect Yvonne will sort that out with you?' 'Let me see how things pan out, as it is quite a delicate matter.' Jim nodded. The meal finished Jim reached for his wallet. Barney wouldn't hear of it, 'No Jim this is on Uncle Sam.' Barney handed his credit card to the waiter who returned with the receipt. Jim insisted on leaving a tip.

Jim declined Barney's offer of sharing his room and caught the late train from Charing Cross. To where he left his car then he eventually arrived home feeling exhausted and crashed next to Jackie.

Jim had a meeting with Langton the following day where he expanded on the meeting with Barney, and what Barney had said about the Russian hit squad.

Langton was not surprised although this also was now getting over his head as well; he shrugged his shoulders, as he pondered, then said 'this was never going to be part of your remit, the murder of Mc Cavity, had opened Pandora's box. I will need to speak with Yvonne, so I can reassess your commitment to the spooks.' 'That would be good guv, cause to be honest, some of the things I have been privy to is pretty deep, even James Bond would be struggling.' Jim smiled as he looked at Langton, who just couldn't let the opportunity go for another dig. 'Are you giving Yvonne one? You are aren't you?' 'Leave it out guv, leave it out, you won't let it a rest will you.' They both laughed as Jim left his office.

His phone rang as he saw the display, it was Yvonne. 'Hi Yvonne, you okay?' 'Yes thanks, I'm meeting with Barney soon, how was the meeting with him last night?' 'It went okay, he explained the situation, he also confirmed that at my level it was fine, it was just that the Mc Cavity situation had opened a can of worms.' 'Thanks Jim; must go I think Langton is calling me so will speak soon.'

Jim looked over the Mc Cavity file again, it was so alien to him not to be turning over every stone to see what crawled from underneath. He just wanted to find who the suspect was and hunt him down, but with a suspected Russian hit squad, or perhaps a CIA or MI5 hit squad in the arena, it was way out of his control. He had been brought into a completely different world, the one where a veil of secrecy, double dealing, and counter intelligence was rife. He was way out of his depth. His life was investigating serious crime, evidence gathering and interviewing suspects. The other life of the spooks was not his cup of tea, although bedding Yvonne was fine; the rest they could keep.

CHAPTER THIRTY-FOVR

Jim had gone to bed having had a few drinks and went into a deep sleep; he hadn't been there for too long when his phone rang. 'What the fuck now?' He said as he fumbled for the phone. He held phone to his ear and said 'this better be good?' In a half awake voice. His eyes were still closed. Then all of a sudden they were wide open, 'what; you sure?' 'Okay be there soon.'

Jim arrived at the taped off part of the track, there was a police car with blue lights flashing, a police officer was standing guard at the access point. 'Hi Jim, the police surgeon has just been, although he was a mess, it didn't need a Doctor to say he was dead.' Jim smiled as he ducked under the cordon tape then walked some fifty yards to the body. He was met by the local uniformed BTP sergeant. 'Hi Jim, I wouldn't normally have called you out for a suicide, it was only when I found this note that, I thought you better be informed.' He handed Jim a note, he looked at the writing through the clear polythene bag under torch light which read. 'So sorry Phil I didn't mean it, I couldn't take any more you hurt me too many times. So Phil Mc Cavity I will meet you in heaven or hell, probably hell for the both of us.' Jim looked at the uniformed officer, 'where on the body was this found?' 'He was holding it in his hand.' 'Did you find any identification on the body?' 'No, nothing not even a receipt, he looks middle aged from what's left of him, it looks like he wanted to die he just stood in front of the train, or that's what it looks like.'

Jim looked at the body, this was no suicide; this was the work of the spooks they had picked up some John Doe from a morgue and made it look like an end it all, then stuffed a suicide note in his hand.

Jim thanked the uniformed sergeant as he went to the local police station. This was probably the work of Yvonne and Barney; so the book got closed with no further investigation. He had to call Langton as part of the requirement although it wasn't a crime scene so to speak, it was still protocol in view of the Mc Cavity murder and the connotations. He arrived at the local police station and grabbed a coffee. He sat in a quiet office and called Langton. 'Yes guv, a suicide note in his hand, stepped out in front of a fast train by all accounts. I don't believe any of it; I suspect the spooks have got some John Doe and made it look like a suicide.' 'That's very sceptical of you Jim.' 'Well that's me guv; anyway just called you out of courtesy, I'm going back to bed unless you want me to stay?' 'No Jim, no point in staying up for the sake of it, I will see you later in the morning.'

Jim got back to bed and spooned Jackie, as he got a lapful of warm bum. Jackie later awoke to her alarm, Jim was still sound asleep, she saw his discarded clothes and presumed he had been called out so let him sleep whilst she showered. Jim finally came to and forced himself out of bed. He heard Jackie in the kitchen and walked in as he yawned rubbing his head as he tried to focus. Jackie looked at him and laughed 'oh my god Jim you do look rough, were you called out?' 'Yeah a suicide I think?' Jim pecked Jackie on the cheek as he took hold of the mug of coffee and slurped a mouthful. Jackie plated up his full English as he shuffled to the table and tucked into his favourite meal of the day. The magic of the breakfast began to work as the lights began to come on, starting at his feet and working up to his head. 'Oh Jack babes that was lovely thank you.' 'You're welcome; I have to keep you well fed so you can feed me later, I so need

229

you Jim; tonight yes?' Jim smiled 'you're on mam, yes.' 'What did you say earlier a suicide I think?' 'Yeah it looks like a guy walked in front of a fast train he had a note in his hand admitting to the murder of Mc Cavity.' 'And you're not sure?' Jim couldn't let her know about the spooks so just said 'no just me Jack, you know what I'm like, always sceptical.' Jackie knew he was lying, but didn't push it any further.

Jim arrived at HQ's, Langton's office was empty, so he checked his tray then commenced his report on the suicide. He called the coroner's office to ascertain if any identification had been discovered, but he was to all intense and purposes still a John Doe.

The post mortem had begun that morning which confirmed that the injuries were consistent with being hit by a train; nothing survives that impact. The part that made him sceptical was the note in his hand. It just didn't ring true; the impact from the train would have torn that from his grip. Still nonetheless he knew that as far as anyone else was concerned it was going to be made to look like a same sex lover's tiff ending up with the John Doe stabbing Mc Cavity in the back then ending it all by standing in front of fast train. The score board was spooks one, Jim nil.

Langton came back and called Jim in; Jim closed the door behind him. 'Okay Jim, I have just come back from the Chief, he is mildly pleased at the suicide, which in effect closes the investigation. I just want you to compile a coroner's report on the investigation of Mc Cavity's death, enough to satisfy any questions, but don't go overboard understand?' Jim looked at Langton and smirked. 'I know the pack drill guv. Well at least the Chief hasn't got an unsolved murder on the forces books?' 'Yes Jim, a clean sheet.' 'I imagine Yvonne will be calling you soon as well?' 'I would imagine she will guv.' Jim left the office shaking his head. He then commenced the investigative report which culminated in the suicide, the note found in John Does hand neatly wrapped the case up.

His phone rang as he saw the display 'Yvonne.' 'Morning Jim, how are you?' 'Fine thanks mam.' 'Bugger off Jim. I understand there has been some movement in the Mc Cavity investigation?' 'Well news does travel fast, doesn't it?' 'Now now Jim, things always pan out in the end; don't they?' 'Yes they certainly do.' 'Right Jim I need you to come to London tomorrow night and have a meal and celebration drinks with Barney and me. I will book you into a room in a hotel.' 'The Savoy?' 'No Jim, not the Savoy.' 'Will I be sharing with anyone?' 'Maybe you never know.' 'Meet Barney and myself at the Savoy at say 3pm then we'll go on from there?' 'Okay, I will be there, but cut me some slack on the time okay?' He laughed as did Yvonne.

Jim went into Langton's office informing him of the meeting the following day and the overnight stay in London. Langton couldn't resist it 'go on then Jim give her one for me too.' Jim shook his head 'give it a rest guv.'

Jim got home, no smell of dinner, but he heard music playing, soft music, not Jackie's normal bopping sounds which she loved to dance to as she cooked. He closed the door hung up his jacket. Then out of the bedroom door Jackie appeared, standing in her black Anne Summers kit, black half cupped bra, skimpy panties, black suspenders and black stockings, she stood leaning against the door jamb 'come here Broadbent.' It looked like the scene with Mae West saying 'come up and see me sometime.' Jim was fixated by her push up bra accentuating her lovely breasts; she backed into the bedroom curling her finger beaconing him into her lair.

She undressed him as she kept pushing his hands away from her as he tried to caress her. Once naked she took hold of his shaft and slowly and sensually moved her hand back and forward as she watched his facial expression. When happy she sat on the edge of the bed parted her thighs as

231

she all but dragged his head down. He then realized she was wearing crutch-less knickers so feasted on her as he listened to her breathing and deep sighs as he drank greedily on her. The night was full of vigour and passion as Jim was taken every which way that Jackie wanted.

They both lazed, panting after the exertions of the long session and just fell asleep in each other's arms not waking till the morning. They both realised they hadn't eaten so ate a hearty breakfast which they both wolfed down. Jim then announced that he might not be home as he had a meeting with the spooks and Barney from the CIA in London, which was likely to go on for a long time, so would take an overnight bag. Jackie was none too pleased, but there nothing she could do.

Jim received a text from Yvonne; you are booked into the Grand Hotel, Trafalgar Square, 8, Northumberland Ave. We will meet you there at 3pm and not at the Savoy as previously stated.

Jim arrived by cab at the Grand, he booked-in and went to his room to place his overnight bag; he was early, so freshened up.

He then went downstairs and looked around for Barney, his bulk couldn't be missed, but he saw Yvonne first in a grey business suit sat at a table; then he picked out Barney as he walked from the rest room. Barney clocked Jim and gave a greeting American style, with a loud 'hey Jim.' He was almost lifted off the floor by the all American football man hug. They shook hands and walked to the table where Yvonne was sat. The greeting with her was far more sedate, which consisted of a handshake and pleasantries.

Coffee ordered they sat and made small talk then they adjourned to a side room. Jim remarked on the oak panelling, with matching tables and chairs.

Yvonne opened up the meeting officially acknowledging Barney; then thanked Jim for attending. Then she made it very clear the reason why they were there. 'Mc Cavity was a double agent; MI5 had recruited him whilst at Cambridge to use his financial skills in the private sector to monitor certain activities on specific foreign government accounts. This he did, and it soon became clear that he was an asset within the organisation. But then sometime later his information and reporting began to go into decline, and what he did provide was of little or no use.'

Then Barney began to talk, 'we in the CIA were looking for a similar person to work for us on similar financial investigations and recruited Ma Cavity ourselves not knowing he was also working for MI5.' Jim could see both were being very guarded in their comments. Barney went on; 'we too after some while saw a marked decline in his reporting, so decided to have him placed under surveillance, which showed that he was also in bed with the KGB as well. He was making dead letter drops and meeting with their handlers.'

Then Yvonne continued; it was like a well-rehearsed double-act. 'We also placed Mc Cavity under a watch and also noted his meetings with the Russians including visits to the American Embassy. That is when I contacted Barney for an urgent meeting.' Then Barney came back into the conversation. 'We never knew he was working for MI5 or we would have never recruited him, but at least we were able to get things sorted out before it got out of hand, you know how you Brits say blue on blue?' That was the cue for Yvonne to finish off 'so Jim that is the long and short of it.' Jim saw his turn looming up.

Jim was dying for his turn and as soon as Yvonne spoke the last word of her sentence he jumped in; 'so who had McCavity killed?' Yvonne looked at Barney she nodded as he nodded back. Yvonne then said 'it appears to have been something like a lovers tiff, wouldn't you say, especially with the guy standing in front of fast train and leaving a note.' Jim knew that this was now the official party line. He raised his eyebrows as he said 'looks like it, my report to the coroner is reading that way.'

Yvonne then said 'okay and that's the way Barney's report and mine will read too; so let's have a nice drink and then some food.' With that they adjourned back to the lounge where Barney ordered a round of drinks which were duly delivered by a smartly dressed waiter. Yvonne signed the chit and gave him a tip. Yvonne raised her glass in a toast saying 'all's well that ends well' glasses raised they chinked them and drank a toast to continue protocol. Then they went for a meal in China town just off Leicester Square. The food was plenty-full and tasty, Barney went to the bathroom. Jim touched Yvonne's leg under the table 'where you staying tonight.' Yvonne looked at him, I was going home, but it's getting late.' 'My room; if we can get rid of Barney?' 'That would be nice Jim.' Barney came back as Jim gave Yvonne's thigh a rub and a squeeze then removed it. Barney looked knackered; Jim commented 'looks like jet lag is catching up on you Barney?' 'You're not kidding, I thought I had cracked it, but it's hit me now.' Yvonne said 'look Barney, Jim and I have some things to discuss on another operation that is imminent; so you go back to the Savoy and I'll meet you in the morning at my office.'

Barney's eyes were showing the signs of getting heavy; although he had wanted to go around Soho with Jim, his legs wouldn't have carried him. They walked to the Square and caught separate cabs.

Jim opened the cab door for Yvonne and patted her bum as she got in. She smiled as he got beside her. As soon as they got to Jim's hotel room they were at each other like teenagers. Yvonne was like a caged animal. Nothing like the cold frosty exterior she portrayed when working. As soon as she got hold of Jim she was like a tigress, she let go all her pent up emotions, she used Jim to the full while she had him; there was always a sense of urgency, as she undressed Jim. She loved to be on top of him controlling the situation and absorbing all of him. She was never into oral sex before she met Jim, but now she loved it; also relishing the pleasure when his head was between her thighs licking her.

In the morning when dressed she looked at Jim and said 'thanks again Jim for a lovely night and also for not asking too many questions regarding Mc Cavity, as far as everyone else is concerned it's put to bed, just like me and you.' Jim smiled 'I like that thought being put to bed by you.' They laughed as Yvonne said goodbye then left.

Jim called Jackie confirming he would be home later once he had fought the London traffic. He wasn't that hungry after the Chinese meal, but he had expended a good deal of energy during the night. He took advantage of the hotel restaurant. After a light breakfast he booked out; he saw the nose to tail traffic of the rush hour so got directions from the receptionist then walked to Charring Cross station.

Jim went to HQ's where he debriefed Langton on the evenings meeting with Yvonne and Barney. Langton looked at him and smiled. Jim jumped in 'no, and before you say it I'm not giving her one.' Langton laughed then said 'that's it then, another successful conclusion to another good job.' Jim smiled although he still knew MI5 had silenced Mc Cavity, but had to let it go. Yvonne wouldn't expand on whether it was CIA, MI5 or even the KGB who had undertaken the hit, although inwardly he suspected she had set it up possibly with Special Forces being involved, who knows certainly not him?

ABOVT THE AVTHOR

Born in the late 40's only a few years after the second world finished with all the hardships of rationing, cold houses windows running with condensation with frost forming on the inside as well as the outside, living in one room for heat. Growing up in the 50's with little or none of the modern comforts of today's modern world, my brother and sister were happy well as happy as you could be. I worked in various organizations including PO as a steward on cruise liners (I must write about that) then on the buildings picking bits of skills here and there and became a jack of all trades certainly master of none. Then joined the police stayed for 30 years mainly as a detective Sergeant dealing with all manner of criminal cases including child abuse rape cases and murder.

Made in the USA
Charleston, SC
31 October 2016